NIGHTHAWKS

MELODY JAMES

First published in Great Britain by M A James in 2008.

Copyright © Melody James 2008

The moral right of the author has been asserted.

All characters in this publication other than those clearly in the public domain are fictitious and any resemblance to real persons, living or dead, is purely coincidental.

ISBN: 978-0-9559850-0-3

M A JAMES.

1995 Amsterdam, Netherlands

There's a smoking café on the Brouwersgracht where a man sits away from the window. He's a noticeable man. His black hair falls down just over the collar of his shirt. He has penetrating blue eyes. He looks sullen and pre-occupied. Joseph: that's his name nowadays. He is thirty-six years old. It's November.

The table in front of Joseph, upon which he rests his elbows, is black and made of metal. On it sits a small white cup half filled with rich espresso coffee from which a twist of steam rises. Next to this is a black ashtray containing the squashed butts of two Gitanes cigarettes.

In his shirt pocket, Joseph's mobile phone vibrates next to his chest. He has it set to silent. He can't stand flashy ring tones. He plucks it out and pushes the button to open the line.

"Piet. Hi. How are you?"

He listens for a moment.

"OK. Give me thirty minutes." He disconnects the call.

Twenty eight minutes and thirty two seconds later, Joseph walks through the revolving door of the ABN-Amro bank on Rembrandtplein. He takes the escalator up to the banking hall and goes through to see his personal banker, Piet: the man who looks after some of his money for him. Piet is a nice man; tall and fair with a comfortable face. He smiles at Joseph, shakes his hand and greets him in English. Joseph has never bothered to learn Dutch in all the six years that he has been here in Holland. He already speaks three languages. He thinks that's enough.

"It's only a little matter, Mr Mason," Piet explains as they sit down on either side of a large grey desk. There is a computer terminal

1

on it and Piet pushes this into a position so that the screen is visible to both of them. "Nothing serious yet, but I thought it would be better to sort these things out before they draw attention, you know."

"Sure Piet." Joseph nods amicably. "I don't mind. Tell me what's going on. Am I still rich?" He speaks English fluently, but with an accent. It isn't his native tongue.

"Pretty much so, Mr Mason." Piet laughs. "There isn't much danger of that changing."

Joseph smiles at Piet.

"It's just that there has been an unusual level of activity through this account." Piet points to the screen where a list of transactions is shown. "It's out-of-pattern, if you understand. This sort of thing might get picked up by people who monitor... you know."

Joseph nods. He is angry. It doesn't show but he feels it inside him. Some people have no common sense, he thinks. Why don't they ever learn? Mucking about again rather than coming through him like they're supposed to. How many times has he told them now? "All right, Piet," he says. "Thanks for letting me know that. I'll sort it out. Don't worry. How's your family?"

"They're very well, Mr Mason. The kids grow every day. Bea's expecting another in March!" He rolls his eyes skywards, shrugging. He looks happy. On the desk, alongside the computer terminal is a pine picture frame. A blonde woman and two blonde children smile out of it with love. "And how's Anna?"

"Oh she's fine, fine," Joseph says evenly. "Writing again."

"I'll tell Bea. She likes to read Anna's books. She'll be pleased."

"I have to go, Piet. Thanks for the information. I need to know these things, as you know." Joseph rises from the chair and shakes

Piet's hand.

Joseph leaves the bank and walks slowly back in the direction of his apartment which is part of a converted warehouse on the Brouwersgracht. Joseph is an artist. He paints abstract pictures. Startling and sought-after, they fetch good prices.

There is the inheritance too – the money he received from the sale of his father's business just after he died, just before they came here. Joseph pulls his expensive leather jacket more tightly around his body and shrugs his shoulders against the bitter wind that's blowing in off the North Sea. He quickens his pace, hurrying across cobble stones and brick-laid pavements. Small pieces of litter are picked up by the wind and whirled around in currents.

His apartment – *their* apartment – is very comfortable. It is spacious and open-plan. Everything is clean and tidy. There is no clutter. Anna doesn't like clutter. She's out today. She likes to wander. When her books are in progress she rises early in the morning and writes until lunchtime. Then she goes out. She walks around the city. Sometimes she takes a train out of town to somewhere quieter. Sometimes she goes out into the countryside. She says she loves the flatness of it. Depressing things appeal to her. Desolation appeals to her. On the wall of her room – the room where she works and where she sometimes sleeps when she feels the need to be alone – there is a big print of a picture that was originally painted by Edward Hopper. It's called 'Nighthawks'. She loves the picture. She says it speaks of space and loneliness. Something like that. Joseph used to like the picture too, but he lost his need for it when he found Anna. He thought she might do the same. Sometimes he isn't so sure of her devotion to him. It worries him.

The living area of the apartment is carpeted in fine Berber wool,

3

the colour of dark cream. The expanse of it spreads out before Joseph as he enters through the heavy narrow door. A wide half-shuttered window looks out to the front of the building, out over the canal. Inside there is not much furniture. A large sofa predominates. It is immensely comfortable, and covered in a fabric that they had printed up from one of Joseph's designs. It is a torrent of colour. It arrests the eye and invites the body. Carefully crafted wooden shelving lines a wall, housing the television, video and hi-fi equipment. There are a few books, but no ornaments.

Joseph uses his mobile phone to make a couple of calls. He sets a few things straight; clears up a few little messes, and then he fixes himself a bite to eat. The kitchen is at the opposite end of the apartment to the front door. Lit by a large roof-window, it usually feels bright even when the light outside is dull. It's spotless. The doors of units and the work surfaces are white. The appliances are chrome as are the handles on the doors and the drawers. Joseph uses a chopping board that is made from a complete slice of the trunk of a tree. He bought it when he was in London. He likes unusual things. Anna says that they get in the way and irritate her. But she loves books. Row upon row of them line the custom-built shelves in her study. She'll never sell one or throw one away.

Joseph cuts himself a few slices of *oude* Gouda, chooses some crackers and spoons pickle onto a plate. It's mid-afternoon. The sky outside has taken on a glower: the violent grey-blue-purples of an Amsterdam winter evening, like those strange paintings by Carel Willinck. Joseph looks out at it. It matches his mood. He thinks he might suggest to Anna that they go out to eat tonight. He wants to drink wine, to recapture the fire between them that has been missing lately. Perhaps over a drink or two she'll relax and talk to him; tell

4

him what it is that troubles her.

Joseph is restless. The time seems to weigh heavily on him. Maybe he should paint or read or check out a few contacts, but he cannot settle to anything. He feels that he doesn't know what he wants to do. It isn't like him to be so aimless. It annoys him.

The telephone rings. It's the one that hangs on the wall in the kitchen, not his mobile. Joseph goes to it immediately, plucks the receiver from its cradle and recites their number.

"It's me." Her familiar voice is flat. It contains no joy.

"Anna?"

"Joe, I'm in Rotterdam."

"What?"

"Rotterdam. I came down here to do some research. I think I'll stop over. I've some more things I want to check out. I'll be home tomorrow."

"Why didn't you tell me?" He feels frustrated. He tries not to shout at her.

"Is it a problem, Joe?" She sounds surprised.

"I was hoping we could go out tonight," he explains curtly.

"We could go tomorrow. That would be nice." It seems to him as though she is trying to sound cheerful. He detects an undercurrent of misery. He thinks he does.

"Sure. OK." He pretends to be relaxed.

"I love you, Joe," she tells him.

He isn't convinced. "Sure. Me too. See you tomorrow." He replaces the receiver with a sharp movement and a weary exhalation of breath. He feels annoyed and confused. It was never meant to be like this.

5

"Just last month, the popular liberal presidential candidate, Luis Galan was gunned down. He had promised to clean up Colombian affairs should he get elected, but he was murdered before the ordinary people of that country even had the chance to state their views…"

The news program on the TV held Harry's attention. These problems down in South America made him feel uneasy.

The telephone rang. Probably Suzie, he thought. He let it ring a couple more times before he picked up the receiver. The phone stood on a small, scruffy, melamine-covered table next to the large, lumpy, ochre-coloured sofa upon which he was sitting.

"Hi," he said, trying still to listen to what the TV presenter was saying.

"Er… Mr Smith?" an uncertain sounding voice asked.

"Sure. Sorry. Harry Smith speaking." He zapped the TV sound off with the remote control and pulled himself into an upright position. It wasn't Suzie, obviously, but female. With his free hand he grabbed the pad of paper and pen that he kept next to the telephone and rested the pad on his right knee.

"I need some help. Er… My name's Tina Philpott. I'm looking for my brother and I understand that you do private detective work. You were recommended to me." Her voice steadied as she spoke. She sounded English to him. Maybe. Harry Smith came originally from New York City. He knew that a lot of his fellow Americans couldn't tell a cockney from a Canadian, but he prided himself on his ear for accents. He had studied these things somewhat. Way back.

"OK, well, maybe we should meet up and discuss the matter ma'am. I should say that I don't always take cases on, and my fees

6

aren't the lowest you might find."

"Yes, I understand that. It's fine. Shall I come to your office?" She sounded vaguely impatient now.

"I don't run an office, Ms er... Philpott." Harry had scribbled down her name on his pad, but he had a little trouble deciphering what he had written. His handwriting wasn't neat. He should have paid more attention to that as a kid, he thought. "Why don't I meet you at the Railroad bar? Do you know that? It's right by the tracks, near the freight-loading area. Say about eight?" He looked at his watch. It was six now. There would be time to shower and shave, and to get a bite to eat.

"Yes. It isn't far from me. That'll be fine."

"How shall I recognise you, ma'am?"

"Oh. Er..." she paused. "I'm five feet six inches tall, twenty-eight years old, long black hair, blue eyes." She quickly reeled off the details.

"Weight?" he enquired absent-mindedly.

"I'm not sure." She sounded taken aback by the question. "Skinny, I suppose." A chuckle followed which was surprisingly deep. There was something about her voice that was interesting.

Harry Smith was thirty-seven years old at this time. It was early September. He was tall, six feet two inches; slim, one hundred and eighty pounds. He had dark brown hair and dark brown eyes. He looked at himself in the shaving mirror which slightly distorted his longish face with its straight nose and neat eyebrows. He raised these and jutted out his chin in order to deal with the stubble underneath it. The creasing of his forehead was noticeably asymmetrical. It used to bother him, but now he no longer thought about it.

Harry was currently renting this apartment which was

reasonably spacious and not expensive. A little before eight o'clock in the evening he drove the automobile around to the railroad, parked it up and walked the short distance to the bar. It was a warm night. He carried his jacket slung over his shoulder.

He spotted her right away. That wasn't so difficult as there were only seven or eight people in there altogether, but even if the bar had been crowded, Harry reckoned he would have noticed Tina Philpott. She sat by a window, preoccupied and unaware of him. His immediate impression was of long, velvet, midnight hair, and a slender, elegant figure; a face with an exquisitely delicate profile. For an instant he thought her beautiful, and then he caught a slight twist in her face and an unwelcoming attitude about her demeanour.

He walked towards her, pushing back his long fringe from his forehead as was his habit, and he looked at her steadily with his clear eyes, his jaw relaxed in a kind of half-smile of greeting that he sometimes practised on himself in the mirror at home when there was no one else around.

"Tina Philpott?" he enquired. She looked up at him quickly, with curiosity and a touch of accusation. Then her face relaxed and she nodded. Her hair moved like tumbling water. Her eyes were the colour of ocean pools, fringed with long, black lashes. Her eyebrows were slim and reminded him of Rita Hayworth's back in those old forties movies.

"You must be Harry Smith." She smiled carefully and held out her hand. Her voice sounded clearer and deeper than it had on the telephone. The faintest trace of some European accent lingered after she finished speaking.

Harry decided that she must be French. Her mouth, which was wide and mobile, looked as though it was designed to speak French.

He shook her hand. Her grip was firm, dry and cool, like a confident man. She looked relaxed now, serious and keen to get on with business. He let her buy him a beer.

"I don't know what you need to know, Mr Smith," she said as he sat down opposite her, sliding into position on the other side of the wooden-topped table. The barman brought his beer over, placing the glass on top of a small round paper mat, and made some comment to Tina Philpott about not being kept waiting long which appeared to confuse her.

"Call me Harry," Harry invited. "Tell me what you can, ma'am. I'll ask if I want to know more."

She hesitated. "I live in England, but my father has a business in Bogotá. My brother has worked for him for many years now and I haven't seen him in a long while. Eight days ago, I got a letter from my brother posted in Mexico. The letter said he had to get out of Colombia quickly, to 'lose himself'. He said he was coming to the States illegally, but that he knew a woman in Phoenix who could get him false papers. He seemed to be asking for my help, but I don't know what to do." She shrugged. There was a slight exaggeration about this movement. Gallic, Harry confirmed to himself. Tina Philpott quickly lit a cigarette. Her hand trembled slightly as she held the flame of the match against the dry tobacco for a moment. "I don't know what sort of trouble he's in. I'm not a detective, Mr Smith… Harry. I don't have any experience of this type of thing." She sounded worried and slightly exasperated.

Harry felt sorry for her. "So you'd like me to help you find your brother and you think he's in Arizona?" he checked.

She nodded. "There isn't much to go on, I know. My great uncle recommended you. He thought we ought to get Joe to England

9

somehow."

"Great uncle?" Now Harry felt confused. And he was nervous about the Colombian connection.

"Yes. His name is Clive Mason. He knows a lot about a lot. He used to work for the British government in some kind of capacity that he likes to be cagey about, and he still seems to be able to find out almost anything."

Harry noticed that her tone softened when she talked of this man. He guessed that she was fond of her great uncle. He supposed the old guy had been some kind of agent, and he wondered why he hadn't just contacted the authorities here and let them handle it instead of sending this woman over. He saved the question. He imagined that Mason had his reasons and he doubted that Tina Philpott knew what they were.

"Your father's business..." He spoke in a low voice. She leaned forward to hear him better. Her hair fell over her eyes and she pushed it back languidly, without a thought. Harry felt a slight disturbance in his chest. He supposed it was a reaction to the nicotine in her cigarette smoke. "What do you know about it?"

"He exports emeralds," she said decisively.

Harry noticed that she was fingering a pure green stone that hung on a fine silver chain around her neck. "Like that one?" he suggested. To his surprise, little spots of colour appeared high on her cheekbones. She looked almost guilty.

"Yes," she said curtly. "Everyone thinks the only business in Colombia is cocaine, but it isn't true."

"Sure." Harry tried to sound sympathetic. "I'm quite aware of that, ma'am, but I'm interested in why your brother didn't leave Bogotá normally. I mean, couldn't he just have walked out and stepped onto a plane?"

Tina Philpott sighed and closed her eyes. She took a long drag from her cigarette, held the smoke in her lungs for a second and then blew it out with a long breath to one side, away from Harry, away from the window. "I don't know anything about the circumstances. I don't get on well with my father, but I can't imagine my brother getting involved in anything illegal. He isn't like that. He's too... well, he was." She lapsed into silence, leaving Harry not much the wiser. He decided to try another tack.

"This woman in Phoenix, do you know who she is?"

"Yes. He gave me her name in his letter and I found her eventually. It took me three days!" She glared out of the window in annoyance. It was dark now outside, except for the daylight-strong arc lamps spilling brilliance onto the railroad tracks here and there. "Her name is Maria." Tina looked back at Harry, suddenly calm again. "She's Colombian. She's married to an American and she lives here legally. She was suspicious of me, but I showed her the letter and that made her trust me, I think. Anyway, she said she got papers for him in the name of Joey Diaz. She said he was headed north, Flagstaff way. That's all she knew."

"So how did she know your brother?" Harry asked.

"Oh I... I'm not sure." Tina hesitated.

Harry thought for a second that he caught some look of deep unhappiness cross her face, but in an instant it was gone, and she looked composed and untroubled. He asked her what her brother looked like.

She reflected for a moment. "A bit like me I suppose. Taller; about five feet ten. Shorter than you. The same kind of hair as mine." She picked up a strand of it to demonstrate and slid her fingers through

11

it. The quality of it caught Harry's attention. He wanted to touch it himself to check. "His hair is shorter, obviously, but... well, I haven't seen him for six years. He might have changed a lot. Sorry."

Harry wanted timescales. Tina had worked it out and written it down. She pulled a small blue notebook out of her bag which was made from black battered leather. The notebook was neat and new, the bag looked badly cared for. She opened the notebook and ran her right index finger down a page.

"I think he came to the States fourteen days ago," she said. "He was with Maria on the twenty-sixth of August, and he left Phoenix according to her, on the twenty-eighth. Today's the fourth of September." She stopped, looking as though she had remembered something, and bit her lip. "So he was probably here about a week ago," she mused.

Harry Smith pondered for a minute or two. "Listen, Ms Philpott. I'm in the fortunate position where I don't have to take every case that comes my way and, to be honest with you, I'm a little doubtful about this one for various reasons. I'd like to give it some thought and get back to you."

She looked disappointed for a moment, and then she masked it. Her voice was steady. "I understand that this may not interest you, Mr Smith, but I can't waste time. The longer I delay, the harder it may be to find my brother. I'm happy for you to think things over, but I'd appreciate a quick decision." The smile she gave him then was neither friendly nor spontaneous.

"OK." Harry nodded. "I'll let you know first thing tomorrow."

He took her contact number and then drove the car back to his apartment. He had offered to drop her at her motel, but she had refused and ordered herself another drink, happy, it appeared, to stay put for a while. There was a message from Suzie on his answering machine. He called her back. She wanted him to go round to her place the following evening. She would cook him something nice, she said. He told her he would go. He felt the odds were against him picking up the Philpott case, but he would wait until morning before he made a final decision. Right now, he was developing a headache, and he wanted to get rid of a persistent image of blue-green eyes that seemed to have burnt itself onto his brain.

Harry Smith got an early night and was up at seven the following morning feeling fit and cheerful. His headache was gone and the sunlight slid in through the bedroom window of his apartment. He looked out and saw that Flagstaff was bright and shiny under a cloudless blue sky. He opened up the window and smelled the freshness of the morning. He regarded himself in a full-length mirror that had begun to develop little brown spots in its silvering, and he was not displeased with what he saw.

He walked lazily into the big living room and picked up his notebook. He opened it at the page where he had written down Tina Philpott's contact details. Hesitating for a moment, he gazed out of the big picture window, unseeing, forehead furrowed in thought, and then he perched himself upon the arm of the sofa and dialled the number of her motel. He asked the receptionist for her room number and waited patiently for her to pick up the receiver at the other end.

three

A train ambles along the tracks towards Amsterdam. It stops wherever it can. She's glad. She could have caught the *sneltrein,* the express, but she likes to travel slowly. At the moment, she would like the journey to go on forever. She can't imagine anything better than being on this train, staring out at the flat landscape, the characters in her current book talking to her in her head, telling her things about themselves that she didn't know before. Once upon a time, she thinks, she would have been eager to get home to him. Once upon a time she might not have made this journey.

Her solitude is familiar to her. It's an old friend. When she looks back on her life she sees that it has always been there. It began when she was born. Her mother hadn't loved her; hadn't wanted her. She knew that, but it didn't trouble her. They get on all right these days on the rare occasions when they see one another. She accepts that her mother has never really been interested in anyone but herself. She has never known anything different. Olga cared for her – the governess. Her only real companion until she was five years old.

She smiles out of the window, remembering her childhood. There are a number of grey herons in a field. Some of them tread carefully around as though they are looking for something they've lost. It's fragile and they're wary of stepping on it, she thinks. Others stand still, aloof, refusing to join in the search.

The train is drawing closer to the city now. She sighs. Soon the journey will end and she will rejoin reality. She wonders what has happened to her life lately. In theory she has everything she wants; in practice, she feels completely empty. It started when she saw that man's face – the man in the café. Four weeks and one day ago, she remembers the exact moment and the shock of recognition. But it wasn't him. It couldn't be. The man is dead. Killed. Murdered. Her hatred for those who did it still burns her. She can't forgive them. She knows that she never will.

The train pulls into the Centraalstation and she waits to get off last. Wearily she pulls on a heavy black sweater that hangs untidily around her thighs. It has lost its elasticity and shape gradually over the years. She doesn't care. Over it she wears a shorter jacket. She catches sight of her reflection in the train's window. Her clothes look a mess. She's had her hair cut recently, shorter than it's ever been. It's shaped around her face with a fringe. She's not used to it yet. Sometimes she doesn't recognise herself when she's caught unawares by a mirror. She got them to put henna on it at the hairdressers. Now it glows dark red in some lights. She thinks it suits her. She hoped the change might brighten her. It worked for a day or two, but the alteration was only superficial – a sticking plaster on a deep, infected wound.

She stops outside the grand red brick station. The square in front of it is a gathering place for the trams with their clattering bells; a tethering place for bicycles strapped haphazardly to over-populated railings. It's not far to their apartment on the Brouwersgracht. She wonders about walking further; about spinning out the time until she has to go back there, but her knapsack is heavy, and it's drizzling with a cold November rain. The sky overhead is leaden and low and so she trudges along the side of the pretty canal until she reaches their building. She expects that he'll be in. This kind of weather makes him moody. He likes the summer and the hot sun. Each year he tries to persuade her to go away with him somewhere warm for the winter, but she won't go. She likes it here, and she likes foul weather. It

15

makes her feel alive. Each year he sulks about it, but he won't go away without her. She feels like crying.

She lets herself quietly into their apartment. She doesn't want to disturb him if he's painting. He sounded cross with her yesterday. She wonders what she's done wrong now. He seems to be angry with her more often than not these days.

She takes off her jacket and her sweater. It's nice and warm in here. She takes her knapsack to her room and unpacks her writing paraphernalia. She hears him come out of his studio into the big living space. He's in the kitchen area making coffee. She knows the noises.

She wonders about him; about how he can switch off from his painting so quickly. He doesn't even mind if she interrupts him in his studio. He knows never to interrupt her when she's writing. He did it once or twice at the start and suffered the consequences. Any distraction from her work will break her train of thought, disrupt her concentration. Even a short conversation can obliterate an idea that's forming.

She looks at her desk. It's large and old, made of mahogany and inlaid red leather. At the back of it, a small rack holds her most used books – two big English dictionaries, a thesaurus, and several volumes on grammar and language usage. Her notebooks are stacked high on its left and one – in which she's developing her current manuscript – is open, her small neat writing covering its pages. She loves the feel of a good black pen on fresh narrow-lined paper and she always writes longhand to start with and types it up later.

Sometimes, when she sits down at the desk in the morning, it feels as though nothing will come, but she's learned her trade now and usually she finds that after thirty minutes or so, the words will start to flow. When she began, years ago, she used to think she had to wait for inspiration, but she soon learned better. She read books on writing and went to workshops and classes when she was in London. When she was eighteen, she got a job in a publisher's office there through some connection of her family's. She liked it. The environment excited her. Authors sometimes came in and she was in awe of them, frightened to speak to them at the beginning. She thought that they must often get aspiring writers bothering them with silly questions so she steered clear and kept her head down. But then one day, when she had been there a year and gained more confidence, a woman came in – an author she particularly admired. She had plucked up courage and spoken to the lady, half expecting a rebuff. Instead the woman insisted she go to lunch with her.

She was taken to an expensive but friendly restaurant and not allowed to pay her share. The woman showed an interest and asked to see an example of her writing. It was she who told Anna that you just had to sit at the page and start. Anna had been excited but nervous of showing such a great woman her own words, but she did it anyway and was offered deeply insightful and constructive criticism as her reward.

For a few years then, the older woman was Anna's mentor, helping her every step of the way with seemingly endless patience. She feels a huge gratitude inside her. The author was elderly and she died four years ago. Anna still grieves for her. She'll never forget her. Every book she writes is in homage to that woman. Her first published novel was dedicated to her. When it came out, they met in the same restaurant and this time Anna paid. They drank champagne and Anna gave her a copy of the book and showed her the dedication in the front and made her cry a little. Sometimes now she still talks to her friend inside her head; still asks her questions. The answers seem to come somehow.

She wonders if the coffee is ready. She creeps out into the living room.

"Joe?" she calls out to him, wondering how best not to startle him with her presence.

"You're back." He responds casually. "Do you want coffee?"

"Yes please." She makes her face smile. His back is to her as she approaches him. She puts her arms around his waist and lays her head against his shoulder.

"Careful," he says. "This water's boiling." He puts down the coffee jug and turns around to face her. "I'm not used to your hair yet," he tells her. "But I think I like it." He touches it, smoothes it with his fingers. Then he kisses her mouth. "I missed you," he says.

Tears prick her eyes, and she holds him tightly to her, hoping to hide her emotion. "I love you Joe."

"Are you sure?" he asks her.

She looks at him. His eyes are searching her for the truth. She hopes they don't find it. She isn't sure what it will be. "How could I not?" she asks. "I don't have any choice."

In the evening, she makes an effort. She puts on black stockings and a black dress that flatters her slim figure. She knows he likes the dress. She puts red lipstick on her mouth and dabs his favourite perfume behind her ears, onto her throat and wrists.

He kisses her before they go out, and feels the suspenders through her dress. "I want you," he says.

"Wait till later," she replies teasingly. "There's plenty of time." She feels better. Maybe things aren't so bad after all. Maybe her mood is lifting. Maybe it's just the book she's writing that's been making her miserable. It's not going so well at the moment, but there's always a difficult stage in a novel and she's sure it will come good in the end.

In the restaurant, they eat good food and drink good wine, but they return to the apartment for coffee and brandies. They sit on the sofa, side by side. She kicks off her shoes and tucks her legs up underneath her. His legs sprawl out in front of him. She is turned half towards him. He sighs and lights a Gitanes.

"I think we should talk, Anna," he says.

"What about?" she asks him. She feels relaxed and quite happy for the moment. She sips her brandy, savouring its expensive taste.

"About us. I feel something is wrong, but I don't know if it's me or you. I think you're hiding something from me."

Her happiness dissipates. She doesn't want to talk about how she feels. She just hopes it will pass and that things will get back to normal. She tries to remember what normality felt like and when it was that it ended. She can't. Perhaps it just faded away. Perhaps it was never there in the first place. "I'm not hiding anything, Joe. I've been a bit down lately though. Maybe that's the problem."

"It's more than that." He jabs his cigarette towards her accusingly. "I know it is. I know you, Anna. You can't fool me."

She shrugs. She can't explain it to him. She can't even explain it to herself adequately. It's just vague, unfocussed suspicions. A feeling of unease. And the man in the café. And the dreams she's been having. But none of it makes sense. She shakes her head. "I really don't know, Joe." She pleads with him to believe her. "I do feel bad, but I'm not sure why. It'll pass, I expect."

"Are you having an affair?" he asks. His tone is firm and even, but he is bristling just under the surface. She can see it. She can't help but smile.

"No."

"Why are you smirking like that?" His anger is showing more plainly now.

"Because it's such a silly idea. Why should I want anyone else but you?"

"Maybe you want to live out some of your literary fantasies," he accuses her.

"I don't know how to convince you." She's tired. She's not enjoying this conversation very much. "I don't know why you're so suspicious of me. I don't know what I've done to cause it."

"What do you dream about, little…" He stops himself before he hisses out the word which throws her back in time for an instant. Is it twelve years now since that day? Her blood still runs cold at the thought of it, but how could it have been any different? She puts the memory aside, focussing her attention on the question. How has she given herself away?

"I don't often remember my dreams," she tells him calmly. "I don't remember any recently."

"Liar!" he spits. "Sometimes you talk in your sleep, Anna."

She feels frightened. What has she said? "I don't know what you're talking about." She tries to be indignant. "I don't remember anything, but in any case I can't control my dreams. I expect it's just a load of rubbish."

"Hah!" He stubs out his cigarette with an angry movement. "I'm going to bed. When you want to tell me the truth, let me know." He rises and strides to the bedroom, slamming the door behind him.

She pours herself another brandy and lights one of her own cigarettes, letting the smoke out of her with a long, sad sigh. She wonders what has gone wrong lately. Why have these ghosts come back to haunt her after all these peaceful years?

four

They met in a diner at eight. Tina Philpott mentioned that she found it odd – meeting for breakfast. She had never done it in England, she said. Harry shrugged and ordered eggs and coffee from the over-bright waitress.

"Guess we don't want to waste time," he said. "Might as well get moving."

"Oh, of course." She looked vaguely embarrassed. Harry wondered why. She cupped her mug of coffee between her two hands, her elbows resting on the table. She sipped carefully from the mug. Harry noticed how she had a habit of twisting up one corner of her mouth. There was a little line around it there. He looked at it with interest whilst they waited for food to be brought to them, and then she saw that he was looking at her, and she tipped her head so that her hair fell forward and hid her face.

"So how do you want to go about this, ma'am?" Harry asked her plainly, in a while, once their breakfast had been delivered and most of it eaten. "See, I can take a look around Flagstaff this morning, make some enquiries and so on, but I'm of the opinion that your brother may have moved on. I may have to go after him."

"I'll come with you," she decided.

"It's not my normal practice." Harry shook his head.

"No, I..." She twisted her mouth. "I can't see any point in me waiting around here for news from you," she explained. "And anyway, I'd go mad with frustration." She had eaten her food quickly and neatly – got it out of the way so that the more serious business of smoking could be begun. She seemed to love her cigarettes. She smoked Marlboros.

22

"I understand," he said, wondering for the third time that morning whether he had made the right decision. "Let me see what I can find out today and take it from there."

She nodded eagerly. "Yes. I'll keep out of your way when you want me to. I just…" for a moment she was as ingenuous as a child. Then she seemed to remember herself and she clamped her mouth shut.

"Now," Harry mused, half to himself. "Is there anything else? Oh yeah, what's your brother's real name, ma'am?"

"Ecuador Josef Byszewski." Her face bore no expression at all.

"Beg pardon?" Harry thought he must have misheard, but she repeated it and he hadn't. The surname sounded like 'be-chef-ski'; she spelt it for him. He would never have thought her Polish. "Ecuador!" Harry raised his eyebrows as he wrote it down in his notebook. "Little unusual. What are you then? Argentina?" He grinned.

"Yes." She looked squarely at him, eyes slightly narrowed.

"Sorry," he said. "I didn't mean to poke fun. It's a pretty name. Your folks were keen on South America, were they?"

"I suppose so." She twisted her mouth, looking vaguely angry. "I call myself Tina Byszewski normally," she explained, suddenly calm again. "Philpott's my married name. Well, it was. I'm divorced." Her cheeks glowed quickly as though she had embarrassed herself with this revelation.

"Me too." Harry nodded. He smiled momentarily at her, feeling an unexpected spasm of empathy. For an instant, their eyes met and hers looked all open to him; all full of warmth. She almost smiled back, but then she snapped off the look and became inscrutable. "I'd like to speak to this great uncle you talked about. Clive Mason, was it?" Harry asked.

23

Tina gave him the telephone number and he left her there then, promising to give her a call later at her motel. He glanced back once as he left the diner. She was staring out of the window, mouth twisted to one side, looking pensive and puzzled. Her long bare fingers drummed softly on the plastic-topped, metal-edged table. A half-smoked cigarette burned in the ashtray creating curls of smoke which drifted upwards, drawn by the draught of the air-conditioning system.

Harry Smith was back in his apartment by nine. He phoned around motels in Flagstaff to find out where this Joey Diaz had stayed. He struck lucky quite quickly. He was on good terms with the owner of this particular establishment. Harry was on good terms with most people actually. In his line of work it paid dividends. He went to talk to the receptionist at the motel. Her name was Sally. When he learned this, Harry smiled, remembering a movie he'd taken Suzie to see earlier in the month starring Meg Ryan and Billy Crystal. She'd loved it. He hadn't been quite so keen, but he'd kept quiet about it. It had been bearable, funny in parts. Sally told him that Joey Diaz stayed one night: August 28th.

"Yeah, I sure remember *him*," she said, giggling, raising her eyes, flirting with Harry. He guessed she could hardly be more than twenty years old. She was pretty, blonde, nice figure. Harry thought he might be quite interested in Sally if she were older. He didn't like his women too young. "His English was real bad," she explained. "He had black hair, about shoulder length, tied back like this." She demonstrated by pulling her own hair back behind her head. Harry caught a nuance of some flowery perfume. He noticed that her bare armpits were clean-shaven. He liked that. "He was slim, but he looked strong," she breathed, dropping her hair and her arms. "Medium kinda height. Oh, but his eyes!" She covered her mouth with her hand and raised her eyes. She giggled again. "Wow! They were so blue. Jeez, they were gor-gee-ous!" She separated the syllables of the word and her voice rose to a squeak. She was almost squirming with delight.

"Did you talk to him much, honey?" Harry asked, smiling at her antics.

"His English wasn't too hot, as I said." She thought for a moment. "He was nice though; friendly. A little jumpy maybe. In fact he asked me not to talk about him, but seeing as you're a friend of Jim's and all, I guess it's OK." She smiled up at Harry coquettishly.

"It's OK," he reassured her. "My client doesn't mean him any harm. Can you remember anything else he said to you?"

"He said I had pretty eyes." She sighed. "I asked him where he was headed. He said he hadn't decided. Probably west. I think that's what he said."

"Did he have a vehicle?" Harry checked.

"Now yes. It was a motorcycle. It was a Harley. See one of my boyfriends had one, so I know what they look like. It was a kind of sandy brown colour. He parked it right over there." She pointed to a patch of gravel just across from the reception area. She had not made a note of the license number. "Jeez, don't I always forget to do that!"

"So he didn't have much luggage?"

"Not much more than a toothbrush, I guess." She smiled suggestively. "He had plenty of cash, though. He paid upfront for his room so I didn't worry too much about taking any details from him."

"Did he go out to a bar or a restaurant while he was here?" Harry asked.

Sally shrugged. "I don't know. I get off at six. I didn't see him again till he checked out next morning. He didn't say no more about where he was going, though."

Harry tried another couple of angles but it was evident that Sally couldn't tell him any more. He worked his way around nearby eating places. He had no luck at the first two. The third was a Mexican café. The walls inside were roughly plastered and painted orangey-pink. Guitars and sombreros hung haphazardly here and there. The tables were made of dark wood, or a good imitation of it, with red place mats on them, and wicker-covered, pregnant-shaped bottles which held red candles perching precariously on castles of wax. The light was dim. Harry sat down at a table and ordered a coffee from the waitress who appeared to be Mexican herself. She was plump, brimming with laughter, and about his own age. When she brought his coffee, he asked her a question.

"Yes, yes," she said happily. "He don't speak much English, but we get along fine in Spanish. Ah, my friend with those *lovely* blue eyes. What a *lovely* man. So sad. So lonely. Missing his family, he was. He *loved* my enchiladas!" She had seated herself opposite Harry on one of the comfortable wooden chairs whose backs hit just the right spot on the spine. Now she rocked backward on it, gurgling with pleasure. "He's going to San Francisco," she confided, rocking forward again. "He said he always wanted to go there. He's on holiday, you see? Travelling around. Seeing the country. Ah! I like my home and my family. I'm happy where I am." She smiled, her eyes full of tearful emotion.

"So, did you talk about anything else, ma'am?" Harry asked politely.

"Actually, he said he's on the run!" She leaned forward further, whispering it with glee. She waved her hands in the air and pursed her lips. "I think he's joking." She nodded, chuckling to herself. "Don't tell no one you seen me, he said. I could get my throat cut, he said." She pealed with laughter, fishing in a large pocket on the front of her brown and cream checked apron and extracting a large white handkerchief with which she wiped her eyes theatrically. "He's *joking*," she insisted. "Ah! He made me laugh so much. He's a one for the ladies, I tell you. There were two pretty little girls over there." She waved loosely at a corner of the room where a bulbous brick chimney housed a pile of unburnt logs. "He was looking at them all the time. Those little girls can't resist, can they? They leave the same time he did in the end, you see. Lord knows what happened after!" She looked scandalised.

"This business about being on the run," Harry asked. "Do you remember any more about that, ma'am?"

The waitress looked at him questioningly. "You don't think he was serious? No, no, he was kidding me. He didn't say no more. Anyway he didn't look scared to me. He drink my wine, he eat my food, he make eyes at the pretty girls. He's *relaxed*. He's not on the run. He's on *holiday*." She emphasized her point by bringing the palm of her left hand down hard and flat on the table.

A little later, Harry found the bar where Joey Diaz had taken the two women he picked up in the restaurant. The bartender remembered the little group, but he hadn't talked to them. He didn't know who the girls were. Harry tried a couple of gas stations on the way out of town towards the west with no luck. He went back to his apartment.

Harry's place had a spare room. It was small, but there was space for a desk, an office chair and a comfortable armchair. These were his own furniture – all he had apart from the TV and the VCR machine. He wasn't a great one for possessions. He liked to be able to move on quickly when he felt like it. He sat at the desk now. It was medium-sized, made from oak. A bunch of files, fawn coloured pouches containing case notes, were stacked up at the back of it. He ought to file them away, he thought. At his left hand was another telephone – an extension on the line. He brushed the receiver with his fingertips absent-mindedly, then pulled his hand back and opened a drawer in the desk; the second one down on the left. After pushing the contents around for a time, he found what he was looking for: a diary. Two pages in from the back was a diagram – a picture of the earth flattened out and showing the international time zones. He checked what it would be in London. Seven or eight in the evening. He dialled the number Tina Philpott had given him earlier. The old guy who answered had a cultured English accent. He sounded cheery and immediately friendly.

"Mr Smith! So glad that Tina got hold of you. I'm a bit worried about her knocking about in foreign parts on her own, but I suppose she's a grown woman now."

"Yeah, er, call me Harry, Mr Mason. Listen, Ms Philpott's given me what she knows but I'm a little cautious about this Colombian thing. There's a lot of trouble down there right now and so on. I wondered if you could tell me any more."

"Not really, Harry. I've been trying to establish if there's anything shady about the Byszewski business for years, believe it or not. I haven't been able to come up with a thing. Either they're extremely clever or they're completely legitimate. I must admit I've a *feeling* about it though. Can't say more."

"Do you have any idea why Ecuador Byszewski should split at this point?" Harry asked.

"The timing is ominous, I agree," Clive Mason mused. "But

again, I've got no information about him being involved in anything else – no political interests as far as I know. My best guess is that he had some bust-up with his father, saw the escalating situation and decided to make a break for it. As I understand it, he was never whole-heartedly committed to the business and was probably waiting for an opportunity to go."

"OK, Mr Mason. Thanks for your time."

"That's quite all right, Harry. I'm sorry I can't be more help. Let me know if there's anything I can do though. Oh and one more thing. I'd like you to look after young Tina. I'd like you to stay with her if at all possible until she leaves the country. There'll be an extra fee for it of course. Would you do that, Harry? She's very precious to me, you know." He mentioned a sum of money which was not trivial.

"Sure thing, sir." Harry replaced the receiver in its cradle and murmured an expletive under his breath. He was wishing he had followed his first hunch and refused the case. That stuff in the Mexican restaurant troubled him. It was weird that Byszewski had said that to the waitress. Had he been drunk? Had she got it totally wrong? Had he been boasting? If it was true then it seemed like pretty reckless statement to make. Maybe he had thought the waitress would keep quiet about him. Harry couldn't fathom it. His mind was not put at ease by what Clive Mason had said either: no evidence, only suspicions. Harry did not want to get caught up in someone else's argument. He liked to keep his head down. He'd got too close to those people once before. He hoped they'd forgotten about him. The last thing he wanted to do was to remind them of his existence.

Harry got up from the desk, stretched himself and loped out into the living room. He stood at the window with his hands resting in his trouser pockets. Could he change his mind now? It wouldn't be very professional. Who else did he know who might be willing to pick up the case? Nobody, to be honest and, in any case, would he really want to admit that he was scared? He could lie. He could make up some tale about family troubles or something. He told himself to calm down. He was getting paranoid. Maybe that's what Byszewski was: paranoid. Maybe that was all. In any case, it would be embarrassing to call Clive Mason back now and go back on what they had just agreed to. He shrugged, laughed a little at himself, and then went out to the kitchen to make a sandwich. Yesterday's washing up still awaited attention. The lack of a dishwasher was a big drawback of this apartment in Harry's opinion.

There was some good ham in the refrigerator. Harry laid a couple of slices on rye bread and spread some mild mustard on top of it. He closed the sandwich and took a large bite out of it as he walked back into the living room. He sat down on the sofa, picked up the telephone receiver and dialled a number. He was still chewing when Suzie picked up the phone.

"Hi honey," he said, trying not to sound as though he was eating. "I'm real sorry, babe, but I just picked up a case. Gonna be out of town for a day or so, so I can't make it tonight."

"Oh, baby! I thought we had things *planned*."

He could hear her pouting, but there was an undertone of good humour. "I know, honey, but business is business. Keep it all hot for me, eh?"

"Sure, sugar," she said.

He could hear a smile in her voice. She was a good girl, Harry thought. Just the thing for him. He pushed the cut off button on the telephone, then dialled again. He made sure his mouth wasn't full of sandwich this time. "Hi, Ms Philpott? OK. Can you be ready to go to

San Francisco in around an hour? Great. I'll pick you up at your motel at one-thirty."

five

He wishes that he hadn't shouted at her, but she makes him so angry with her denials – her sudden inexplicable lies. They used to be the whole truth to one another. Of course, there are things they don't discuss. His little deals. Not so small any more in fact. But they aren't important. They're his business. They don't affect her. They're nothing to do with her.

He lies awake in the big empty bed, hoping that she will come to him and break the silence, but he expects that she won't. She has her pride too. Her stubborn streak. They're too much alike in that way. He expects that she has gone to her own room to sleep. The wedge between them goes deeper. Joseph feels a sense of panic. Since he was a child she has been the only one he truly loved. He always knew they would be together when the time was right. He thought it would be permanent. Now his certainty is gone. What would he do without her? What would his life be?

He turns onto his side and tries to sleep. He has a business meeting in the morning, and he wants to be alert for it. He looks at the clock by the bed. It is small and square with luminous white numbers and hands. It's two a.m. Outside, the city rests. This city never sleeps. He wonders whether to get up for a while; whether to go for a walk. How can he make himself tired? His body feels weary, but his mind won't slow down.

He remembers the first time he left her. When his father took him away to work. Far away. He remembers how she cried. She was fourteen then; a picture of innocence. But the picture was an illusion. She had lost her innocence a year before, and shared its loss with him. Oh, how he remembers that time. It was his fifteenth birthday and they were alone together in her room. She had shown herself to him, and let him touch her, and she had demanded that he do the same. They hadn't fucked then, but later, up by a pool, clear and deep, reflecting the sky and the purple mountains, out on a slab of rock, heated by the summer sun, naked, silent, she had let him put himself inside her. Oh, the first pleasure of it. The thought of it arouses him now. He wants her. He remembers the feel of her suspenders earlier in the evening. He wants her. He gets up, pulls on a dressing gown; thick towelling coloured a deep dark blue. He goes to the door of her room and knocks softly.

"Anna, are you awake?"

There is no reply. He knocks more loudly. He will not be put off.

"What is it, Joe?" She sounds weary, but not as though she has just woken.

"Come to bed with me."

"I'm tired."

He opens the door to her room. She is in the single bed there. As he enters the room, she props herself up on an elbow. He sits beside her on the bed and strokes her hair.

"I'm scared of losing you, that's all," he says.

"You know it isn't possible."

"Things change." He shakes his head. "Why should we be any different in the end? We're ordinary people in our hearts."

"Speak for yourself!" She laughs at him. "Maybe it's you who wants to leave, Joe. Is that what's really scaring you?"

"I wouldn't know how to go." He shrugs. "And I promised I would never leave you again. You know I keep my promises."

"But you mustn't keep them despite yourself, Joe. If you want to change your mind, you must do it. Staying with me when you no longer love me won't make me happy."

"How can you think that I don't?" he demands it, but not unkindly. "Come to bed with me Anna."

She looks at him for a moment, making her decision. Then she gets out of her bed and goes with him into the big bedroom where she takes off the long tee shirt she's wearing, leaving herself naked. She lies down on the bed and he comes to her, running his hands over her, down her, inside her. Soon, he is thrusting into her, and she is moaning and clawing at him in pleasure.

When she comes, she cries out his name, and then he sleeps with her cradled in his arms, his worries gone from him.

In the morning he feels bright. Tired but peaceful. They breakfast together with no sign of tension. She seems more at ease to him; more content. He makes a promise to himself to look after her; to make sure she knows she is wanted; not to let his other interests interfere or come between them. He must always remember what his priorities are.

"I have to go out for a while this morning," he says. "I'm seeing some guy about a possible exhibition in London."

"Could we go there?" she asks, looking interested. He knows that she doesn't much like long-distance travel, but she likes England.

"I don't know." He frowns. "The negotiations have only just begun."

"It would be nice to go to London," she sighs.

"I'm wary of it."

"I know," she nods. "Old memories."

It's cold today but not raining. Joseph heads down to the New South. He is meeting these people at a fashionable address. It's a large house backing onto the Noorder Amstel Kanal, just off Beethovenstraat. The owner is a collector of fine art. He owns two of Joseph's paintings and a small gallery on the Amstel. There are three men in the meticulously appointed sitting room of the house. Three sofas are arranged on three sides of a square with a large square coffee table in the centre. The table is fashioned from wood that is almost black, but its top surface is inlaid intricately with mosaic tiles glazed in orange and blue. The colours of the sofas match these precisely: one orange, two blue. They are well-made, elegant, expensive and uncomfortable. Joseph sits down on a blue one, at ease, accepting the cup of strong black coffee he is offered. He lights a Gitanes. An ashtray is provided.

"I have some calls to make." The owner of the house excuses himself and leaves Joseph with the two other men. They introduce themselves. Frans, who is Dutch, dark-haired, and intelligently bespectacled, sits on the orange sofa. Carlos, Spanish, sandy-haired with vivid laughter lines etched into his face, sits on the blue one opposite Joseph. Carlos smiles constantly. It seems to be the natural set of his face. Frans is more earnest.

"How can I help you?" Joseph asks with a smile he saves for business.

"We're doing some trade with the United Kingdom," says Frans. His eyebrows rise in conspiratorial seriousness.

Joseph nods. "I understand. Good prices."

"Excellent at the moment," Carlos agrees. "Worth the effort, but the money is a problem, as you're aware."

"Have you got a commodity?" Joseph asks.

"We have two outlets," Carlos tells him. "Art is one, but it can move a little slowly. Machine parts are better."

35

"We need help with finances," Frans adds. He seems less relaxed than Carlos, but maybe the Spaniard's smile is misleading.

"Of course." Joseph shrugs. It's the reason he's here. He knows that already. "You will know that I can help in this matter." He looks at each man in turn, and they offer confirmation. "I have access to a large spread of accounts throughout Europe, and I can put you in contact with similar facilities in the Americas. For a price, I can set up a suite for you, and advise you how to deposit funds. I will also make sure that these cannot be traced back to their origin, and arrange for you to draw monies, as we shall agree in advance, without attracting unwanted attention. My services aren't cheap, as you know, gentlemen, and I need access to all your accounts in order to control security." He takes a sip of coffee and draws on his cigarette. He has made the same speech many times before. They never turn him down. He's the best there is.

Carlos contemplates him for a moment. "We would like you to work for us," he says. "Your reputation is outstanding, and we need good security."

"Of course," Joseph says. "Shall we discuss the specific terms now, or would you prefer to arrange another meeting?"

"Now will be fine," Carlos says. "I would like to take some specifics away with me and come back with a final agreement in, say, a week's time?"

Joseph nods. They talk in some detail about what will be done and how much it will cost. The sums of money involved are not the largest he has dealt with, but they are large enough. Joseph will take a percentage as his fee. He will never have to worry about where his next crust is coming from. Then again, he never has.

At midday, he leaves the house. A few yards away, in a shop

doorway, a man is lighting a cigarette with a petrol lighter. The man is tall with dark brown hair just turning grey at the temples. Joseph hardly notices him. He is deciding whether to take a detour via the Albert Cuypstraat market. On the whole, he finds it too down-at-heel for his tastes, but he knows a stall where the cheese is excellent, and they are running low at home. He doesn't think Anna will remember to buy some.

A little later, Frans and Carlos leave the building. They shake hands out on the street, and Carlos hails a conveniently passing taxi, which stops. He gets in and is driven away. Frans approaches the man in the doorway and they walk off together, onto Beethovenstraat, and to the north, talking.

six

She asked if there was time to drive to Phoenix. She said she would rather do that than take the plane. Harry said he didn't mind. The drive would take around three hours or a little more, so they would be there in plenty of time to catch the flight out to San Francisco which was due to leave just before seven thirty. He had booked their seats by phone, using his credit card, and called ahead to a motel he knew where he had reserved two rooms for the night. He kept a careful note of his expenses.

On the way out of her motel, he told her what he had found out; summarised it. He was reluctant to repeat what he had heard about Byszewski being on the run. He wasn't sure how she would react to that. He mentioned it anyway. She looked worried.

"Do you think he was joking?" she asked him.

"The waitress was certain of it." Harry considered. "I guess you know him better than I do, though. What do you think?"

Tina put her hand up to her forehead and pushed her long hair slowly back over her head. She looked perplexed. "I used to know him well," she said softly. "But we've been apart for years. I don't know how he might have changed. Close contact with my father might have turned him into a monster. No, no, he couldn't be like that. He was so honourable, so loyal, so…" She shook her head, and then her face became placid. "I'm sure he was joking," she said decisively. "He'd never do anything that would cause him trouble. I know that."

"OK." Harry shrugged. He wasn't so sure. He didn't have the kind of confidence in her brother that Tina seemed to, but it wasn't his place to judge. "We've only got that waitress's word that he went off to San Francisco. I know it isn't much," he said. "I've called a couple of contacts in the other big towns round here, but I thought you might like to go over and have a snoop round there. It's a nice city. Worth a look."

"Yes." She agreed eagerly. "Yes I would. I'll feel much better if I'm doing something."

She had bought a pick up truck when she arrived in Phoenix. It cost her hardly anything she said. She hadn't completed any paperwork, hoping that she might be out of the country before it caught up with her.

"You need to be careful of that," Harry warned her. "If they get something on you, they may not let you back in another time."

"Oh, I don't suppose I'll want to come back." She shook her head.

"Hey, it ain't that bad is it?" Harry felt annoyed. On the whole, he thought the States was a pretty nice place to be. He hadn't been anywhere else, mind.

"No... Oh no, I didn't mean I didn't like it." Tina looked up at him quickly. A worried little frown knotted her forehead. "It's just that I'm so scared of flying, and it's such a long journey. I don't know if I could stand it again."

"Safest form of travel." Harry smiled at her reassuringly. She didn't look convinced.

He took the keys of the pick-up from her, told her he would sort it all out later and opened the passenger side door of his newish Ford for her. She smiled at him with a mixture of gratitude and uncertainty.

Thirty minutes or so outside Flagstaff, Harry Smith asked Tina Philpott if she would mind if he switched off the radio in the car. She said she didn't mind at all.

"So tell me about yourself," he invited pleasantly, glancing across at her with his friendly half-smile.

"Oh, you wouldn't find my life very interesting, Mr Smith," she replied.

"Where are you from originally?" he asked.

She thought for a while. It was hardly a difficult question to answer, but she seemed to be unsure of what to say. He thought that maybe she hadn't heard him, and he was about to repeat himself when she spoke.

"I was born in Switzerland, but my father's family came from Poland originally – hence the name. My mother is French. She still lives in Geneva."

"Your parents are separated?" Harry continued.

Again she hesitated. It seemed to Harry that she was carefully constructing her answer – rehearsing it to herself before she let it out. It was a weird, disorienting habit. It made him feel wary of her. He didn't know whether to believe what she said.

"Only geographically," she eventually replied. "They've always been that way."

"Odd thing, your pop working in South America," Harry observed.

"Why?" she asked him quickly and defensively.

Harry recoiled a little and shrugged his shoulders. "Long way from home, I guess."

"My grandfather was in partnership with a Colombian," she sighed. There was an impatient note in her voice. "The Colombian had no children so our family inherited the business. I don't know a lot about it. I've never been very interested in it quite honestly."

"Just the two kids then: you and Ecuador?" Harry asked.

He could feel agitation coming from her now. "Do you mind if I smoke in here?" she asked him. He shook his head. She lit her cigarette with quick, sharp little movements, opened the window, blew out the smoke with a fast puff. "I expect you mean well," she said. "But I really don't like talking about my family very much."

"OK. Sorry." Harry was driving on an empty straight road. He turned to look at her. She was gazing out of the side window. She looked far away and infinitely sad. The curve of her cheek looked downy-soft. He wanted to run his fingers over it; to comfort her somehow. She was unaware of him, caught up in some painful memory or other. He turned his eyes back to the road and wondered how long this journey might feel if they had to make it in silence.

After a little while, she spoke again, volunteering information as though she had taken pity on him, or felt sorry that she had shunned his enquiries before. "There were four of us: Venezuela, Bolivia, Ecuador and me. I'm the youngest. It was Bolivia's birthday yesterday and I forgot. Damn!" She was scowling, angry at herself.

"Guess you had other things on your mind," Harry offered. She looked at him with surprise, as though she had been talking to herself and forgotten that he was there. She bit her lip and blushed just slightly.

"I moved to England when I was sixteen," she explained carefully. "My mother's sister, Christine, and her English husband live there. I stayed with them for a couple of years, and Clive got me my citizenship. I still share a flat with Chris's daughter – my cousin Caroline." Harry fancied that the tone of her voice lightened when she mentioned her cousin. "Anyway, what about you?" she asked him. The tone of her voice suggested to Harry that she was merely being polite.

"What about me?" he repeated playfully. "Oh, I don't like to talk about myself too much."

Tina turned to look at him. He could feel those turquoise eyes on him. He wondered if she was angry now. She seemed to be so unpredictable. A smile that he was trying to suppress quivered around his mouth.

"Well!" she said in a tone that was as dry as the desert. "If that's true, then you're the first American I've met who doesn't, Harry Smith!"

He snatched a look at her, fancied he saw a twinkle in her eye, and grinned broadly. She chortled in response, and suddenly he felt happy. The tension between them had relaxed. Harry was surprised at how good he felt about that.

"I find it strange," she explained. Suddenly she seemed eager to confide in him. "At home, people don't normally tell you much until they know you. It's different here, isn't it?"

Harry nodded. "I guess we're more open about ourselves generally," he agreed. "Can't see the harm in it."

"No," she said. "I'm just not used to it. I quite like it, I think."

"So, do you think of yourself as English, then?" Harry asked.

"I'm more that than anything else. I don't feel Swiss. After all, neither of my parents is. I like England. It's my home now."

"And Clive Mason, is he a real great uncle?" Harry felt curious about the old guy.

"He's sort of half of one." She twisted her mouth. "He's my father's mother's half brother. Their mother married twice, you see. First to a Pole, and they had two children, one of whom was my grandmother. Then that husband died and she met an Englishman and married him. Clive's their child. After a while, the two Polish children moved back to Poland. I don't think they got on very well with the stepfather. Anyway, Clive himself told me that. My father never talked much about his family. Well, he was never there much!" She tutted in indignation. "It was father's brother – my uncle Peter – who told me about Clive originally. Peter lived with us, you see. He…" She stopped. Harry looked and saw that she was biting her lip anxiously. He guessed she thought that she had said too much.

"It all sounds pretty interesting to me despite what you said earlier," he remarked kindly.

"It was all before my time." She shrugged. "It has nothing to do with me. My life before I went to England was one great big yawn. We didn't even go to school like normal children. Father would have kept us locked up in a dungeon if he could."

"Really?" Harry was taken aback by the sudden venom in her voice. "Why do you think that was?"

She shrugged in the exaggerated way that she had. "How should I know? He's mad. I expect he thinks we'd have been kidnapped or something. He always thought he was something important."

This little piece of information filed itself alongside the 'on the run' story in Harry's brain, and made him feel uneasy once again. Emeralds were a lucrative business and Bogotá could be a dangerous place, but the fact that Byszewski senior had kept his whole family in Switzerland *and* stopped the kids mixing outside seemed a little excessive. Still, maybe the whole family was paranoid. More worryingly, maybe they weren't.

"How long has your brother been in the business?" he asked.

"Since he was sixteen. That's about fourteen years." She let out a little gasp of surprise. "It doesn't seem that long," she

43

murmured.

"Did you keep in touch?"

"Yes, by letter mainly. We saw each other a few times after he'd gone, but after I went to England, it... it was more difficult. He came to my wedding. I..." She lit another cigarette and drew very hard on it as though it might help get rid of some unwanted emotion. "I haven't seen him since then."

"Were you close?"

"Quite." She sucked on her cigarette again. "We were good friends when we were little. He looked after me to an extent. I always had such great faith in him. I still have!" She sighed and leaned her head on her hand, her elbow resting on the frame of the car window, cigarette held between her first and second fingers. "I want to be there for him this time."

"We'll do our best," Harry reassured her.

He told her a little about himself: that he came from New York City; that he had studied psychology at college. When he mentioned it, he noticed that she looked at him warily. He laughed. "Hey, it's OK," he said. "I already forgot most of it. Don't worry. I won't try to psycho-analyse you."

"I'm glad to hear it!" she sighed with relief. "I once knew a man who took a psychology degree. He was always trying to stick some label on you. I ended up being scared to speak to him!"

"Well, I guess people do fit into psychological types to an extent," Harry considered. "In my job, I meet a lot of folks and there are some basic behaviour patterns. You could categorise people."

"Hmm. I think people might not like to be categorised," Tina said sternly. "Everyone likes to think they're unique, don't they?"

"Oh, for sure. Of course they are." Harry felt scolded. "But you know there are some fundamental similarities that help us to get along with one another and so on."

"I suppose so," she said sceptically. "So what sort of personality type do you have me down for then, Harry?"

He looked across at her. One of her fine eyebrows was raised. Her eyes looked like pieces of lapis lazuli; their green content seemed to alter with the quality of the light. He fancied he saw mischief dancing in them.

"I would not be so bold, ma'am," he grinned.

"Coward," she told him.

"Correct," he replied.

They both laughed and then she asked him to tell her about his own family. He shrugged.

"Not much to say to be honest. Mom and pop still live in New York. Got one brother, five years older than me, lives up in Portland in Maine. He's a cardiologist. Married, three kids."

"Do you get to see them much?" Her questions seemed genuine now. The politeness of before had been replaced by honest curiosity.

"Not a great deal. Charlie – that's my brother – and me, we were never that close, and to be real frank about it, I can't stand his wife."

"Why's that?" she asked. He glanced at her. Her face was open and eager to hear his answer.

"Well… she's one of those women who just won't shut up. She tells you what to do all the time, and, if you do manage to get a word in edgewise, everything you say… she's done it and been there, and she's done it and been there bigger and better than you have." Harry felt himself getting a little worked up just with the memory of it.

Tina laughed quietly. "I've met people like that too," she said.

"Hmm, perhaps I'm coming round to your idea of psychological types after all. What about the children though?"

"Don't feel like they're anything to do with me. I never had a lot of interest in kids. Never had the desire to create them anyhow."

"Me neither." She shuddered slightly as she said it, he noticed.

They grew quiet then, each occupied with their own thoughts. Harry felt light, but wary. He found himself drawn to this woman even as a part of him pulled hard in the opposite direction. She wasn't his type. He knew that.

Harry turned up the air conditioning in the car. They were headed down into the valley now; into the searing desert. The Arizona sky spread out before them, enormous and relentless. September storm clouds were gathering on the horizon. They were piling up, growing perceptibly larger by the second, black and threatening, as big as mountains. Tina pulled off the light cotton sweater that she was wearing and flung it onto the back seat. She was wearing blue jeans and a thin red vest. The vest was loose, but Harry could see the shape of her small breasts clearly defined under it. She lifted her spun-silk hair away from the back of her neck and her armpits showed little specks of black where the shaved hair had begun to grow back. Harry tried to put his thoughts elsewhere. He searched for something boring or unpleasant to contemplate because he had become slightly aroused and it really wasn't very convenient.

seven

In the afternoon she calls round to her friend's apartment on the off chance. She isn't pleased with herself today. Her mood is colouring her writing. Her main character began to suffer from her own lassitude and depression this morning and she had to throw two hours' work away. That annoys her. She likes to treat her writing as a professional job of work, not a soul-baring catharsis. She tries hard to be as non-autobiographical as she can, but sometimes she finds her self hidden there in her words and she chides herself for sloppy thinking.

Mari is in with her corn-coloured wavy hair and strong blunt features. Anna loves the look of her. She seems to be so real and right, where sometimes Anna thinks her own face too delicate of structure with no character to define it.

"Anna!" Mari smiles with white teeth and good skin. "Come in. I'll get some coffee going."

"I don't want to disturb you if you're busy," Anna says.

"I've only got housework to do." Mari grimaces. "You're a fine excuse to put it off. Don't stand in the cold. Come into the kitchen."

Anna follows her through the bright, beautiful rooms which are scattered with interesting objects in wild colours; bold statements of a definite taste.

Mari becomes preoccupied for a while with the intricacies of her coffee making machine. The kitchen is cheerful; predominantly pine, with walls painted in sun-bright yellow, a few leafy green plants and the odd splash of something in brilliant blue. A smell of fresh toast lingers.

Anna sits down at the kitchen table and fingers a magazine left lying open at a page of horoscopes printed in Dutch. She decided to learn Dutch soon after they came to Amsterdam. Joe told her it wasn't necessary, but she wanted to do it. She thought it rude not to try to communicate with people in their own language in their own country. Joe didn't care about that. It doesn't worry him. She wants people to like her, if she's honest, and she thinks Joe is a trifle arrogant. He doesn't care whether people like him or not. They seem to though. Or perhaps it's just respect. He has an air about him that seems to command respect.

Mari teaches Dutch as a foreign language at evening classes. It doesn't pay much, and she works at an office during the day where she's an administrator for a shipping company. Her flat is rented. Mari says the people in her office are all men, and they mostly talk of sport – mainly football. They like computer games. She says she's dying there. The evening classes help her stay sane. It's how she and Anna met. Anna went to her classes, but she didn't do very well in that environment so she asked Mari to give her private lessons. She had learned English quite easily when she went to London, but she was younger then, and surrounded by family who spoke it all the time. The private lessons with Mari were fun, and the women became good friends. Anna thinks she's still not very good with Dutch, but now she can get by. Sometimes she insists that they talk in it – she and Mari – so that she can keep in practise. Not today. She doesn't feel she wants to expend the energy required today, and Mari speaks English almost perfectly.

How's Joe?" Mari asks, once the machine's all set up and brewing.

"He's all right," Anna replies. "A bit moody. I think that's my

48

fault."

"What have you done?" Mari demands, coming to sit opposite Anna, who shrugs.

"I'm bound up with writing, you know. " She pulls her face into a dismissive expression. She doesn't really want to burden Mari with her worries, but they feel so close to the surface at the moment. "What about you? How are things?"

Mari pulls the corners of her generous mouth downwards. "Not so good, I'll admit it. I don't know what to do about Jan. I thought he was going to leave his wife but the last few weeks I haven't seen much of him. I'm scared that he'll stay with her now."

"Oh, Mari." Anna feels sympathetic. "Have you talked to him about it?"

"No. I'm frightened to bring up the subject. Here. Have a cigarette." She pokes a packet towards Anna who takes one and lights it with a match, and then does the same for her friend. "It's a mistake – getting involved with a married man – isn't it?" Mari says, blowing out smoke in a white-grey cloud.

"So they say. But you can't necessarily choose who you love, I suppose."

"I don't agree. I could have stopped it earlier, before I got so close to him. If I had denied myself a little pleasure to begin with, I would be all right now."

"But you might have seen it as a missed opportunity," Anna suggests. She likes to concentrate on Mari's problems. She thinks too much about herself these days.

"I would have felt better about myself," Mari insists. "It would have been a strong thing to do. Now I feel pathetic."

Anna shakes her head. "It's horrible to be powerless, but I

always think of you as strong."

"If I was, then I would leave him." Mari frowns sadly. "I can't face solitude at the moment, even though it's all I've got most of the time anyway. The promise of him occasionally seems to be better than nothing at all. I want him to break it off so that I can't blame myself for doing the wrong thing. Did you ever leave someone for no one, Anna?"

Anna considers carefully. "When I was married before, I left my husband and there wasn't another man around at the time. But it took me about two years to make up my mind to do it!" she adds in disgust. "I felt bored and out of place with him, but I didn't know if I should expect anything more."

"I'm not bored with Jan," Mari admits. "I'm just traumatised with him."

"Just suppose he left his wife and was available all the time," Anna suggests. "How would you feel then?"

Mari thinks about this. "Ecstatic at first. That's all I can see. I can't tell what would follow. I can't imagine it. That's why I'm not a writer. I can't put myself in another place." She gets up to pour out coffee into yellow mugs and there are some moments of silence. Intense thoughts like violent weather batter the two women. "You're so lucky," Mari says in a while as she sits back down in her chair. "Joe's so devoted to you."

Anna gulps down a surge of emotion. She knows she could take this opportunity to talk. "He troubles me," she admits. "I feel there are things he does that I don't know about. We seem to have lost some closeness recently."

"What sorts of things?" Mari asks with interest.

"I don't know." Anna shrugs. "Sometimes I think it's women,

but that's nothing new. I don't think he's ever been entirely faithful to me. It isn't his nature, but it doesn't mean anything. I don't feel threatened by it. But there's something else now. I'm not sure how long it's been going on." She shrugs again, and drags on her cigarette. She blows out the smoke in a long slim stream. "I'm not making sense, am I?"

"You do seem to be a bit down," Mari tells her. "What a pair we are! Maybe we should drink some wine and drown our sorrows."

"I want to go back to England," Anna says, surprising herself. "I remember feeling whole there for a while; content and peaceful. I wasn't completely happy, but I felt easy in my mind. At least it seems that way when I look back. Maybe it wasn't so good." She feels exasperated with herself, searching back through memories, trying to find a tranquil moment in her life; a moment without cares. She remembers one, so fleeting, but it leads to other, painful thoughts. She thinks she grasps an idea. "It seems to me that happiness can't be an aspiration. It seems that it comes once in a while for a few hours or days, and then turns into normality. It sounds depressing, but how could it ever last longer?"

"I'm afraid you might be right," Mari says thoughtfully. "Have you talked to Joe about your worries?"

Anna shakes her head. "I can't. It surprises me, but I just can't do it. It would seem like an accusation and, if what I suspect is true, I don't know where it might lead, what ghosts it might revive. I don't want to think about it." She takes another drag on her cigarette.

"Will you tell me what it is?" Mari coaxes her.

"No." Anna looks at her friend kindly, she hopes. "I'm sorry. There's too much baggage attached to it, Mari. The explanation would take too long. Besides, I could be wrong."

51

"I think you should talk to him." Mari nods.

"Yes. And you should talk to Jan," Anna tells her in retaliation. "Tell him what you want."

Mari rolls her eyes and sighs in agreement.

On her way home, Anna sits for a while by the side of the canal, huddled against the encroaching cold in her big sweater and her jacket. Over on the other bank, a couple of small boats are moored. An old man is pottering around on one, doing nothing much except being in a place he likes. She watches him without seeing. She tries to follow through the implications of her thoughts, but they all lead to the same inevitable conclusion. She can hardly bear to think any more. Whatever subject she starts with, she always ends up in the same place. It bores her with its pervasion, this worry. Maybe she should simply accept what she believes to be true, and carry on. But she knows she can't. It feels like such a terrible betrayal. A broken promise from one she thought incapable of such a thing.

She remembers his promises when he left her the first time, so ardent and certain, and her awash with misery, feeling that she had lost her life. But she had not. It was hard at the start. Minutes dragging by like days, and everything in monochrome; tiredness and no sleep. But gradually she had recovered. That was when she started to write. She remembers her first efforts with fond embarrassment and she smiles. And he had come back, though not to stay, not for many years, not until she had almost lost all hope of him. At first he had returned for holidays, and they had been together as before, but then came that terrible time in France. The shock of it grips her stomach, and the shame, and the hatred.

On the other bank of the canal, a tall man is walking. At first Anna, deep in her memories, does not notice him, but something attracts her attention – the wheezing squeak of a coot, or an oil-starved bicycle wheel – and she looks up. By this time, he is walking away, but there is something familiar about the back of him; about the way his hands rest in his trouser pockets; about the length and lope of his gait. She feels her heartbeat quicken, and she watches him intently as he moves further and further away. She feels a great urge to follow him, but there is no bridge nearby and, if he turns away down a side street, her pursuit will be in vain. Besides, it isn't him. She knows that. The man is dead. And even if he weren't, he wouldn't be here. And after all this time, how could her memory be accurate? She pulls her gaze away from the figure, by now too far away to be remarkable. She stands up and begins to walk towards her home, closing her eyes for a second to blink away the tears that come too easily these days.

eight

Harry Smith had done too much flying to bother being scared of it. He had no particular fear of heights or depths or enclosed spaces or crowds. He wasn't over-fond of snakes, but he concentrated on disliking the poisonous ones. He considered it prudent to avoid things that liked to kill you.

Tina Philpott, after she had overcome her original frostiness, seemed happy to chat to him. She still seemed to be easily embarrassed and a little reserved in certain ways, but she appeared to be getting more comfortable. But then, as they approached Sky Harbour airport in Phoenix, as the signposts alongside the highway indicated it was getting closer, Harry could sense her tension growing, and she spoke to him less and less.

He picked up their tickets from the airline desk, and then checked in. She was quiet throughout. They walked together to a café where Harry got a bite to eat. Tina did not want any food. She ordered a glass of wine and sat silently opposite Harry while he munched on a tortilla. At length, they made their way to the departure gate and sat waiting for the call.

"I'm sorry, Harry," she said, turning to him suddenly, eyes like saucers and the strain showing in her jaw. "I'm not being rude. I know it's irrational. I just hate it. I can't talk. I'll be all right when we get there."

"No problem." He smiled at her. "Tell you what. If we crash, I'll let you off my fee." He meant to reassure her, but her eyes widened even further. She looked horrified. "Sorry," he mumbled. "Bad joke."

She turned away, staring straight ahead of her, and then she closed her eyes.

A few minutes later a stewardess came and instructed them to board the plane. Harry could see that Tina was holding herself rigid. He felt sorry for her, but he wondered why she had wanted to come with him if it caused her this much grief.

Throughout the journey – which was hardly more than a couple of hours long – he stole glances at her. She was tense and white, everything shot through with adrenaline. At one point he felt an urge to put his arm around her; to hold her and calm her, but he knew it would be neither appropriate nor helpful. Even if they had been closer, she would have to deal with the fear herself. He could not take it from her.

He saw her turn to the window as the plane began its descent. Now she seemed to be excited, or rather she exuded that odd sort of excitement bordering on terror induced by an over-exhilarating fairground ride. As they approached the runway, he could see her relaxing. When the wheels touched the tarmac, she clasped her hands together and laughed softly with the sort of sound he had only ever heard from women in his bed before. She turned to him, eyes shining with elation. He realised that he was staring at her.

"I *love* landing!" she exclaimed, bubbling over with relief.

"Hey, I thought that was the most dangerous part," Harry laughed.

"Oh, well, I don't claim to be logical about it," she smiled. "I'm just so glad to be back on the ground!"

Harry chuckled, and they gathered together their sparse luggage and disembarked. It surprised him that Tina seemed to have come all the way to the States with just a small roll-bag, but that was all that she had with her now. No cases to check in and out. He supposed that she wasn't planning to stay long. Nevertheless, most of the women he had known needed three suitcases just to get through the weekend. Tina's approach impressed him. He liked to travel light himself.

They took a taxi to the motel, bought hot coffee in plastic cups from a machine, and went to their separate rooms.

The following morning, Harry was awake at seven as usual. He showered and shaved, then called through to Tina Philpott's room at seven-thirty.

"Tina? Hi. You awake?"

"Hardly." Her voice was deep and husky with sleep. Harry felt a frisson slip through his flesh at the sound of it. It surprised him.

"Sorry," he said. "I thought we should get going fairly soon – get on the trail. Meet me at eight by the coffee machine?"

"All right," she said.

They snatched a quick breakfast and then went to call on an old acquaintance of Harry's – an ex-cop who had set up on his own as a private eye. He called himself Steven J MacArthur these days. He had a shiny brass plate on his office door advertising the fact. He had a nice leather chair and a big mahogany desk. He had an attractive secretary and a distinguished kind of look about him. He had short, wavy, mid-brown hair, an aquiline nose, grey eyes and a permanent smile.

"Hi Harry, old pal." Steven J MacArthur greeted him with a strong handshake. "And who is this pretty young lady?" He smiled ingratiatingly at Tina.

"Tina Philpott, Steven J MacArthur." Harry introduced them. He noticed that Tina had gone very stiff.

"Pleased to meet you, Mr MacArthur." She smiled carefully.

"You too, honey. Call me Steve." He put his hand on her back and propelled her to one of his visitors' chairs. Harry thought he saw her flinch, but he wasn't sure. Tina sat very upright in the chair, a kind of fixed, polite look on her face.

"Well, old pal, how are things over in downtown Flagstaff?" MacArthur asked. "Always plenty going on here," he continued without waiting for a reply. "Murder, robbery, arson, you name it. Real hotbed. Plenty of work. You oughtta come over, Harry. You make-a a lotta money, hah?" He put on a bad Italian accent and grinned a little wider. "Course, I keep in touch with the boys, you know. Never hurts to know what's going on in terms of crime et cetera. At the end of the day it always comes down to who you know, eh Harry? It's good to keep a few contacts. Honey, can I get you some coffee?" He suddenly addressed Tina whose attention appeared to have wandered.

"Pardon?" she said in surprise. She looked at Harry questioningly, then back at MacArthur. "Oh, yes please. Can I smoke in here?"

"Sorry honey. No smoking policy." MacArthur shook his head, corners of his mouth turned down as he pointed to the wall where a sign backed up his statement. "Besides, it's *real* bad for you in terms of your health, baby. Maybe it'll do you good to go without for an hour or so. At the end of the day, you know, heart disease... lung cancer... emphysema." He shook his head and tutted, then pressed the button on his intercom and asked his secretary to bring them coffee.

Harry noticed that one corner of Tina's mouth had begun to twitch. He gathered that she wasn't very interested in MacArthur's advice. He allowed himself a tiny mental chuckle. "Yeah, uh, about my call yesterday," he said. "Sorry to bother you and so on, but we're trying to move quickly here as I said, and the more enquiries we can run in parallel, the better."

"Well, sure thing, Harry. I understand that. Understand we're after your brother, honey. Up from coke city, huh?" He cackled to himself.

Tina issued MacArthur with a polite smile. "I think you'll find that the cocaine cartel is more active in Medellín than Bogotá," she told him.

"Well, hush my mouth!" MacArthur put on a big expression of surprise. "Brains as well as beauty. You wanna watch that one, Harry. Hah!" He cackled again. "Course you had some old contacts with them guys, didn't you Harry? When was that?" He looked at Harry expectantly.

Harry was taken aback. He wasn't sure that he wanted Tina to know about that. "Yeah that was way back," he said dismissively.

At that moment the secretary came in with coffee. By the time she left again, MacArthur seemed to have forgotten about Harry's past.

"Course, I'm right in the middle of a *real* messy one at the moment," MacArthur said, sipping his coffee from a green cup with a gold rim, his little finger carefully crooked whilst a large chunky signet ring adorned its neighbour. "You wouldn't believe the things that go on. Not for the ears of young ladies." He smiled in a kind of sickly way at Tina. "Even if they do have coke-dealing families! Hah!"

Tina looked murderous.

"Yeah, well, if we could just…" Harry tried to rescue the situation.

"Course, at the end of the day… money," MacArthur stated. "It's what it comes down to, Harry, pal. They just wanna get all they can. They get vicious, you know, honey." He turned to address Tina. "Vengeful. It ain't a pretty thing."

Tina's face had taken on a glazed expression of polite disinterest. She sipped at her coffee sedately and nodded occasionally when MacArthur addressed her.

At around eleven, they emerged from Steven J MacArthur's office onto the street. As soon as she was outside, Tina lit a cigarette and smoked it furiously. She finished it in less than two minutes, and then lit another which she drew on more calmly.

"So, he's an old friend of yours, is he?" she enquired of Harry in an icy tone.

"Acquaintance," he corrected her.

"My God! I was very nearly bored to death in there," she said crossly.

Harry looked at her. Her forehead was furrowed into an angry knot and her eyes were sparking at him, challenging him. He grinned. "I guess he does tend to tack around the subject somewhat," he admitted.

"Tack around the subject?" Tina said incredulously. She shook her head and muttered something like: "complete waste of space," half under her breath.

"I gather you didn't like him too well then?" Harry was grinning broadly, but Tina apparently wasn't seeing the joke.

"I'm glad you find it amusing that we've just wasted about two hours talking to that... that man," she spat. "We're supposed to be looking for my brother, not catching up on your old... acquaintances." She glared at him.

Harry grew more serious. "Calm down," he said gently. "I know the guy's a little... well, some women like that kind of thing I guess, but he did get us some information so our time wasn't completely wasted."

"What information?" Tina asked with a pout.

"The fact that none of the shipping or airline companies have received any bookings in the name of Diaz," Harry explained patiently. "That's quite helpful to us. It suggests that your brother hasn't left the country at least, and that he's still travelling by road. He may still be here."

Tina bit her lip. For an awkward moment, Harry thought she might cry. She took a deep breath. "I'm sorry Harry. I didn't mean to get angry with you," she mumbled. "I just found it very frustrating having to be nice to Mr MacArthur."

Harry didn't say anything. Tina had her head tilted forward so that her hair partially hid her face, but he could see that her cheeks were glowing red underneath it. He kept silent a moment longer, until she looked up at him sheepishly, squirming with embarrassment. He looked back at her, looked her in the eye, tried to keep a straight face, but a corner of his mouth twitched and gave him away.

"That's OK, honey," he said, smirking despite himself.

For a second, she looked utterly furious, then she burst out laughing and punched him gently on the arm. "Don't you *dare* call me that!" she giggled and Harry joined in with her laughter as they walked off down the street.

Later, Harry found himself alone in a bar, a small beer in front of him, his notebook open on the table, pen poised above it. Tina had returned to the motel, having been put off by the MacArthur experience. She said that she might wander out sometime and take a walk around the city. They had arranged to meet up again at six. It was mid-afternoon and Harry didn't feel that he was much further on with the case. He had jotted everything down that they'd found out so far and it didn't amount to a great deal. No one he'd so far spoken to had heard anything of Joey Diaz; there was no clue about where he had stayed. Maybe he hadn't come here at all. Perhaps Harry had been wrong to drag them out here. He wondered how Tina would react if he had to tell her he had made a mistake. He did not relish the prospect. She seemed a little volatile, to say the least. That stuff with MacArthur for instance. Harry didn't think he was *that* bad. The guy had just been trying to be friendly after all. Some women did seem to get offended over some trivial stuff.

Harry thought about Suzie. She was a good-tempered girl. She liked to have fun; enjoyed a laugh. Sure, they didn't have many deep conversations, but who needed that? Harry preferred to discuss serious things with guys, if he was honest. He found them to be more logical. He wondered whether Tina was a feminist. She had been married. That didn't mean a lot. She seemed to be pretty fond of her brother. It was odd that they hadn't seen each other for so long. He wondered why that was.

Harry pulled his thoughts back to the immediate problems he had to deal with. It was none of his concern what Tina Philpott's particular views were. She was his client and he preferred to keep his relationships with his clients on a purely professional level.

Harry looked around. He was the only person in the bar. It was a small place with green walls, green chairs and green baize on top of the tables. It had a slightly worn look about it overall. A tired feel; it had seen better days and could do with an overhaul. There was an ashtray close to Harry's right hand. It had the Camel cigarette logo embossed on it. Harry gazed at it for a while, lost in thought.

"Like another beer?" The bartender came by. She was small,

with short, white-blonde, spiky hair and dark eye make-up. She put him in mind of the actress in that British film, Breaking Glass. What was her name? Hazel O'Connor: that was it. Her nails were painted black and her lips maroon. She looked to be in her mid twenties. She had large breasts. Harry glanced at these. He was fond of such things.

"No thanks," he said. "Too early in the day for more than one."

"Not according to some guys. Mind you, we're pretty quiet at the moment. What's your line?"

"Oh, uh, doing a little snooping."

"Oh yeah?" She looked interested. "Who you after then?"

"Guy named Diaz. Joey Diaz," Harry told her.

She shook her head and pursed her lips. "Ain't heard of that guy." She was leaning on his table with her left hand. Her breasts hung slightly to that side, attracted by gravity. Harry thought she had no brassiere on. He could just make out her nipples through the cloth of her tee shirt. "I'll keep my ears open though." She stood upright.

"He may have moved on by now," Harry said.

"Everybody's always movin' on." She shrugged. "You ought to talk to my friend O'Brien. He knows every damn thing goes on in this city."

"Hey, that wouldn't be John O'Brien by any chance?" Harry grinned. "I heard he'd moved over this way."

"Sure! That's the guy. You know him?" She looked surprised.

"I had a vague acquaintance of that name a while back," Harry admitted.

"He's kinda short, kinda weasley-featured. In here most nights. He's after some Polish guy currently. Can't remember the name."

"Oh, right, well the description fits the O'Brien I know. Maybe I'll drop by later; renew old friendships."

"Hey, I wrote it down." She rushed away and disappeared behind the bar for a moment. She emerged shortly, clutching something. "You ever heard of this?" She showed him the piece of paper in her hand. It was white, four inches square with a little round hole in the top left hand corner. Across it was scrawled one word: 'Byszewski'.

nine

A week later he meets them again. Everything will be arranged. No money changes hands. No pieces of paper are signed. Nothing is written down. There will be no tangible evidence of this transaction.

After the business is completed, Joseph decides to have lunch in an Italian restaurant on the Lange Leidsewarstraat. There are red and white checked table cloths and a bright atmosphere. Joseph chooses a light pasta dish with garlic bread and bottled water. There are not many other diners in. The waiter is friendly. He knows Joseph. He has seated him at a table placed with discretion in mind, away from the window and the centre of the room, over next to the wall in a corner. Joseph prefers this. He toys with the idea of a glass of wine with his meal, but decides against it. He prefers to drink alcohol late at night, before sleeping. It makes him sluggish during the day, and he cannot bear to be under par. Joseph is seldom ill, but even the hint of a head-cold will throw him into a foul mood. He will go swimming later in the afternoon, once his lunch is digested. He swims fast and strongly. It keeps him fit. He is proud of his body. He lights a Gitanes while he waits for his food to arrive and pours water from the bottle into a glass from which he takes a sip.

It's a bright day. The sun shines, but the wind is laced with ice. People out on the street smile at the blue sky, their faces bare between woollen hats and scarves. A family of four sits around a table by the window: mother, father and two children, perhaps eight and four years old. A boy and a girl. The ideal set. The children are well-behaved although intermittently the younger one will let out a loud noise, excitement overtaking her, but then she will put her hand across her mouth and make her brown eyes round with contrition, acknowledging her mistake. The parents are proud of their little ones. It's easy to see it. There is love apparent in the group; a wholeness and a quiet happiness. Joseph wonders how life might be with children. He knows he's too selfish to be a good father. Besides, Anna wouldn't contemplate it. A child would probably come between them. They would both be jealous of it; the attention it took from the other. He smiles to himself. What a pair they are! Still children themselves at heart; spoilt and self-centred in their way. He thinks they are very alike.

The waiter brings Joseph his food and offers him parmesan cheese and black pepper to top the pasta. Joseph accepts these and begins to eat. He is in no hurry. He can relax and take his time. He's pleased with the morning's deal. Now he can get to work and set it all up. That's the enjoyable part. That's where the interest is. Joseph likes to think up something different for each new client. He's proud of the ideas he generates; his cleverness. His father taught him well. He appreciates that.

Joseph notices a man sitting half-hidden in another corner. He didn't see the man come in. He must have been there all along, or did he arrive whilst Joseph was preoccupied with his thoughts? Joseph is annoyed with himself. He should be more observant, he thinks. It's not like him to miss things. He's not a day-dreamer like Anna. She can get completely lost in her head, but Joseph thinks this is a luxury that he cannot afford.

He can only see the man's hands, which are holding a copy of the London Times in front of his face. A little dark hair is visible. Joseph judges that the man is taller than himself. As the man turns the pages of the newspaper, Joseph catches glimpses of his face. There is something familiar about it, but he cannot place it. Has he seen the man before? Maybe he just reminds him of someone. The man looks at Joseph, perhaps aware of the latter's attention. He makes no acknowledgement, no sign of interest or recognition. He moves his eyes back to the page of his newspaper as he folds it neatly into a small square which he lays on the table beside the plate topped with pizza that the waiter brings him. He cuts the pizza carefully into segments, then lays down his knife and fork and picks up a piece in his left hand to eat it. He appears to be pondering over a crossword puzzle. He has picked up a pencil with his right hand and he writes something down. He glances up at Joseph again; looks longer this time as if to question the curiosity of which he is clearly aware. Joseph turns his head, casually moving his focus to the family in the window. The man looks down at his crossword. He eats his pizza quickly, then orders coffee before Joseph does the same.

Later, when he leaves the swimming pool complex, in the late afternoon, Joseph thinks he sees the man again. He's sure he catches sight of him. He thinks the man is watching, standing on a street corner, hands thrust down into the pockets of well-cut loose trousers, rolled up newspaper tucked under his arm. The street is crowded and a mass of people pass in front of the man obscuring Joseph's view. And then he is gone. He's slipped away in the bustle and Joseph did not see him go, nor notice the direction of his departure. Joseph feels uneasy. Is he being followed then? By whom? He moves in circles of mistrust. The people he deals with are, by their nature, duplicitous. If someone is checking up on him then what are they looking for? Which side of the law are they coming from?

Joseph takes a tram-car home, although he despises public transport. He is not comfortable, batched up with random samples of humanity in the clanking, swaying carriage. In his teenage years he sometimes travelled on buses driven by lunatics at break-neck speeds to foil bandits. The experience remains with him, stark and scary. He learned to drive and tried to put it behind him, but Amsterdam was not designed to accommodate the motor car. He doesn't drive much here.

She's not around when he gets in so he takes himself into the studio. It's well organised and clean – unlike the common conception of an artist's lair. The walls are painted pure white. There are two large roof windows and some very bright electric lighting for the darker months of the year. Two easels stand in separate corners and between these numerous paint tubes hang in bespoke racks: oils and acrylics. He doesn't work in watercolours. He thinks them too feminine. Jars of painting media – linseed oil and liquin and the like – are lined up neatly on shelves. Brushes are stored in wide drawers in a chest made from beech wood, all sorted by size and shape and application. He uses paper palettes and throws the used one away at the end of a session. It's all neat with no mess. He clears up spills immediately. Interrupting the flow of his work is not a problem for him. He thinks himself disciplined and meticulous. He prides himself on it.

He regards his current half-finished work with curiosity but no passion. The other things in his life are crowding his mind and all he sees in front of him is a blur of clashing colours. He stares for a time as the fog of his thoughts starts to clear. Moodily, rather irritably, he pulls a tube of ivory black oil paint from the rack and squeezes a fat worm of it onto a fresh palette. He goes to the chest where the brushes are stored and extracts one which is long and thin-tipped. It's shaped like a wedge of cheese and made from some synthetic material. When he bought it he liked its look and feel. He buys brushes often and throws them away directly their bristles start to splay.

Going back to the canvas, he dips the brush into the undiluted paint and begins to outline sections of colour with a narrow black border. Almost immediately, the painting takes on a new clarity and a sort of Japanese flavour. He's pleased with this. He repeats the process on different areas of the picture. For the time being, the attention and dexterity required ease his mind. He finds that he can concentrate on the movement of the brush and the consistency of the lines of paint to the exclusion of everything else. It often happens this way. He wonders if this is what is meant by 'art' – this absorption. He's sure it isn't. He's heard other painters talk of getting up in the middle of the night, niggled sleepless by some aspect of their work. That never happens to him. When he walks out of the studio, he forgets about it. To paint, for him, is always a deliberate decision. It serves purposes: it fills his time when he's nothing else to do; it clears his mind when he's pondering on some accounting problem; it calms him when he's had an argument with Anna; it occupies him in the hours when she's out walking or absorbed in her writing.

He has made a mistake. He glares at it in anger for a moment and then rushes to the turpentine bottle. He soaks a small sponge in the smelly liquid and douses the area to remove the errant paint. It leaves a dirty grey stain. He works at it, trying to eradicate the error, but it won't go back to its pristine state. All right. He will have to try to incorporate it somehow. It's not a disaster. Nothing's ever that bad. Perhaps it could lead to something that might even enhance the work. He stands back and considers it carefully. He decides he will introduce larger areas of blue-grey at appropriate points. Quickly and methodically, he works out where these should be, and then he mixes a new colour and makes delicate changes in precise positions. He's pleased now with the result. The new dark areas are good. They add gravitas to the painting and suit his mood. They make a strong statement. Later, he could overlay them with a thin red wash; layer them up and give them a depth like Mark Rothko's work.

He laughs cynically, quietly. If only those art critics knew how easy this is for him, they would cast him aside as a charlatan. Anna doesn't know it either. She thinks everyone's like her, but he knows better. Her work is her life; it comes from her soul. She thinks his painting is the same, but he can see that she's confused by the way he can leave it aside so easily. He doesn't talk about it much with her. He doesn't want her to know the truth of it. She doesn't talk much of her writing with him. Sometimes he wishes she would. He thinks he could help her, but she thinks she must work it all out for herself. When he reads her books, he finds that her characters are invariably sympathetic people. They're well-drawn and well-rounded, but too kind, he thinks. Even the ones who are supposed to be bad have their cruel natures explained by some awful event in their past – an abandoned or abusive childhood has hardened them against the world. Most often they are redeemed by some challenge that they face. He thinks he could tell her a thing or two. He's known people in his time who have had loving families, good friends and comfortable lives. Yet these men could hang another upside down and set fire to him if crossed. Oh, he's known pure evil in men, but he can't tell her about it. He loves her innocence and her trust in humanity. There's a part of him that can't bring himself to destroy it.

He hears the front door of the apartment open. She's back. He stops painting, folds up the paper palette and throws it into the large shiny dustbin that's there for artistic waste. He cleans the brush he's been using and stands it in a special rack for drying. He glances at the painting. He considers that it looks interesting. He switches off the lights in the studio and goes out into the living room, shutting the door behind him.

She cooks dinner for them. She is a gifted cook. She takes pride in most things she does, but she's not over-adventurous in her ways. Sometimes, if she finds something difficult, she will give it up rather than look a fool. Joseph is still worried about the man he saw earlier. He managed to forget about it for a while when he was painting, but now the concern has returned. He tries to persuade himself that he's imagining things; that there's no problem, but he doesn't succeed. He frets, but he can't talk to her about it. If he told her, she would want to know more and there are things he won't tell her. She wouldn't understand his reasons. Sometimes he doesn't understand them himself, but he's tied up with it now. They don't like it if you try to resign. It's a job for life.

He eats the food she lays before him, insisting that they sit at the table tucked away in a dining area which is screened off from the main room by a curtain coloured blue and gold. A blind made from the same material is pulled down over the window which looks out of the back of the apartment onto other dwellings. Anna says that the metal component parts of the many fire escape staircases out there make it look like a prison. She doesn't like to look out that way. She prefers to sit near the big window at the front, overlooking the canal. She can gaze out of it for hours. She pleads with him to join her at the little table there.

"I don't want to be on show," he tells her.

"Why? What have you done? What are you afraid of?" Her tone is light, but he thinks he catches accusation lurking. Maybe it's his own guilt that makes him hear it.

"Nothing at all." He shrugs. "You know I don't like it."

"How's the London show coming along?" she asks. Again he wonders if she suspects him.

"I don't know if it'll come off. The people don't strike me as reliable. We'll have to wait and see what happens."

"That'll be a pity," she sighs. "I keep thinking about London lately. I seem to be getting obsessed with it. Sometimes I really miss the place. And the people. I remember what it used to be like this time of year. Always raining. Always dark."

"Another miserable city!" he states blankly. "And you know it's difficult for us there. We gave all that up when we came here, Anna. Family. Friends. It was part of the deal. Getting rid of the past."

She sighs again. "Sometimes I wonder if you can. It's always there in your mind, isn't it?"

"What are you saying?" He is worried now. So many implications in so few words. "Would you rather have your old life back?" He looks at her steadily. Her eyes look shifty to him. It's a straight choice in his mind: England or him. She can't have both. She knows that.

"Some of it was good," she says after a moment. "But I always wanted you more. Waited all those years. I couldn't give you up, Joe."

"I'm glad to hear it." He nods, eating some of his food. "How's the book going?"

"All right." She shrugs. "It's a slog at the moment, but I'm about halfway through. Not too bad. Listen! Let's go out later. I'd like some beer tonight."

"Oh, would you?" He grins at her. The spark of her old self is there, and he responds to it with a quick jolt of joy.

71

"Yes. The Café de Doelen," she decides, smiling with self-satisfaction.

"Can't you choose somewhere with a bit more class?" he complains good-naturedly.

"No. I like it. It feels comfortable."

He shrugs, giving in to her. He doesn't mind. He likes to see her happy.

Closing time is one a.m. on weekdays. They wander home. She's a little bit drunk. She drinks the local lager beer in half-litres, used to pints when she was in England. He drinks smaller quantities. He can't stand hangovers. He likes it when she gets tipsy. She's affectionate then and often happy. She giggles at a man who asks them for money as they cross the Damrak. Joseph tells her off in a kindly way, and she looks contrite. He gives the man five guilders. It's nothing to him.

"Sorry," she says. "I'm drunk!" She looks surprised.

Joseph laughs at her. "It looks that way," he says, nodding.

She looks at him. She narrows her eyes and curls up the corners of her mouth. He hasn't seen her do that for a while. He grabs her and kisses her right there on the street. She breaks away from him and runs away giggling. He catches her in a moment. He is much faster, much stronger than she. She is bubbling with laughter.

"You used to do that to me when we were young," he tells her. "Usually at the most inappropriate times."

"It was always accidental," she says with feigned innocence.

"Oh, was it?" he says sceptically. "I think you've been bad practically from the moment you were born."

"I had no role models to teach me otherwise," she says indignantly. "It came quite naturally."

"That's true," he says. "Come home with me. I want to fuck you."

"Oh all right," she sighs. "If you must." And then she puts her arms around his neck and kisses him sexually before they walk off quickly in the direction of their apartment, their arms each around the other's waist.

The tall man with dark hair sees them unlock the front door of the building and slip inside, only concerned with one another. It's been a long day for him. He's tired but he can rest tomorrow for a while. He feels sad. He knew the truth before he came here. The old man told him because he needed to know in order to do his job, and because of the past. Nevertheless, he realises now that there was a hope in him that things might have changed. He sees that this is not the case. He hunches his shoulders against the cold, pushes his hands further down into his trouser pockets, kicks at a piece of litter that lies innocently near his feet, and then makes his way back to his rented apartment, not far away. He doesn't know what the outcome of all this will be. It's a job that he would rather not have done.

ten

Harry got back to the motel at four-thirty in the afternoon. He gave MacArthur a call, listened to what he said, and decided that maybe Tina Philpott did have a point after all. MacArthur's secretary had been checking out motels for him, and had established that Joey Diaz stayed at the Vagabond Inn on Van Ness for two nights. He called there but the receptionist asked him to try again in the morning when the manager would be in. She wasn't authorised to deal with enquiries, she said. Harry didn't mind. He had an interesting evening planned. He wondered if Tina was back from her wandering yet.

Whistling quietly to himself, he sauntered out into the corridor, along and across to her room. He knocked softly on her door.

"Who is it?" she called.

"Me. Harry," he said.

"Hang on."

He waited for a little while and then she opened the door. He went to speak and failed. She was wearing a tiny pair of shorts – jeans sawn off at the tops of her legs – and a white tee shirt which clung to her damp skin. Her nipples stood out clearly through it. She had her hair twirled up in a towel on top of her head. Harry's mouth had gone completely dry.

Her face reddened slightly as he looked at her. Her hands made little self-conscious movements as though she hadn't realised how exposed she was before and was now trying to cover it up or apologise for it. "I was having a shower," she explained nervously. "I... there doesn't seem to be a bathrobe... sorry. Er... come in." She turned around and led him into the room. The shorts barely covered the cheeks of her backside. She couldn't possibly be wearing anything under them. Harry felt like he needed a nice cold shower himself.

She sat down on the bed, one leg bent over the edge of it, straight in front of her, the other crooked slightly to one side. Harry thought he caught a glimpse of black pubic hair. He wasn't sure. He tried not to look. She rubbed her hair with the towel and let it fall down all mussed and tousled up; all full of sex. She looked up at him expectantly. He pulled his brain into gear.

Harry explained about the Vagabond Inn. She looked pleased.

"So," she said dryly. "MacArthur does have a use after all. Or rather his secretary does. I've a feeling we might have got more sense out of her altogether."

Harry shrugged and let the comment pass. He told her about the encounter in the green bar. Her expression grew serious and worried. "So someone else is looking for him," she concluded. "I wonder if it's father. I bet it is. Why can't he just leave us alone!" She thumped her fist down lightly on the bed. "Always poking his nose in."

"Maybe he's worried about you," Harry suggested.

"Hah!" She leaned over to a small cabinet by the bed where a cigarette packet and a large box of matches lay. She plucked a cigarette out of the packet. Her long fingers manipulated it elegantly, placed it between her lips, and then she lit it, putting out the flame of the match with a deft flick of her slim wrist.

"Anyhow, I'll go along this evening and see what I can find out," Harry said. He found his attention was constantly distracted by the movements she made.

"Can I come?" she looked up at him hopefully.

"It wouldn't be a good idea." He shook his head. He was still standing, loitering at the end of the bed. He felt awkward. He didn't think he could sit down next to her on the bed. There was a chair – a comfortable looking recliner covered in soft yellow fabric – but it was on the other side of the room. Besides, she hadn't invited him to sit down. He pushed his fringe back out of his eyes, then scratched the back of his head. His left hand was in the pocket of his trousers. He shifted his weight onto his right foot. "See, if you look anything like your brother, O'Brien may get suspicious. Also, he might not want to say too much in front of a stranger and so on. It's best if I go alone and make up some story about why I'm in town."

"Maybe I could hide somewhere. You know, a darkened corner or something." She seemed to be only half serious. "Sorry, I can see it's a bad idea." She smiled up at him apologetically. "It's just that, being here, I'll wonder what's happening... you know."

"I know it'll be real dull," Harry sympathised. "Maybe you could go see a movie. There's a theatre not far from here."

"Hmm. I like the cinema," she mused. "But I don't think I could concentrate. I may as well get a pizza or something; spend the evening staring at the TV." She shrugged and twisted her mouth into a wry little grin.

"Yeah, well, whatever. Listen. Depending on what time I get back, I'll give you a call. It it's early enough, we'll go for a beer, huh?"

She brightened visibly. "Great!" she said enthusiastically.

Harry stopped off in a burger joint on his way to the green bar. He ordered a large burger, large fries, large coke. He seemed to have an appetite on him this evening for some reason. As he ate his food, he thought about Tina Philpott again. So much for keeping things on a professional level, he chastised himself. What was it about her that caused such a reaction in him? Usually he liked women built rounder, especially on the upper levels, but there was something about her, about the way she moved. She had a kind of innocent sensuality, and the look in her eyes sometimes when she wasn't trying to hide herself... She seemed vulnerable in some respect, no matter how she tried to hide it, and it reached inside him somehow. When Clive Mason had asked him to take care of her the day before, Harry had agreed to it without really registering it. He had thought no more about it. Now, he found that he wanted to carry out Mason's wishes. He felt protective towards her.

He took a long draught of coke, felt the bubbles rise back up in his chest and belched softly and politely. The burger bar was garishly lit, the fluorescent tubes making the worst of people's complexions. Harry looked around, thinking he could be anywhere in the States, thinking how alike these places all were. He felt odd this evening. Out of place. It was as if something had shifted inside him, but he didn't know what it was. He felt a strange kind of restlessness in himself; a dissatisfaction, but he didn't know why or where it had come from. He wondered for a moment whether there was something more he wanted out of life than what he had.

Harry finished his food and walked out into the dark evening. It was eight-thirty now and the street lamps were shining, their lights haloed by a very fine mist that hung in the air dropping the temperature down by a couple of degrees. Harry felt a chill run through him. He was only wearing light clothes, but he wasn't sure that the shudder had anything to do with the atmospheric conditions. In the distance he heard police car sirens start up, sudden and ugly. A cable car passed by, clanking upwards, and out of it came a woman's voice, raised in delight: "He's in love!" she exclaimed. Harry looked up quickly to catch sight of the words' source, but he could only see the face of a man looking out in his direction. A Latin-American looking man. A good looking man. Perhaps thirty-five years old.

Harry strolled on up the hill in the direction of the Green bar.

eleven

Her head aches a little bit the next morning, but she doesn't mind. She likes the reality of a hangover. Later, when the light has gone from the day, she meets Mari in a café where the walls are painted black. There are several large frameless mirrors hung on them, and the tables are made from shiny metal. Mari has come from her office. She is smartly dressed, but the day tells in her face. She looks tired. They drink coffee. They smoke cigarettes. The saucers under their cups clank on the surface of the table. The atmosphere in the café is chilly and smoky. The sounds are harsh and sibilant. The syrupy smell of sweet pastries mixes with the acrid tobacco.

"I've seen Jan a couple of times recently," Mari says in response to Anna's enquiries. "I asked him what his plans are in a roundabout kind of way. Nothing too overt. No ultimatums. I'm not brave enough for that."

"So what did he say?" Anna is eager to learn.

Mari shrugs. "That he needs time."

Anna is sceptical. "Oh, really?" she says ironically. "How much time? How long have you been seeing him now?"

"About a year," Mari moans. "I know, I know. Don't tell me how foolish I am. I know it already."

"It's him I'm annoyed with, not you."

"What about you?" Mari asks. "Did you talk to Joe?"

Anna shakes her head. "No. I'm worse than you. I didn't even have enough courage for that. The trouble is that in my case, talking about it can't change anything. If what I believe is true…" She raises both hands in front of her, palms upwards in a gesture of hopelessness. "Nothing I can say will change things."

"Maybe it isn't true," Mari suggests. "Maybe he could put your mind at rest."

"Perhaps." Anna nods, but she doesn't have much hope left in her.

"I'm going to go skating at the weekend," Mari says more brightly. "Will you come?"

"All right." Anna smiles. She likes to skate. She learnt to do it when she was quite young. She has an idea. "Mari," she says, reaching out, touching the other's hand. "How would you like a holiday?"

"Oh, I'd love one," Mari sighs. "I haven't taken much leave this year. An odd day here and there. There hasn't been a good reason to go away."

"I want to go to England," Anna says. She's getting excited at the prospect. "Joe won't come with me, but we could go. Just a short break – a few days, perhaps a week."

"The weather is no better than here." Mari frowns.

"I know," Anna admits. "It would just be a change of scene. London's brilliant. Especially in the rain." She smiles remembering it. The shiny streets and bright shop windows.

"You're an odd one." Mari laughs at her. "Anyone else would want to fly south for the winter."

"So you don't fancy it?" Anna is disappointed.

"I didn't say that." Mari wags a finger at her. "It would be good to get away anywhere, quite honestly. I'll come with you if you like. When shall we go?"

"I don't know yet. I'll have to talk to Joe about it." Anna is nervous of this. "I've a feeling he might object, so…"

"Why should he mind?" Mari asks.

"Oh, he doesn't like me going off without him," Anna says. It's half the truth at least.

"Poor little boy!" Mari makes a face, pushing out her bottom lip, turning down the corners of her mouth.

"I know," Anna giggles. "Aren't they all?"

He's been out all day. She doesn't know where and he doesn't tell her. That's all right. It's quite usual. They don't pry into each other's every move. There isn't any need. She can see he's tired. He looks troubled. She wonders whether she should leave this discussion for another day, but she's eager to put things in motion. She doesn't want to delay. Nonetheless, she lets him eat in peace. She waits a while before she mentions the subject.

They are sitting on the sofa. He is drinking a small brandy. He likes to do that with coffee after an evening meal. He swirls the brandy around the bowl of the proper glass and regards it curiously.

"I saw Mari this afternoon," she tells him. "She's a bit low."

"She should pack it in with that guy," he says emphatically. "It's stupid to carry on. He'd have left his wife by now if he was going to."

Anna knows that Joseph likes Mari. "Yes, I know," she sighs. "But it's easy for us to say, isn't it?"

He shrugs. He lights one of his Gitanes, narrowing his eyes against the smoke. "I wouldn't put up with it," he states.

"We talked about going away for a short break. Me and her. I know you're busy, so…" Anna falters.

He looks at her sharply. "I see," he says. "You won't go away with me for the winter, but you're happy to accompany your friend off on some jaunt."

"It's not the same thing," Anna explains. "It would only be a few days. I thought it would cheer her up; make her feel stronger."

"How altruistic you are," he says flatly.

"What's the problem?" she asks. "Do you mind?"

"I suppose not," he says, but she doesn't believe him. "Where will you go?"

"England," she states. She has been wondering whether to lie, but has decided against it.

He glares at her. "You can't!"

"Why not? There's no harm in it, surely?"

"You believe that no mistakes will be made?" He looks annoyed now.

She thinks his objections are partly due to jealousy. Her closeness to the others doesn't please him. She thinks he likes to keep her away from them. "I can cope," she says.

"You can't go," he tells her decisively.

She feels her anger returning. It's a feeling she hasn't had much in recent years. She remembers when it used to be more common. Maybe it has been smouldering constantly at the bottom of her. Maybe it's just been biding its time. "You're going to stop me then." She states it coldly and lights a cigarette for herself.

"You're going whether I like it or not?" he counters. "Why are you so stubborn about this, Anna? You know it's dangerous."

"I'm not the stubborn one. You'd keep me locked up if you could."

"That isn't true," he tells her. "You can do whatever you like, but this is different. You know it is. How can you be sure that Mari won't find out? And if she knows, what will she do? You can't be sure, Anna. It's too much of a risk. Or don't you care anymore?"

"And you, I suppose, never take any risks!" It's out of her

before she can stop it. She's furious with him. The thing he talks of seems trivial to her compared to what she suspects him of doing.

"What do you mean?" His eyes have turned to ice.

"Nothing," she mumbles. "I didn't mean anything." She doesn't want this matter out in the open. She can't stand to think about it. She doesn't want to know the truth. She wants to be able to fool herself for part of the time that she is mistaken.

He takes hold of her arm and holds it uncomfortably tightly. "I think you did mean something, Anna. I think we'd better have a serious talk about this."

"You're hurting my arm," she tells him. "There was a time when you would never have hurt me, Joe. There was a time when I believed that you loved me."

"Don't try to change the subject." He says it angrily, but he loosens his hold on her. "What risks do you think I take?"

She thinks quickly. "You sleep with other women," she says. "You can't think much of me if you need to do that." She sees that he relaxes slightly.

"I have done once or twice," he admits. "It doesn't mean anything. You know that."

"But why do it then?" she asks. She knows he does it more often than he says. She knows it isn't really important, but it's a convincing complaint.

"It's a challenge." He shrugs. "It doesn't affect us at all. You shouldn't worry about it."

"So it would be all right if I slept with other men, would it?" She asks, narrowing her eyes at him. She never has. Not since they've been together this time.

"It would be a different thing," he tells her. "It would mean more to you."

"Oh, I'm glad you know me so well," she declares. "Better than I know myself, evidently!"

"Are you planning it then?" he asks her. "Is that what your little jaunt to England will be for? Renewing old friendships?"

"Don't be ridiculous," she says. "I'm sick of your double standards, Joe. It seems to me that you think you should be free to do exactly as you please and that I should do as I'm told!"

"Women are different," he explains curtly. "Everything is tied up in the emotions. There's no rationality."

"Rubbish!" she shouts. "How dare you assume you know how I feel! How dare you! Women are not all the same any more than men are. If you think that, you're even more stupid than I thought!"

"You're simply proving my point," he says calmly. "I can't see why you're getting into this state, Anna. You seem to be determined to fight with me."

"I'm getting into this state because you won't trust me and yet you expect me to trust you," she says angrily. "Anything you do is all right; justifiable; not to be questioned. But you treat me like a child. You want to own me. You're so full of yourself that you think the whole world is yours to do with as you please. Well I'm a separate person from you, Joseph Mason. I'm entitled to do what I like with my life and I'm going to England whether you like it or not."

He stands up. "As you wish," he says coldly. "I'm going out. Maybe I'll find some more amenable company."

She watches him leave. Neither of them says another word. She feels spiteful towards him but, once he is gone, a niggle of doubt worms its way into her mind. Has she gone too far? Should she go to England despite his objections? What if he's right? She smokes a cigarette and wonders when he'll come back and apologise to her.

twelve

It was nine thirty in the evening and no sign of O'Brien yet. Harry sipped at a glass of beer, making it last. The character of the bar had changed now. Smoke hung in a grey-brown pall just above head level, held in place by the low ceiling and the lack of adequate ventilation. There were a comfortable number of people in there at the moment but more were arriving by the minute and soon, Harry thought, it might get stifling. The air was already dense with the cigarette fug and the citrus reek of over-worked deodorants which almost, but not quite, obscured the underlying smell of sweat. The clientele was mostly male. They were, on the whole, nondescript types of men. They were badly dressed, many of them; not shabby but inelegant and clumsy. They wore trousers that didn't fit, and shirts that were too tight across expanding guts. A few wore hats, shiny with age and hair grease. Harry didn't think himself a particularly vain man but he liked to dress reasonably well. He felt out of place now in loose pale khaki chino trousers and his good linen shirt.

In a far corner of the bar, a badly made up transvestite sat with two male companions, one of whom was short and balding and full of theatrical exclamations which kept his listeners sporadically amused. Harry wondered idly why some men liked to dress as women. He couldn't see it himself. Still, what other folks did was up to them.

"Here's my friend." The bartender, still working well, had changed into a sparkly short dress for the evening shift. Her legs didn't really suit it, and she had wisps of curly brown hair nestling in her armpits.

Harry turned around and saw a man approaching. He had a thin, twisted little nose on a thin, beady-eyed face. The trousers he wore hung on him badly – the crotch of them had clearly never made contact with the crotch of him. His green-grey tweed jacket was too wide across the shoulders. It had leather patches on the elbows. He took off a trilby hat and smoothed his few precious strands of hair across the top of his shiny little head.

"Geraldine, my one and only love, have you got a glass of the old black for me, darlin'? The mists are getting up outside. Fair reminds me of old Dublin town."

Harry remembered O'Brien better now. He had never been entirely certain that the exaggerated Irishness wasn't a fake. He had a vague recollection of someone telling him that O'Brien had actually been born in Chicago, but the man himself was insistent that County Dublin was his place of origin.

"Friend of yours here, O'Brien." The bartender nodded towards Harry as she operated the tap to dispense Guinness into a tall straight glass.

O'Brien looked at Harry for a moment without recognition, and then he raised his eyes with a big cluck of the tongue, held out his hand and creased his face into a mischievous smile. "If it isn't old Harry Smith!" He said. "Bejazus, it's been a few years."

"Around seven of 'em if I'm not mistaken." Harry grinned back at him.

"Seven damned years!" O'Brien shook his head and leant on the bar next to Harry who was seated comfortably on a bar stool. "Time flies, as they say, don't they Harry? Tempus fugit."

"Indeed it does, old pal. How are you doing these days?" Harry raised his glass to the other man who lifted his own freshly delivered one, torrents of bubbles still streaming upwards in it.

"I'm doing pretty damned fine, and cheers to you, Harry."

87

O'Brien took a slurp out of his glass, leaving himself with a creamy-coloured moustache, which he licked off his upper lip with relish. "So tell me now, Harry, what is it brings you back to these parts now? Bejazus, they're a queer lot in this town and no mistake. Never a dull moment at all. Always something to be lookin' at."

"Oh, I'm snooping around on a case and so on." Harry nodded. "Looking for a guy. Some matrimonial kind of bust-up. You know the type of thing."

"Don't I just, Harry? Don't I just. People are forever getting themselves into a right old pickle. Now me and my good lady, we've been together twenty-two years come this Christmas, Harry. Twenty-two years, if you believe me. I don't regret that marriage. We go along all right the two of us. She doesn't interfere with me, if you get my meaning. She knows I like a glass of the old black, and she doesn't complain. That's the sort of woman you want now, Harry."

"Sounds pretty good to me," Harry agreed.

"Now, have you got yourself a girl, Harry? You used to be married, didn't you?"

"Oh way back now." Harry shrugged. "Can't say it suited me too well."

"No? Well, the married life isn't to everyone's taste, I suppose." O'Brien considered this for a moment, and then reached into his jacket pocket and extracted a packet of cigarettes. He offered one to Harry.

"No thanks." Harry held up his hand, the palm towards the packet.

"Now I had you down for a smoker, Harry, that I did." O'Brien regarded him, frowning slightly.

"Trying to give up," Harry said.

"Well, it's a terrible habit, but it gives a little pleasure to me," O'Brien sighed. "Tell me, Harry, do you ever bet on a horse at all?"

Harry admitted that he didn't.

"Lord alone, man, do you have no vices at all?" O'Brien laughed. It was a rasping sort of noise, cultivated through years of nicotine abuse. "I'm a man for the horses myself. I like to have a flutter. If you fancy it, you know, I know an excellent man for a tip. Now he comes up with the goods nine times out of ten, and maybe more than that. An excellent man. I could give you his name."

"Thanks for the offer, pal, but I'm not much of a gambling man." Harry pursed his lips and shook his head.

"Oh, now you're telling me and that trouble you were mixed up in as I remember it." O'Brien winked at him.

"Yeah, well, that was kind of accidental, if you get my drift, O'Brien. I had no idea of the consequences of that particular case."

"No? We've all got to watch out, to tell you the truth, Harry, and if you want to know it, I'm looking for some fellow come up from that part of the world just now. Doing a little bit of investigation. Keeping the old hand in."

"Yeah?" Harry showed a casual interest.

"These people do get themselves into a pickle, don't they just, Harry?"

Harry nodded. "I guess. This some drug-trafficker, then?"

"Who's that then?" O'Brien asked innocently.

"They guy you're looking for," Harry explained.

"Now why would you want to know that?" O'Brien grinned at him.

Harry smiled back, shrugged his shoulders, and indicated to the barmaid that he wanted another beer. He got a top-up for O'Brien at the same time. The Irishman had been drinking quickly, gulping down the dark liquid between sentences. "Oh just interested in stuff, you know," Harry said accepting a small glass of light beer from the bartender. "Can't keep the professional hat off and so on."

"It's our curiosity that gets us into trouble, isn't it Harry? Can't keep our damned noses out of anything. Well, if you want to know, it's a man by the name of Byszewski I'm looking for. Me and half a dozen others."

"Don't sound like no Colombian to me," Harry remarked

"Now I'm not saying I know anything about his origins." O'Brien shook his head and then gleefully grabbed his topped-up glass of Guinness from the bartender's hand, his eyes following it around until they faced front and he could take a great draught from it, screwing up his face with pleasure. "You're a top man there, Harry. And if you should change your mind about the horses now, I could assure you of a win, indeed I could."

"You're a generous man, O'Brien," Harry said, wondering how he might lead the conversation back in his desired direction.

"I've never been called mean," O'Brien admitted. "Never that. Many other things though. Indeed I have."

"Must be an important kinda case you're on with all those guys involved," Harry mused.

"Oh, now, I dare say it is." O'Brien pulled himself into a more upright position and stuck his chest out a little. "I dare say it is. It's a wealthy kind of a man who's running it, if you understand me Harry. A man with a lot of money. It's not supposed to have come from the drugs now, that's the thing they're saying, but bejazus they wouldn't admit to that if they had an ounce of common sense between their ears now would they, Harry?"

"Guess not," Harry agreed. The bar was very crowded now. People jostled past regularly and the thick atmosphere made breathing a hazardous activity. Harry longed to get out into the fresh air but he couldn't leave yet. "There's been some trouble down there just lately, I hear," he said.

"Oh, yes, I did hear about that, but I don't think this is a political thing." O'Brien shook his head and took another ecstatic swig from his Guinness. "More of a family crisis is my understanding of the matter, Harry. A little mix-up to be resolved. I don't think there will be any guns blazing about this one. I don't think there'll be any bodies off the bridge, if you understand me."

"The cops aren't getting involved then?"

"Bejazus no. We don't want them damned boys poking their noses into it. It's only a family matter, Harry. It's not a criminal case, so I'm told."

"You had any luck yet?" Harry continued, moving slightly to one side as a large, bearded man, dressed mainly in leather and smelling strongly of some spicy sort of aftershave, tried to get past him.

"Well now, I shall be honest with you, Harry, and say I haven't come up with a thing as yet. There's a man called Juan who's acting as an intermediary, if you understand me, Harry. He's a shifty little fellow to be sure. He's not a man I'd necessarily trust to tell the truth, but he came to see me a week or so ago and he tells me that his boss can pay very well for information about your man, Byszewski. Very well indeed, I might say. It's a tempting kind of an amount. I won't lie to you about that, but I'll tell you something, Harry: there's not a hair of him in this town. I keep my ears open, Harry. I'm an observant man. There's no one of that name been here lately."

"Why do they think he came here then?" Harry asked.

O'Brien shrugged. "It's no good asking me the question, Harry. I'm not the man to answer that one. I think they're probably looking in all the big places in this part of the country; around the south west, if you understand me. They tell me that Byszewski came up over the border. They don't know where he went after that. If you ask me, I might as well be chasing wild geese!" He cackled and lit a cigarette. "Bejazus, there's a crowd in here tonight," he commented. "Look at them all crammed in. It's not usually this packed, Harry. I prefer a bit more space around me on the whole, I don't mind saying it."

"I'd sure go along with that." Harry nodded. "Is there a quieter place near here?"

"Well now, I'm sure there may be," O'Brien said with resignation. "But it's not everywhere that sells my tipple, Harry. The old black's not as common here as in the old country."

Harry acquiesced and, seeing that O'Brien had managed to guzzle down most of his drink already, signalled to the bartender to bring more. His own glass was still quite full. Because of the heat and the fug, it was tempting to drink quickly, but Harry resisted the urge, keen to stay alert for any useful information O'Brien might provide.

"You're a prince of a man, Harry," O'Brien told him.

"Cheers." Harry raised his own glass, and then took a sip of his beer. It was getting warm and beginning to taste quite sour. "So this Byszewski's not a trafficker then?"

"Well they don't say so," O'Brien said. "I heard the trouble was all to do with a woman," he confided, leaning closer in towards Harry. "I heard that your man Byszewski is a bit of a one for the ladies. Apparently he got himself involved with some girlie who was already tied up with a big man in one of the cartels down there." O'Brien pursed his lips and sucked air in noisily through them. "They don't like that kind of thing, Harry. They're not reasonable men like you and me, are they? They're not prepared to live and let live, if you understand me. Especially not to let live!" He rasped and wheezed with laughter for a while. "But they say that your man's father – the dad of the Byszewski – has sorted it all out after the boy ran out. And it's the dad who's trying to find him and get him to go back. The prodigal son. All is forgiven. Do you understand me, Harry?"

"Sure." Harry nodded. He wondered how much truth there was in the story. It sounded just about plausible. If it was true then there didn't seem to be much danger after all, and it explained why Byszewski had been worried about pursuit. On the other hand, if everything was as above board as O'Brien had been told, then why not just alert the authorities and let them find Byszewski and deport him as an illegal immigrant? Why bother paying private eyes large sums of money for information?

"Now tell me, Harry," O'Brien was saying. "You're showing an uncommon sort of interest in this thing. You're a man with a nose for information, if I'm not mistaken."

"Sounds like an interesting case." Harry shrugged. "Most of the stuff we deal with is pretty dull, wouldn't you say, O'Brien? Pretty run of the mill?"

"I'll agree with you on that point, Harry. I think you have it right there. There isn't a lot of an interesting nature in our line of work, although the average man might believe otherwise. The man on the street might think we have an exciting job to do, Harry. The truth is very different, I'll agree with that."

After another hour, Harry made his excuses and left the bar.

The cool night air outside made him feel dizzy momentarily, but he took several deep breaths, felt better and headed off down the hill towards the motel. He was pleased to be free of the fug of the place, and relieved to get away from O'Brien's chatter. O'Brien was a nice enough guy, but Harry found him wearing after an hour or two. Several glasses of Guinness and a couple of tots of Irish whiskey didn't exactly quell his garrulousness either.

Harry bought himself a coffee from the machine in the reception area of the motel which had hard-textured brown carpet on the floor and beige paint on the walls. There was no one around. A sign on the desk instructed him to ring a bell if he wanted service. In one corner was a cigarette machine; in another, two video games flashed and tweeted. Harry was carrying his room key. He checked the change in his pocket, paused for a moment and then shook his head and walked determinedly off towards his room.

It was almost midnight. Harry switched on the TV and flicked through the channels until he found a movie to watch. He remembered then that he had said he would call Tina when he got back. It was too late now, surely? She would probably be asleep. Besides, he had had enough beer. The taste of it still felt cloying in his mouth.

He lay back on the bed, still clothed, hands behind his head, coffee next to him on the bedside table. He looked at the TV screen and tried to pay attention to the movie. He felt alert and awake, restless and irritable. He wanted something. For a time he fought with himself, arguing the pros and cons in his head. Then, at length, somewhat angrily, he got up off the bed, picked up his keys, some dollar bills and loose change from the top of the dressing table, and let himself quietly back out into the motel corridor.

thirteen

He sits on a leather-topped barstool, fingers touching a tall glass containing dark beer. The bar is on the Prinsengracht where there are several to choose from. He likes this one though. There is an intimate and expensive feel to it, with its Tiffany lampshades and solid old oak and leather furniture. Its clients tend towards the erudite. Two acquaintances of his sit close by. They are discussing the work of an author they know. The writer is well thought of, highly regarded and admired by the intelligentsia. Joseph thinks that Anna writes better books than this other author, but he keeps this opinion to himself. His friends would consider him biased but he wouldn't agree. The last one she wrote, published earlier in the year and now selling quite well, was intricate in its plot. It was set here in Amsterdam, a love story at its roots, but much more than that in its execution. He read it after it was published. She won't let him see her books until they get into print. She thinks it will be unlucky if he reads a draft and besides, she says, a book has more authority once it has a proper cover and can be bought in shops.

He thinks that she has special descriptive skills; she writes with elegance and sparsity. The author that his friends talk of now uses long flowery passages which irritate him and hold up the plot. He thinks Anna is very clever in this respect; she can capture the essence and feel of a scene in just a few well chosen words. Her books always end unhappily though; or maybe philosophically would be a better term. She uses star-crossed lovers who harbour dark secrets. He smiles to himself. Dark secrets. It's only too obvious to him why she likes that idea, but her non-happy endings make him feel uneasy. He wonders if her deepest self comes out in her writing. He wonders if she believes that they too will end unhappily. He wonders if she will somehow engineer things to make it so. He's told her that her books would make good films, but that Hollywood prefers things to end on an upbeat note. She says she can't change it; that it wouldn't be right; that life is not a movie and she won't write differently.

Sometimes he wonders if she should give it up. He sees how much it takes out of her. When she finishes the first draft of a new story, she is inconsolable for a while. She says it's like the end of an affair. Occasionally, when she is actually writing, she seems completely lost in the story and he feels that he hardly exists for her. He doesn't much like it, but what else would she do? He can't imagine her working in an office again and he doesn't want her to. She's a beautiful woman, though he knows she doesn't think so. In an office, men would flock to her, he thinks. There's a chance that one of them might appeal to her. He hates the thought of that: men ogling her; making sexual remarks about her to one another. The idea of it angers him. He couldn't tolerate it.

They have plenty of money. She doesn't have to work, but he can't tell her not to. He knows, besides, that her writing is the most important thing in her life – more important than he is in the end. He is jealous of it in a way, but then again, it's not the worst thing. It can't make love to her or take her out to dinner.

His own art is nothing like hers. He harbours a little contempt for what he considers to be the pretentiousness of the artistic establishment. They call his pictures 'art', but he knows they are only paintings. The act of it doesn't capture his soul, it's merely a matter of placing a brush on a canvas and seeing what flows out. He knows all about the golden ratio – the way of proportioning a painting to make it more aesthetically pleasing to the eye. He measures it out each time he starts anew as mathematically correctly as he can. His paintings are calculated but not felt. Critics wax lyrical about the power and the depth of his work; they go into raptures about the meaningful essence of his brush strokes. He doesn't disabuse them of their notions although he knows they are false. He knows what he has to do to make a painting sell and he executes it with precision. He is cynical about it. He finds it relaxing to paint, for sure, and it's easy for him. Inside himself he laughs at the awe his work inspires in others. He sees them as foolish and easily taken in. It's little more than a hobby to him; a dabbling, whereas Anna's writing involves the whole of her being; it's the meaning of her life.

He is thinking about her. Why can't she see his point of view? She's right though. Sometimes he does think he knows her better than she knows herself. In fact, he's certain of it. He thinks she disagrees with him because she wants to assert her self. She takes up a contrary point of view out of principle rather than pragmatism. He sighs with frustration.

"What's with you tonight, Joey?" Guus is young – in his late twenties. He has curly brown hair, twinkling eyes and a new girlfriend every week.

"Nothing a few beers and pleasant company won't cure," Joseph replies. "I'll buy you another." He signals for the barman to refill their glasses.

In a corner, two women are lounging, talking lazily. One of them looks over now and then. A couple of times she catches Joseph's eye. On the third occasion she smiles slightly at him. She has light brown hair which is smooth and shiny and hangs to her shoulders. It sparkles with copper tones under the dim lights. Eventually she comes up to the bar to buy drinks. She looks to be in her mid twenties. She has orangey eyes and beige skin. Her eyebrows are strangely dark. There is a small gap between her front teeth. She stands next to Joseph who offers to pay for her drinks.

"You think you can buy me, eh?" she says, but there's a smile on her face.

"What do you think?" he asks her. He looks into her eyes, imagining things she wouldn't dream of. He sees her begin to melt. It seldom fails. Only Anna could ever resist him. Only she could turn the tables.

"I think you have a nerve!" She is trying to maintain her dignity.

"What's your name?" he asks.

"Heidi," she says, accepting drinks from the barman and handing over a garish note in payment.

"I'm Joseph," he tells her. Out of the corner of his eye, he sees his two friends smirking. "Would you mind if we joined you?"

"I'll have to ask my friend," Heidi states. She walks to her table. She is wearing tight jeans around a bottom that is just a touch too heavy for the rest of her. It swings from side to side as she moves. Joseph watches it. Heidi speaks to her friend. Guus has turned to look at the women. The other man, Willem, who is gay, looks bored. He drinks his beer quickly.

"I'm off," he says, draining his glass. He glances over to where the two women are still in discussion. "Backsides like elephants!" he says in disgust. Joseph and Guus laugh and shake his hand as he leaves them.

A few minutes later, Guus and Joseph are invited to the women's table. Guus smiles with his prettiest twinkle at Heidi's friend, Julianne, and they find a common interest in some item of obscure Dutch literature about which they begin to talk animatedly.

"Shall we go somewhere quieter?" Joseph asks Heidi in a while. She likes art, but she doesn't know much about it. She reads books, but prefers light fiction. She works in a travel agency. She likes foreign travel, sandy beaches and cocktails at twilight. Joseph has discovered these things. She knows nothing about him yet.

"Where do you suggest?" she asks. She has a habit of flicking her hair back off her shoulder with a quick movement of her head. It is vaguely attractive, but might become irritating on a long acquaintance.

"We'll walk a little, find somewhere." He smiles at her as though she is the most desirable woman on earth.

They amble, seemingly randomly through darkened streets, although Joseph knows exactly where he's going. He buys her cocktails in a bar on the Spuistraat. Jazz music plays in the background, but nothing modern or experimental. Her pupils are dilated with the darkness and the alcohol. She can hardly take her eyes away from Joseph's face. He touches her a few times as if by accident. He sees that she doesn't mind. It grows late. At last she looks at her watch.

"I've got to go," she says. I have to get a bus, and I've got to work in the morning."

"I'll walk you to the bus," he says, a picture of chivalry.

Outside the bar, she lurches into him, a little drunk from the cocktails. He steadies her, and she moves in towards him, welcoming the arm he puts around her. He turns to face her, pushes her hair back with his free hand and kisses her gently. She responds to him like fire, passionate and eager.

"Stay with me," he whispers.

"Oh, I can't," she whines, but in a while she doesn't object when he books a room in an expensive hotel nearby and has champagne sent up. It comes in an ice bucket under a lacy cream serviette with tall chilled glasses on a silver tray. How could she resist? A room decorated in burgundy, pink and green; chocolates for love on the pillow. She eats the chocolate, guzzles the champagne. He takes off her clothes and licks the pink nipples on her full breasts, puts his fingers down between her thighs and feels how excited he has made her. He pours some champagne onto her little rounded belly and then licks it off. Some trickles down further. He follows it with his tongue, down into folds of damp skin. Giggling, she kneels up above his face as he instructs her, and lowers herself down until his tongue can penetrate her. She moans and works herself onto him. Then she waits impatiently while he deftly unrolls a condom onto his penis.

"You don't need that," she says. "I take the pill."

He thinks how stupid she is. "There are other risks besides babies, Heidi," he says, smiling, parting her legs and slipping inside her. She gasps with pleasure. He has never in his life trusted a woman with precautions. Except for Anna. He pulls back. "Turn over," he tells her.

"I'm not sure I like it," she says.

"Please. For me."

She does as she is told and he runs his hands over her fleshy bottom, squeezes it, parts the cheeks of it, sees his penis enter her. The sight and feel of it together are so exciting, but he holds back a while, moving slowly in and out, then thrusting harder as she cries out with pleasure or pain, or maybe both.

Soon it is over. She hasn't come. He begins to finger her, to help her complete the transaction, but she pulls away and wants him

100

only to hold her. He complies although he doesn't much want tenderness.

"Tell me about you," she says. Her head rests against his shoulder, her hand on his chest touching black hair not there in his youth. The amount of hair on his body increases with age. He doesn't much like it, but supposes it is inevitable.

"Oh, you wouldn't find my life very interesting, Heidi," he says with a sigh.

"Where are you from?" she persists.

"I'm French," he tells her. It's half the truth. It's the safest nationality to be. He reaches out to take a sip from his glass of champagne. He has only drunk a little bit of it. This sip is to wet his mouth. He doesn't want any more to drink. It's very late. Heidi is settling down as if to sleep. He gets up from the bed and goes to the bathroom where he washes himself meticulously, removing all the traces of her, all the evidence of sex. He wants to be cleansed now. It's for himself he does it. It's not for Anna's benefit. He thinks about Anna. He wonders if she's asleep yet. He smiles. There's no guilt in him. He can't see the need for it. This is just a piece of recreation like a game of tennis or a swim. A game. He always wins it.

When he comes out of the bathroom he begins to dress himself. Heidi's orange eyes are closed, but the little noises his clothes make rouse her and she props up her head on her hand, leaning on her elbow. She flicks back her hair and her breasts bobble prettily. She looks puzzled.

"Where are you going?" she asks.

"I have to go," he says sorrowfully. "It's all right. You can stay. I'll pay the bill."

"I'm not a whore!" She sits up straight. Her hand moves across

101

her breasts to her throat. Her eyes look angry. She pulls the sheet across her to her waist.

"Of course not," he tells her. He sits down beside her, strokes her hair and kisses her cheek tenderly. "But I brought you here and you can't afford this room. You have such pretty eyes, Heidi." He pulls her to him and kisses her on the mouth although he wants to be gone.

"You asked me to stay with you," she complains as he gets up and pulls on his leather jacket.

"Well, I'm sorry," he says kindly. "But I've got to go. Wife and kids at home."

"Bastard!" Her eyes are wide and hurting, her mouth open.

He smiles at her and goes down into the foyer. He settles the account with a credit card in the name of Dupont – his mother's maiden name – and walks out into the bitter night. There is snow in the air. Not much, but it dances around, reluctant to reach the ground, flickering copper and blue in the haloes of street lights.

He stops for a moment outside on the pavement, pulls on gloves, winds his scarf around his neck and sniffs the brilliant cleanliness of the night air. Out of the corner of his eye, he thinks he sees a tall figure skulking in shadows on a nearby corner. He turns sharply to look more closely and then strides to the spot to inspect the area, looks up the street and down, but there's no one to be seen. And yet, as he turns to resume his homeward journey, he thinks he catches some faint trace, some lingering aroma of American tobacco hanging there in the snow-spangled air.

102

fourteen

"You're a creature of habit, Harry Smith," she said. "I can tell."

Harry looked at his travel alarm clock. It was seven thirty a.m. precisely. He understood what she meant, chuckled, arranged to meet her by the coffee machine at eight, and hung up the phone.

"Sorry I didn't get back to you last night," he said as Tina approached him in the foyer. "I was pretty late getting in."

"Oh, that's all right. I was quite tired anyway," she said brightly. She was more demurely dressed this morning in blue jeans and a red tee shirt with a scooped neck. Nothing to distract him from business, except for a kind of sly look in her eyes when she glanced at him. But she didn't glance at him much. In fact she seemed reluctant to look him in the eye. She dropped her head when he looked directly at her, looking somewhat agitated and uncomfortable. Harry wondered why.

In the diner – half a block or so away – they ordered eggs and coffee and sat either side of a small table covered with a blue and white checked table cloth next to a window. Tina poured herself a glass of water from the jug provided and gazed out at the pleasant morning and the few people who were passing by.

The waitress brought them coffee. Tina was holding her glass between her two hands. She put it down on the table and picked up the coffee mug instead.

"I drink tea at home," she remarked suddenly. Until that moment she had been quiet and the silence between them had just started to make Harry feel uncomfortable. "But I ordered some the first day I was in the States and it was terrible!" She made a disgusted kind of face.

"Hey, you're just an old stereotype at heart, ain't you?" Harry teased her playfully. She laughed, caught his eye, and then coloured slightly and looked away again. Harry wondered if he had done something to upset her. She didn't sound upset. Perhaps she was embarrassed about the clothes he'd caught her wearing yesterday. "Anyhow, guess I'd better fill you in on progress," he said, trying to be business-like.

"Yes. Tell me immediately." Suddenly she had changed again, looking at him directly now, relaxed, calm and in control. He felt nonplussed. The waitress brought their food and Tina began to eat it with quick, neat little bites. She chewed quickly. Harry ate more slowly, savouring each mouthful. The eggs were good; over easy just as he liked them. Tina's were scrambled with white toast.

"OK. I ran into my old buddy, John O'Brien last night. See, I happened to be in San Francisco doing some snooping around on a matrimonial case and so on."

"Oh yes?" She interrupted him. "Investigating adulterous goings on in seedy motels, eh?"

"Something along those lines." Harry nodded. He winked at her and pushed his hair back out of his eyes. She smiled.

"What I want to know," she asked, her left elbow resting on the table and her empty fork pointing at him. "Is how you know all these people? I mean, do all the private detectives round here know each other?"

"No, well, we don't *all* know each other for sure, but if you've been doing it a while you do tend to get acquainted with quite a few guys. You know, we can help each other out now and again."

"Yes but San Francisco isn't exactly next door to Flagstaff, is it?"

"Not really, but I've only been in Flagstaff a year or so. I used to work over here a while back."

"I see. Sorry, you were saying about this man, O'Brien. You know him from when you were here, do you?"

"I knew him in LA. I was there before, same time he was."

"Oh." She looked interested. "So how many different places have you worked?"

Harry considered. "Four, five maybe. Hey, is this some kind of inquisition?" He laughed.

She looked surprised, and then bit her lip. "No," she mumbled. "I'm sorry. What did O'Brien say?"

"Only joking, I don't mind," Harry said kindly. "O'Brien offered me some good tips for the races it so happens."

Tina raised her left eyebrow. "Oh really. Well, I trust you didn't let that information go to waste."

Harry looked at her quizzically. "To tell the truth, I ain't much of a gambling man," he told her. "But John O'Brien's of Irish stock, or so he'd have you believe. He's a man for the horses himself." Harry attempted an Irish accent for this final sentence. He didn't think it was too bad an attempt.

Tina had just taken a gulp from her mug of coffee. Her eyes widened at Harry and she made a big effort to swallow what was in her mouth, then she burst out laughing with a deep, chortling noise that was rich and a little dirty. She shuddered with it. "That's a *terrible* accent," she gasped. "I know Irish people, Harry, and they do *not* talk like that!"

"O'Brien does," Harry said, feeling slightly miffed.

Tina smirked at him.

"Now where was I?" he asked himself.

"Getting some tips for the races," Tina said.

"Well, you've gotta start someplace." Hurry shrugged. "Can't exactly leap straight in with it. You gotta allay a guy's suspicions."

"You could have discussed philosophy and politics," Tina suggested with a grin.

"Oh sure! With an Irishman!" Harry said ironically. "I'd have been there all night. Anyhow, we're getting off the point here."

"I don't know that we've actually been on it yet," Tina said cheekily.

"Hey! Gimme a break!" Harry acted exasperated. In fact, he was quite enjoying himself. He fished in the pocket of his jacket which he had hung over the back of his chair. He pulled out a packet of Camel cigarettes, flicked one out and put it into his mouth. Tina raised an eyebrow and offered him the services of the lit match that she had just used herself. "Don't say a word," he warned her. "I was attempting to give it up, but I'm working under pressure here. A great deal of provocation."

Tina giggled and made a contrite sort of face. Harry drew on the cigarette and let out the smoke with a great sigh of satisfaction.

"Jeez, that's better," he said. "Don't think I was designed to be a non-smoker. Anyway. O'Brien." He got his thoughts into order. "Yeah, he told me he's looking for a guy called Byszewski. Can't be too many of 'em about, I guess. It's your pop who's looking for him. Apparently he wants him to go back and so on."

"I could have guessed that," Tina twisted her mouth and frowned. "But how did he get hold of O'Brien? Surely father wouldn't know any private detectives in San Francisco? He's never even been to the States as far as I know. Mind you, I haven't wanted to know much about him. Maybe he has been here."

"I don't think he knows O'Brien. Some guy called Juan is coordinating the search for him," Harry explained.

"What did O'Brien know?" Tina asked.

Harry told her what O'Brien had said about the trouble her brother had encountered. He thought he saw a spasm of some kind pass across her face when he mentioned that it had been to do with a woman, but if it was there she masked it quickly.

"Do you know what happened to the girl?" she asked in a flat voice.

"No I don't. And I'm not sure your brother should go back. After all, we don't have any proof that any of this is true. It may just be a story designed to keep everyone calm. And frankly I wouldn't trust any member of a drugs cartel not to change his mind about whether or not he's got a grouch against some guy."

"You know this from personal experience do you, Harry?" Tina narrowed her eyes at him. Harry had thought she hadn't been paying much attention to Steve MacArthur when he mentioned that. It seemed that he had underestimated her.

"Would you trust them?" he asked her.

"I don't know any," she said. "But I suppose I wouldn't. I don't really know much about it at all. I've always tried to avoid finding out, you see. I didn't want to know. I was..." She winced and looked worried. "I was scared for Joe. You can't help hearing things though, no matter how you try to block it out. I was scared of what he might find himself mixed up in."

Harry nodded. "I can understand that."

Tina looked uneasy. "So they know he's been in San Francisco?"

"No, they don't know that," Harry reassured her. "As far as I could make out they don't know anything. O'Brien didn't know what name he's using and I sure didn't tell him. He's looking for Joe Byszewski so he hasn't come up with anything yet. They're looking all over the south west. I guess they just picked a guy in each of the cities to check around locally."

"So they'll be looking in Phoenix?" Tina said warily.

"I guess so." Harry shrugged.

"Oh no. They're bound to find Maria then." She sighed, and closed her eyes. "She used to work for them, or rather she said she had 'some dealings' with my family a few years back." She was leaning on the table with her elbows, cupping a fresh mug of coffee between her hands, rocking back and forth just slightly.

Harry thought for a moment. "You didn't tell me that before," he said.

She looked at him quickly. "I suppose I forgot." She bit her lip.

"I asked you specifically how he knew her and you said you didn't know," Harry reminded her.

"Did I?" she asked, looking troubled. "I must have thought it wasn't important."

Harry knew she was lying. He knew that she had deliberately withheld that information for some reason. Would he still have taken the case if she'd been honest about that? It was hard for him to say now, and maybe it wasn't such a big deal in itself, but that wasn't the point. If she had lied to him once, then how could he trust her? He contemplated this and her whilst smoking his cigarette. She had put down her mug. Her right elbow rested on the table, while her hand cradled the side of her face. The fingers of her left hand played about nervously with the mug's handle and she stared down at it fixedly. She looked a picture of dejection, but he didn't feel sorry for her. Not just at the moment. Right now he was more concerned for himself and what he had gotten into. He didn't feel very happy about it.

"So," he said at length. "Is there anything else you forgot to tell me, Ms Philpott? Any other items of information that you didn't think were important?"

She looked up at him sharply. He saw hurt in her eyes. "What difference would it have made?" she asked defensively.

"You assured me that your whole family business was above board," Harry said firmly. "That phrase: 'some dealings' implies something different, wouldn't you say?"

"I don't know." She hung her head down. "I was desperate for help," she said quietly. "I didn't know what to do. I didn't want to say anything that might put you off. I'm sorry."

Harry looked at her, but she wouldn't look back at him. Her eyes were fixed downwards, staring at the table. She looked as though she might cry. He leaned back in his chair and sighed. He looked to his right, out through the big picture window at the automobiles that had begun to block up the street outside. It was nearly nine a.m. He felt disappointed. He felt that he had been tricked and he felt let down. He had fallen for her play-acting. She had lied to him blatantly and deliberately. He couldn't trust her. He wasn't sure what to do next.

fifteen

It's two in the morning and he's still not home. Anna lies awake in the single bed in her room. A roof-light above her head looks out into the stars above the city. They twinkle, fade and then reappear as clouds pass by on ephemeral journeys. Looking into the night reminds her of London when she first went there. Since then she's loved rooms in roofs. She remembers the glow of that other city, fighting and winning against the darkness. A thousand nights spent waiting whilst hope receded. Is this what she waited for? This half-life of suspicion and betrayal? What was it that she kept alive in her soul all those years? A fairy tale? A romantic illusion? An everlasting affair straight out of a trashy piece of women's fiction? She curses herself. Why didn't she escape him while she had the chance? Why didn't she make a separate life for herself then? She knows the answer, of course. He's part of her, like an arm or a leg. She can't cast him off. It isn't an option.

Sighing, she rises and goes out into the big living room. She makes a pot of coffee. It's hardly the thing for a sleepless night, but her life isn't governed by clocks now. She lights a cigarette while she waits for the coffee to brew, and wonders what to do. She can't write – her brain prefers mornings for that activity. Reading doesn't appeal. She doesn't watch much television, only sometimes CNN on satellite; sometimes the BBC for old times' sake. She puts a compact disc into the machine. It's a recording of 'Take Five' by Dave Brubeck. It seems to evoke the right sort of mood for this hour. She sits herself down, or rather sprawls along the sofa. She closes her eyes and lets the music fill up her mind.

She is woken by the sound of the apartment door opening. The compact disc has finished playing. She glances at the clock displayed in luminous green numerals on the video recorder. It is three seventeen. He is standing at the end of the sofa, regarding her with no emotion.

"Oh, hello," she says in a manner as off-hand as she can muster. "I've been asleep I suppose."

"I'm going to bed," he says.

"Surely, you've only just got up!" She laughs without mirth.

"You like to assume you know what I do."

"All right. Come here and make love to me then."

"While you hate me?" he says in exasperated surprise. "No thank you. In any case, I'm tired."

"So where have you been?" she persists.

"Don't question me, Anna," he says sharply. "You know I don't like it." He turns and walks off to the bedroom while she glares at the back of him, imagining how she might take revenge.

Intermittently fuming and dozing, she whiles away the rest of the night on the sofa. She makes more coffee at eight when he emerges from the bedroom looking tired and troubled. He lights a Gitanes impatiently. Things irritate him. She can tell. She has no sympathy. She doesn't believe he deserves any. He hardly speaks to her as their paths cross in the kitchen and at the eating table.

"Oh what a fine mood we're in this morning," she remarks with syrupy sarcasm.

"I don't know what you expect of me," he retorts. "When it's clear that you don't give a damn about our relationship."

"This is new!" She acts ironic enthusiasm. "How have you come to this conclusion, pray?"

He shrugs. "You're obviously not bothered about the

111

implications of visiting England. I thought you were happy here. Happy with me, with us. I'm not enough for you, I suppose."

"That's rich," she snaps. "Coming from one who fucks every little floozy who melts under his baby blue gaze. I've seen it Joe. You can't resist the effect you have on them. It's pathetic."

"It's unimportant." He states it plainly.

"As is my going to England for a couple of days, I would say." She is talking through gritted teeth to stop herself from screaming at him.

"It's not the same thing at all." His voice is calm and condescending while her anger grows by the second. "What I do – it's just a game; a momentary flirtation. What you want to do will put our whole existence in jeopardy."

And what about the other thing, she thinks, the other thing he does, but still she can't say it, even in the full torrent of her temper. Still she can't quite tackle the truth head on.

"I thought you wanted me," she says instead. "All that time we had to be apart and all those other women. You told me they were there because you couldn't have me, but it wasn't true, was it?"

"I didn't marry anyone." He shrugs. "I kept my promise even when I thought you didn't care. Unlike you, Anna. What are your promises worth, eh? What are your convictions? Do you have any? They change by the day, don't they? Depending on your mood of the moment. Today, I'll make a promise, tomorrow, who knows? I'll change my mind if I feel like it!" He mimics her. She wants to kill him. It would solve a lot of problems.

"Oh, shut up," she tells him. "Every time you want to get the better of me, you bring up the same thing. I'm sick of it. How many times must I apologise? How many 'hail Marys' must I say? It's so facile, Joe. My one mistake gives you an excuse to do anything you like. How very convenient for you." She is boiling with anger. He looks at her as though she's a poisonous snake.

"I have to go out," he says without any feeling. "I'll see you later."

And soon he is gone and she is alone again in the apartment that she's beginning to despise. Once upon a time it felt like an exciting hideaway; now it feels like a prison. She sits awhile and thinks, unable to write until she's regained some equilibrium. She remembers her marriage. David was a kind man; kinder than Joe. He wanted her to marry him; he wanted that commitment. She gave in to his request with reservations.

But it hurt Joe so badly. He turned up on her wedding day, coming across oceans, thousands of miles to tell her how much she had hurt him. The pain she felt lingers still somewhere inside her; that desolation; the certain knowledge that she had finally lost him. Would things be different now if that day had never happened? She doubts it. She always looked up to him. He was her hero. But now she sees that he's a human being like any other. He's fallible. Is that what life's about, she wonders. Failure? How disappointing.

She remembers David, loyal and tender. He loved her and she could never love him back the way he wanted. Not with that spectre in her psyche, this promise of never-never land in her childish mind. Life seemed simple then, with hindsight. The fact that she was bored with it she now sees as her own fault. All she can remember is a sense of peace; of calm and tranquillity. Oh, how she yearns for that. How she yearns for an ordinary life.

sixteen

Finally she lifted her face. Harry, still looking out at the street but too bound up in his own thoughts to be seeing much, caught the movement but didn't turn his head.

"I suppose you want to drop the case now," she said quietly.

Harry said nothing. The waitress came by with more coffee. He accepted it more out of habit than desire.

"I did lie to you about that," she said. "The way Maria used the words made me think that there might be something shady going on. I suppose I didn't want to believe it myself. I mean, I could believe anything of my father, but not Joe. Not Joe." She repeated the last two words with a sigh and her eyes closed.

"Tell me why you dislike your pop so much." Harry had noticed the sneer in her voice every time she mentioned her father. He wondered what the man had done to deserve it.

She bit her lip and dropped her head forward. "He was rarely there when I was young," she said quietly. "He shut us up in a big remote farmhouse in Switzerland, didn't like us to mix with other people, and he left us there to rot. We could go out – of course we did – but it wasn't a very normal childhood.

"I didn't feel wanted. Venezuela was always special to them, being the oldest. I suppose she was born while they were still in love. Bolivia was very independent. I don't think she gave a damn what they thought about her. She looked different to the rest of us. We took after mother, but she was more like father in appearance. I thought she got special treatment too." Tina paused for a moment to light a cigarette. Harry noticed that her hands were visibly shaking as though talking like this was truly traumatic for her.

"When I was allowed to go to England, I asked father if I could go to university if my studies went all right. He told me that he didn't see the need for a 'pretty girl' to get such an education. He told me to get married and have babies!" Her voice rose indignantly. "Can you believe that?" she demanded of Harry, her eyes raised now and glaring at him. He didn't answer but found that, despite himself, he was smiling slightly at the look of outrage on her face. "And then," she continued, jabbing her cigarette towards him. "The next thing I know is that he's agreed for Bolivia to go to college in Geneva to train as a teacher! Bastard!" She let out a stifled, high-pitched little growl and gulped some of her coffee down.

"Of course Ecuador, being a boy, could do no wrong, *and* he used to defend father. He just couldn't see my point of view. Boy, did that make me angry!" She had worked herself up into a state now, reliving all the injustices of her youth. Harry could see it. He had to admit that he found her a little comical when she got indignant. Her Swiss-French accent got stronger and gave a funny twist to her words. "And father used to come home once or twice a year and shower us with gifts and platitudes. Then, as soon as he could, he'd be back off to Bogotá and his wonderful business.

"When Ecuador was sixteen, father took him off to Colombia to join the business. It had always been planned, but it was terrible! Venezuela had already gone to England by this time. Bolivia and I weren't close. Joe was my best friend, my *only* friend come to that. I was devastated when he went. I felt so lonely. I hated father for taking him away. I still do." She shrugged and looked down at her hands. She had stubbed out her cigarette a moment before and now they were splayed out on the table in front of her.

"Maybe it wasn't such a bad thing," Harry said softly. "Maybe

115

you needed to get a little independence. What would have happened if Joe'd stuck around? What would you have done then?"

She frowned. "I don't know. I don't like talking about it... even thinking about it much. I find it quite painful, even now.

"Harry?" She looked up at him. Her eyes looked troubled but honest as though she was begging him to believe her. "I really want you to help me. I'm so sorry I lied about Maria. I shouldn't have done, but we'd only just met. I wasn't sure of you. There's nothing else that I haven't told you as far as I know – nothing relevant to this anyway. I honestly don't know if my family is caught up in anything illegal. I don't know what to say to convince you."

"Well." He drained the last of his coffee. "We got an appointment to keep at a motel. I ain't promising anything after that, mind. We'll see how it goes." He stood up, stretching himself slightly. Tina, with something of the air of a grateful puppy about her, paid their bill and scurried after him out onto the street.

Later, in a pretty plaza with water cascades and lots of green foliage, they met a woman. At the Vagabond Inn, the manager had told them that he had employed a temporary receptionist for the week during which Joey Diaz had stayed as his usual full-time one had gone on vacation. Nobody else there remembered the man, so Harry traced Jane Gray through the agency which employed her, and they arranged to meet her for ten minutes or so in her lunch hour.

It was a balmy day. The two of them sat on a bench in the appointed spot. Tina twirled her hair up on top of her head with her hand, holding it there for half a minute or so, letting the air get to the back of her neck. She had her eyes closed, face up towards the sun, looking blissful at the feel of it on her skin. Harry watched her. Sometimes she seemed so unaware of herself, so natural, like a child.

At other times she would be trying to hide everything about herself.

A tall woman in her mid-twenties approached them. Harry recognised her from the description she had given him and stood up to meet her. She had sleek, short, red hair, strong bones and a handsome face. She had green eyes and a wide business-like smile. Harry introduced himself, and then Tina who stood now too and shook the other woman's hand. He explained that they were looking for Tina's brother.

"I thought you looked familiar," she said to Tina. "There is a kind of resemblance. Yes, I remember Mr Diaz. He spent two nights at the Vagabond Inn while I was working there."

"Did you talk to him at all?" Harry asked.

"As a matter of fact, I did." Jane nodded. "Spanish is one of my languages, you see, so he was grateful to have someone to chat to, I think."

"What did he say?" Tina asked eagerly.

"I suspect much of it wouldn't be relevant to your enquiries." Jane smiled. "He's something of a flatterer, isn't he?"

Tina looked down at her own feet, and Harry made a non-committal sort of noise, encouraging Jane to continue.

"He asked me to go to dinner with him, but I do have a partner, so I didn't feel it would be appropriate. In any case, I wasn't sure I trusted him... sorry," she apologised to Tina who said it was quite all right, with a little hint of irony in her voice. "He seemed kind of jumpy," Jane continued. "Looking over his shoulder, you see? That kind of thing makes me nervous about spending time on my own with a person.

"However, I did have quite a long conversation with him over coffee and a sandwich one lunch time. He talked to me a little about

117

his plans. I guess you guys would be interested in that?"

Harry and Tina both nodded and waited for her to continue.

"Let me see…" Jane thought for a moment. "He told me he was waiting for his sister – you, I guess – to get in touch with him through someone he knew in Phoenix. He said that you lived in England and that it might take a little time so he was travelling around in the meantime taking a look at the country. He was kind of cagey about why he was here in the first place and why he was waiting for you. When I asked him questions, he tended not to answer them directly. It was off-putting to be honest."

"He didn't mention leaving the country?" Harry prompted.

"No, I don't recall that," Jane replied. "My impression was that he was spending a couple of days looking around the city, and then he would drive back to Phoenix via LA. It was just kind of tourist stuff and his plans were pretty vague, you know. He definitely gave me the impression that he thought you were going to contact him in Phoenix. I think that was the only part of the conversation that would interest you." She smiled pleasantly at them. Particularly at Tina.

"Has anyone else asked about him?" Harry checked.

"Not to my knowledge," she said, shaking her head. "At least no one has asked me except you two."

"Did he have any idea when he'd get back to Phoenix?" Tina asked.

Jane frowned slightly, thinking, stroking her square chin between the thumb and forefinger of her right hand. "Hmm. Not really. He didn't say anything specific. I guess a week. Ten days maybe. He didn't seem to be in a particular hurry. I thought he was killing time in a way. I got the impression he hadn't wanted to sit around waiting in Phoenix for some reason. He didn't say anything specific about that though, it was just a feeling I got."

"So he could be back there now," Tina said after they had left Jane. "If he left here on the 31st."

"Looks like that's where we're headed," Harry agreed.

"She was nice," Tina said.

"Who?" Harry murmured, preoccupied with planning the journey back in his head.

"Jane."

"Oh, yeah," he said. "Not my type really." He glanced at Tina. She wasn't looking at him. She was walking beside him, head held up, a little smile playing at the corners of her mouth. Harry wondered what the hell was going on in that head now.

At the airport, later that afternoon, when an unseasonable fog had descended on the city, Tina Philpot turned taciturn again. She hadn't spoken to Harry much since they checked out of the motel, but he understood now that it was nothing personal. Their flight was delayed for an hour. Harry spent the time mooching around, looking at the shops and the people, while Tina sat in the smoking area of the departure lounge looking morose and unapproachable.

At length, their flight was called. Harry walked over to where Tina was sitting. "Come on scaredy-cat," he said softly. He smiled gently at her. "We'll be there before you know it."

She stood, looked up at him with something approaching terror on her face, and then she relaxed slightly and smiled weakly. Unconsciously, Harry found himself moving towards her, offering himself as protection. His right arm began to raise itself as though he would put it around her, draw her to him and comfort her, and she too seemed to move in, ready to welcome this. And then they both remembered themselves and what they were to one another which was little more than strangers. They looked away from each other and started walking quickly towards the departure gate.

The flight was smooth and uneventful. When the aeroplane touched down in Phoenix, a huge, contented sigh escaped from Tina Philpott. As she stood up she stretched herself massively and let out a tiny, delighted laugh.

"You're a strange one," Harry told her. He couldn't help smiling at her change in mood. "Just a while back I thought you might die of fright. Now look at you. Happy as a cat."

She looked at him, slightly startled, as though she had forgotten he was there. Then she smiled widely and laughed again. "Sometimes I think the fear is almost worth it because it feels so good when it stops!" she said.

"Crazy woman!" Harry grinned and shook his head.

"Well, maybe I am." The words came out of her softly, like a sensuous purr. Harry had been looking down at his bag, concentrating on the closure of a recalcitrant zipper. Now he looked up at her sharply. There was a soft, languid smile on her face. Her blue-green eyes seemed to be drinking him, beckoning to him. For a moment, after she lowered her gaze to her own bag, he continued to stare at her, mesmerised. And then she looked up at him again, expecting that he would be moving out of the way, down towards the exit, and the naked desire had gone and been replaced with ordinary warmth. Harry pulled himself together and they disembarked without speaking again.

They picked up Harry's car and drove to the Ramada hotel in the north of the city where the receptionist told them that she could only accommodate them for two nights. A convention was starting Saturday, she said. They would be full for a week after that. They considered this and decided to stay, hoping that two nights would be enough. Then they drove over to see Maria.

It was eight thirty in the evening, hot and dark. Maria answered her front door in response to the bell. She came out, shutting the door behind her. She lived in a single story house with a noisy air-conditioning system on a decent estate. It had nice gardens with the palms and cacti that were ubiquitous in Phoenix. No doubt there was a pool out the back.

"Ah, you again," she said to Tina. "I told you I wanted to be left alone." She looked annoyed. She was short, not much more than five feet tall, with light brown skin and eyes bright and black like pieces of recrimination. Harry thought she had a nice figure. Good breasts. He liked his women a little taller generally though. A sudden thought came to him that he wasn't sure what the hell he liked any more, but he dismissed it. Harry was certain that he knew his own mind well. He thought about Suzie for a moment then. It struck him that he ought to start thinking about her some more. He hadn't called her since he left Flagstaff. Still, it was only a couple of days. It seemed longer somehow.

"I'm really sorry to bother you again," Tina said calmly and compassionately. Her tone reminded Harry of the first time they met: businesslike, diplomatic and firm. He gathered she didn't like Maria. Dislike would be too strong a word, though. Disregard would fit better. "I've heard that my brother has come back, or is due back here," Tina explained. "I wondered if you'd seen him again?"

"No. I hope I don't too," Maria said grumpily.

"I understand," Tina said. "But I think he might contact you. If he does, would you tell him I'm staying at the Ramada until Saturday. Here's the address and my name and room number." She scribbled them on a piece of paper. Her handwriting was small, basically neat but with the odd unbalancing flourish. Harry wondered what one of those handwriting analysts might make of it.

"OK. I'll tell him if he calls." Maria took the piece of paper and turned to go back into her house.

"Could I just ask, ma'am, whether you've had any other enquiries after him?" Harry asked.

"Yes," she replied wearily. Harry noticed that Tina stiffened. "A woman came, but I said I didn't see him. She said she works for his father. She leave her number to call too, but I thought I won't bother unless he comes again."

"I'd rather you didn't call her," Tina said earnestly. "I'd like to talk to him first."

"Whatever." Maria shrugged. She gave them the other investigator's name and number. It was another name that was familiar to Harry. They wished her good night.

It was almost nine thirty when they got back to the Ramada.

"Fancy a beer?" Tina asked casually as they walked past the entrance to the hotel bar.

"Er... yeah." Harry suddenly wondered if it was wise. "Listen. I should give my girlfriend a call. I'll join you there in a while. OK?" He watched her face, fancied for a second that there was a reaction, but it was instantly masked and replaced with a polite smile.

"Sure," she said lightly. "I'll fetch a book to read while I wait."

The bar was large and dark and almost empty. Harry looked around for Tina Philpott and spotted her in a corner, hidden away, immersed in her book, half a small glass of beer on the table in front of her. He got himself a drink and went to join her.

He had not spent long talking to Suzie. She had sounded pleased to hear from him and delighted that he would probably be back in a couple of days, but he hadn't been able to think of much to say to her. Every time he thought of something, it seemed to have a lot to do with Tina Philpott so, after having inadvertently mentioned her twice, he had checked himself and tried to think of unrelated topics, but there hardly seemed to be any. The conversation had sort of petered out.

Tina greeted him with her business smile. There were four chairs around the table. Harry sat down opposite her, a chair between them on either side.

"So," she said. "I suppose we sit and wait for Joe to come to us now."

"I guess so," Harry agreed.

"But what if he doesn't?" she mused, half to herself.

"I could do some checking around while we wait," Harry said, trying to reassure her that he was still worth having around. He could go now, he thought. He could leave her here alone to wait for her brother. But then there was his agreement with Clive Mason that he would stay with her. And he didn't want to leave her alone.

"What if he changes his mind about contacting me?" she asked. "What if he goes off somewhere else on a whim? How long should I wait?"

Harry shrugged. "Is it likely he'd do that?"

She twisted her mouth. "Not really, I suppose. He always stuck to his word; kept his promises. Not like me." She bit her lip. "Oh, God!" she said suddenly. "Everything seems so *uncertain*. Last time I saw him we had a dreadful row. I've no idea how he'll react to me now." She lit a cigarette with agitated little movements and then leaned back in her chair, running her hand through her hair. She was wearing a black dress now. It was straight and simple. It left her arms

123

bare and came down to her knees. Her legs were skewed out to one side, crossed at the ankle, slim and tanned. On her feet she wore soft black slip-on pumps, like ballet shoes. She tapped on the table with her fingers.

"But you said that was, what? Six years ago?" Harry checked.

"Oh, Joe could bear a grudge for twenty years if it suited him," she said crossly. "He expects everyone to be as perfect as he is."

Harry wondered what Tina had done to upset her brother; what it was that made her chastise herself like this. He remembered something. "So you had a big row at your wedding," he said. "That can't have been too nice."

"It wasn't," she said flatly. "How's your girlfriend?" The question was asked cordially, like a query about the weather from a person you'd just met. It took Harry completely by surprise.

"Oh... she's OK." He shrugged. "I figured I should let her know I was still alive and so on."

"I suppose she has to put up with you being away a lot, does she?" Tina asked.

Harry felt unnerved by this line of questioning. "Some," he said. "She's used to it. We don't live together or anything. It's quite a casual thing." He wondered why he was telling Tina this. It wasn't his style to talk about his relationships. Especially with another woman.

"You're not into heavy commitments then?" Tina continued, smiling.

Harry thought she was being impertinent, but he wasn't sure how to put her off. Actually, he wasn't sure he wanted to. "Nope. One marriage was enough for me." He grinned.

The bartender came by with two more beers for them. They

124

both watched silently as she placed full glasses on fresh paper mats and took away Tina's empty one. 'Thank yous' and 'your welcomes' were exchanged, and then she left them alone again.

"I don't know that I'm really cut out for it myself," Tina considered. "Marriage, I mean. I didn't seem to be very good at being part of a couple. It seemed too restrictive somehow – as though I was being overwhelmed. My husband was nice enough though. It wasn't his fault. He was a good friend to me."

"Can't say I saw my wife as a friend." Harry thought about it. What *had* she been exactly? Well, just a wife.

"Why did you marry her then?" Tina asked. She looked genuinely curious.

Harry shrugged, feeling a little embarrassed. "I guess I was in love. What other reason is there?"

Tina smiled at him. "Personally, I don't see how you can really love somebody if they're not your friend as well."

"I guess we're different there," Harry said hoping to tie up the conversation and to move on to something less intimate. "Don't know that I know any women I'd call friends," he admitted.

"Really?" Tina leaned towards him, catching her hair as it fell forward and pushing it back, tucking it behind an ear from where, strand by strand, it immediately started to escape again. Her eyes flashed at him, looking vaguely suspicious. He felt a certain quickening of his heartbeat that he'd noticed coinciding with any move she made towards him over the last couple of days.

"Yeah well, I suppose I don't feel entirely relaxed in women's company." He knew he was on difficult ground here, but ploughed on regardless. "It seems like there's always some emotional undercurrent there. With a guy, you know, you can just be yourself. With a

125

broad..."

"Broad?" Tina looked daggers at him. "What's a broad?"

"See what I mean?" He laughed a little. "See I don't mean anything by that term, but you take it that way."

"What way?" Tina countered. "Now you're making assumptions about how I feel." She spoke calmly with no hint of annoyance. Harry had a feeling that she was a cat waiting to pounce, and that he was the prey.

"Maybe." He shrugged.

"Anyway, I agree that women are different from men," she said, surprising him. "In general, women are more emotional, more intuitive. Men are more physical, more logical I suppose. But that's a generalisation, isn't it? And anyway, I don't see why that makes it impossible to be friends. Sometimes there's an undercurrent perhaps. I'm sure I've had male friends where I've felt perfectly at ease though. Mind you they were the ordinary ones – guys who didn't think they were God's gift to women." She scowled slightly.

"I wonder how they felt about it?" Harry said. "They probably thought you were stringing them along, hoping you might notice them someday."

Tina's eyes widened in surprise. "Oh no. Oh dear, I hope not. You've made me feel guilty now." She bit her lip. She seemed to be genuinely surprised by the idea. Harry was sceptical though. Surely she knew how she looked?

He laughed. "I don't believe you."

"It's true," she insisted. "I really hadn't thought that. Anyway, I shouldn't think they felt that way at all. It isn't very likely."

Harry thought it was very likely indeed, but he wasn't going to indulge her in overt flattery. He felt that the conversation had gone

126

quite far enough and he didn't want to encourage it any further. Harry didn't want to have to blame himself for anything.

He noticed that she had almost finished her beer. They were small glasses and she was drinking more quickly than him "Buy you another?" he offered.

"No." She shook her head. "I'm tired. Flying really knocks me out. I need to get some sleep." She stood up.

"Well, I think I may have one more," he said.

"I'll see you in the morning then." She smiled at him, looking genuinely warm towards him. But there was a hint of something else too; an echo. It reminded him of the look of her on the plane earlier. He tried not to think about that.

After she had gone, Harry went to sit at the bar. He ordered another beer and looked at a bank of television screens which were set up high, near the ceiling. Silently, they showed a football game. Harry preferred to watch baseball if he had the choice, but he'd choose a good movie over sport any day. The bartender chatted to him. She was pleasant and professional about her work. Harry thought that he would much rather be talking to Tina. He wondered what she thought of him. He shouldn't care about that, though, should he?

"Penny for 'em?" the bartender said.

"I think they'd cost a good deal more than that," Harry grinned.

"Well if it isn't the divine Harry Smith!" A familiar female voice greeted him. It was a very young-sounding voice and it came from a face that was the same age as his own. A rather glamorous looking face surrounded by immaculately coiffed blonde hair and sporting a cute retroussé nose. Her name, he knew, was the one he'd seen earlier that evening. The one printed on the card that Maria had shown him.

seventeen

"There are a couple of things I need to discuss with you, Mr Mason. It's rather urgent." Piet has called Joseph on his mobile phone. Joseph isn't pleased. He is in a business meeting with Carlos and Frans, sorting out a few final details and making sure they have all the information they need.

"Give me an hour, Piet," he says calmly. He never lets his emotions show when he's working. It's vital that all his business contacts have complete confidence in him. Tantrums don't inspire trust. He finishes his interview with the Spaniard and the Dutchman. He doesn't rush anything. He makes sure that everything on the agenda is completed to his satisfaction and to theirs, and then he takes his leave and makes his way to the Rembrandtplein. He wonders what the trouble is that Piet seems to be so worried about. He isn't too concerned. The ABN-Amro accounts are only minor ones. Small fish.

"Mr Mason, I hope I didn't disturb you with the call." Piet is profuse with apologies. "But we needed to talk right away. I didn't want to…"

"It's quite all right, Piet," Joseph tells him, smiling in a friendly way. "Just fill me in on the details. You know I need to be kept right up to date all the time."

Piet looks relieved. "OK Mr Mason. It's the Vaquez accounts. There's a problem," he explains. The tone of his voice changes from conciliator to business confidant.

"Nothing but trouble," Joseph tuts. It's the same client who's given him problems in the past. They like to think they know better than he does; that there isn't any risk. Or maybe they like a little risk, enjoy a little gamble. In his opinion there's quite enough risk as it is. He tries to minimise it, but it's still there. There isn't any place for complacency. "Have they been raiding funds again?" he asks, keeping his voice light and reasonably cheerful.

"No." Piet shakes his head. "After our last meeting, things quietened down, but I think we may have moved too late on it." He points to his computer screen. There is a memo displayed on it from the head of security at the bank. It's an instruction to put a stop on the Vaquez accounts. They are under investigation. No more transactions will be supported. "I can't do anything about this," Piet explains ruefully. "There's no way around it."

"I see." Joseph's mind is racing. Damn them, he thinks. His heart is beating more quickly than normal. He hates the feeling. He needs time to consider this problem. "What does this mean exactly, Piet? Is it an internal audit?"

"I don't know, Mr Mason," Piet says. "Security won't give out any information at this stage. Personally, I doubt that it's internal. We don't usually stop accounts unless the holder requests it. I can't see any reason to do so, unless a card had been stolen, or they were in unsecured debt, but if it were anything like that I would know about it. My suspicion is that we've had outside instructions on this one."

"And where would they come from?" Joseph asks.

Piet shrugs. "Government auditors, the police, Interpol. It depends what the problem is."

Joseph considers. "Could you find out any more, Piet?"

"I could try, Mr Mason. I don't want to put my head on the block."

"Of course not." Joseph remains outwardly perfectly calm. "Just find out what you can and let me know. In the meantime is there anything we can do to minimise trouble?"

Piet frowns. "I can't see there's much. I mean, these accounts are quite autonomous. Nothing else should be affected, but there's clearly some difficulty that your people should be made aware of."

"Yes." Joseph nods. "OK Piet. Well, thanks for the information. Let me know as soon as you get anything else on this, won't you?"

It's lunchtime. Joseph doesn't feel very hungry. He buys a *broodje,* a bread roll filled with cheese, and he takes it with him to a small room he rents on the first floor at the back of a commercial building on the Utrechtsestraat. The room contains a desk, a chair, a computer, a telephone and modem, a printer and a dedicated fax machine. All the bills for this 'office' are paid in another name. Not Mason. Not Dupont. Very few people know about this office. Anna has no knowledge of it.

Joseph makes himself some strong coffee and eats his *broodje.* Once he has finished eating, he lights a Gitanes and dials a long telephone number. When the call is answered, he speaks in Spanish.

"Hey, Eduardo, what's the weather like?" He exchanges pleasantries. The conversation continues for a while in this vein, and then, when he considers that enough convention has been followed, he explains the problem. He isn't very pleased with the response. "Listen, my friend," he tells Eduardo. "There's nothing I can do here. I'm going to have to withdraw support. I can't put my other clients at risk. You understand."

He listens for a while to some angry words. "Eduardo. Calm down, my friend. It's only a little money. Forget it. Let it go. It's not worth the trouble. I'll try to find out some more, but I need a little time. My terms are always the same, Eduardo. I can't carry on trading accounts that draw attention. You'll have to bear this loss. I'm sorry, Eduardo, but it comes with the package, my friend."

Joseph sees that a fax is coming through. It catches his attention, and he misses some of what Eduardo says.

"Sorry, my friend. Could you say again? Bad line," he says. He listens. "I understand. It's a piece of shit, but we have to be careful, otherwise we lose the whole operation. Give me a couple of days, eh? Don't try to touch the ABN accounts in the meantime."

He puts down the phone and pulls the thin shiny piece of paper out of the fax machine. He reads it with growing unease. It's from Geneva. A man there wants to talk to him. As soon as possible. Another problem.

Joseph phones Switzerland and speaks to the man. He'll have to go there. He arranges a meeting in a couple of days. Damn this, he thinks. He doesn't need it at the moment. He calls the KLM office and books a flight to Geneva. Then he calls another number. There is no reply. He dials again. This time the call is answered.

"Hi Frans. Joe Mason here. Listen, something's come up. I'm going to have to delay your set-up for a couple of days. I'll be available again early next week so I'll give you a call when we're all clear to go ahead. OK?"

This is bad, he thinks. Stalling on a new client is unprofessional, but he has no choice. He really needs to check things out before he goes any further. He pours himself another coffee. Smokes another Gitanes. He wonders whatever made him get back into this lousy business. He promised her he wouldn't. He promised both of them. But he missed the thrill of it; the constant vigilance. When they first came here to Amsterdam, life was easy for them. There was plenty of money in the bank from the sale of the business,

131

his paintings attracted immediate interest, and her writing was going well. It was all very rosy: a life of contentment. And them together after all those years apart, in the way they wanted at last. A new birth certificate for him, a marriage certificate for them and a ring on her finger. He thought it was all he wanted.

But it seems that he isn't cut out for a life of ease. He has spent too many years on a knife-edge of intrigue. At first he resisted the temptation to go back to it, but opportunities kept presenting themselves. For three years he held back, keeping his promise. Then one day a little deal. Very small. Just a tiny favour for an old friend he came across by accident. And it stayed that way for a while. A little dabble here and there, just to keep his hand in; just to add a little spice to life. But he was good. His reputation grew. The favours got more frequent, and now he is in deep. As deep as he has ever been. A promise well and truly broken. Smashed to smithereens.

Joseph walks home in the middle of the afternoon. The weather is milder today. A breeze blows in from the south. The low sun comes out, emphasising the stark trellising of the winter-bare trees against the pale sky. It glints off pallid water where lazy bright-eyed gulls sit bobbing on wavelets. Joseph wonders what kind of reception he'll get this time. Maybe she'll be out.

She's on the sofa, smoking. She's wearing a silky dressing gown in cream. It clings to her body, around the curve of her hip, around the cheeks of her backside, slimmer than Heidi's. The thought of the other woman leaves him cold now.

"I've been sleeping," she explains. "I'd better get dressed." She seems to be even. Not angry or spiteful just at the moment. He goes and sits down beside her on the sofa. He feels guilty. Not about Heidi. About the other thing: the broken promises that she doesn't know about. She looks up at him with a question on her face. He can't tell how she's feeling. He looks back at her. He sees all of his past in her eyes. He sees the pain he has brought her all her life. It makes him want to cry, but he's forgotten how to. He hasn't cried for twenty years. He takes her hand and kisses each of her fingertips.

"Go to England if you want to," he says. "I trust you. Of course I do. Nothing really matters to me except that you're happy, Anna. You know that."

"Do I?" she asks, but the question's a soft one. There's no bitterness in it. "What's the matter with us, Joe? Why do we fight so much these days?"

"Because we're so damned stubborn!" He smiles.

"That's true," she admits.

He kisses her mouth, and she puts her arms around him. He holds her close to him. For a while they lie together on the large sofa, cradled in each other's arms.

"Don't ever leave me, Anna," he whispers.

"No," she replies. "I never could."

Later he tells her that he has to go to Switzerland. He's concerned that she'll take it badly, but it's all right. For the moment, she is soft towards him, and she accepts his explanation that he's seeing an art dealer.

"Will you see anyone else while you're there?" she asks casually. "You know. The family." She winks at him and they both laugh.

"I shouldn't think so," he says. "They were never very interested in me."

"You might meet one on the street by accident," she says, eyes wide with mock concern.

"I'll stay off the street." He nods. "I'll travel under cover of darkness."

"A practice of your shady past," she laughs. Does he detect an edge to that? In hidden corners of his soul, he knows that she suspects the truth of him. It hurts him. He grins back with a wicked look.

After they've eaten in the evening, he makes love to her. It starts so slowly and takes so long. It's filled with gentle caresses and the most sensuous of touches. They know each other's pleasures so well. She makes him feel almost delirious with his desire; his love for her. How can she be jealous of anyone? Nothing could ever be like this. Sometimes he just wants to fuck, but with her it can be an act of worship; a transcendent thing. There isn't any comparison.

In his arms she sleeps, twitching like a cat in her dreams. Her hand curls and flexes against him. Gently he takes hold of it and draws her nearer. And then she murmurs something: a word filled with longing. It's hard to decipher. And then again, a little louder, a little clearer. A name, not his own, and an ugly, threatening fear grips at his heart.

eighteen

"Hi Julie." Harry smiled. "Can I get you a drink?"

"A martini would be divine," she said, perching herself elegantly next to him. "I just got back from New York," she told him. "Spent a couple of days shopping."

"Oh yeah?"

"You know I can hardly help it, honey. Anyhow, shouldn't really. Got a few jobs on currently, but nothing too problematic. How about you, Harry? I thought you were up in Flagstaff now?" Julie Jefferson picked up her martini and sipped at it beautifully – several times in quick succession. It was clear to Harry that she had tried to model her look on Marilyn Monroe's. In Harry's opinion, she'd missed by a mile. She was good-looking enough in her way, but the shade of her hair was too harsh, the colour of her lipstick too garish, the set of her jaw too masculine, the look in her eyes too greedy. She flashed him a wide, brilliant-toothed smile.

"I'm investigating a matrimonial case," Harry told her a little uncomfortably. "It ain't very interesting I'm afraid. Some guy ran off. I'm looking for him. You know the sort of thing."

"Oh sure." Julie nodded. "Let's not talk shop though honey. I mean, long time no see. What's been going on with you?"

Harry shrugged. "Things are pretty quiet, pretty run-of-the-mill," he said. "Much the same as ever."

"You always were a simple soul, Harry." Julie took another half dozen sips of her martini. It was all but gone. "Hey, get me another martini, Melanie sugar. That one didn't touch the sides."

The bartender obliged.

"So is this a regular haunt of yours?" Harry enquired.

135

"That's right," Julie agreed. Her blonde hair bounced shinily around when she moved her head. "I don't live too far from here. I kinda like it. It's kinda quiet. Good service."

Harry felt relieved. He'd had a suspicion that Maria had told Julie about him and Tina, but evidently not. "So," he said. "Anything exciting been happening in your life?"

"Not till five minutes ago, honey!" She winked at him and laughed in her little-girl voice. "Never could resist a pretty face."

"Not sure I appreciate being called pretty." Harry frowned.

"Sorry, honey." Julie slapped the back of her left hand with the fingers of her right. "You know I got married?" she asked.

"No?" Harry felt relieved again.

"Yeah," she said sadly. "Barely lasted six months. What *is* it with you guys? Can't you be domesticated? Think I'm better off with my dog."

Harry cleared his throat. A rather unsavoury image had just presented itself to him. He flicked a cigarette out of his packet and lit it.

"Now that is *so* bad for you, honey," Julie scolded him.

"Yeah, yeah." He grimaced. "Smokers know that better than anyone, Julie."

"Then why do it?" she persisted.

"Death wish," he said a little curtly. He wanted to get away from her. He found her cloying and overbearing. He had made a mistake back when they first knew each other and he wished he hadn't. He wanted to get himself a coffee and go to bed, but he knew where his duties lay. He wanted to find something out. He wondered how he might do it.

Julie was describing her flight back from New York to him.

136

There had been problems. One of the plane's engines had failed.

"Must have been scary," Harry sympathised.

"Oh, I just looked around for the nearest hunk to hang onto," Julie smiled. "It wasn't so bad. I don't think there was any real *danger*,"

"My…" Harry stopped. He'd been just about to say something unwise. Something about Tina. "Got in from San Francisco earlier myself," he said.

"Such a cute city," Julie said. She examined a polished nail quite closely, checking for chips. She shifted in her seat, uncrossing and recrossing her legs in the opposite direction. She ran a bejewelled hand down her shin to her ankle, leaning forward and revealing a deep cleavage. "Not a bad little journey either." She sat up straight again, picked up her martini glass and swirled the liquid round in it.

"Hey, I ran into an old buddy of yours out there," Harry said as though he had suddenly remembered. "Back when we were out in LA. D'you remember John O'Brien?"

Julie was leaning now on the bar with her elbow, propping up her head with her hand. Her crimson, pointed fingernails intertwined with the metallic blonde curls of her hair. "Had other things on my mind in those days honey." Her eyes narrowed lasciviously. "I remember *you* in LA, Harry. Now that was kinda nice."

"Long time back now," Harry said rather abruptly. He noticed that he was sitting with his own legs crossed, sort of coiled in on himself, protecting everything. He wandered what those body language experts might make of it. He didn't think the interpretation would be too difficult.

"Great shame," Julie sighed.

"Yeah, it was funny running into O'Brien again," Harry mused.

"Hasn't changed a bit."

Julie thought, toying with her glass, running an elegant finger around its rim. It was almost empty again. Harry signalled to the bartender who made another one up and brought it over. "Angel! You're clearly *aware* of a girl's needs. Goodness, I knew that already didn't I, honey?" She leaned across and pinched Harry playfully on the thigh. He wished she would shut up about that. "Anyhow, who did you say?" She sipped her fresh drink. "O'Brien? No, I can't say... oh, now, yes. That dreadful little Irish man. Ugh! Never did like him."

"O'Brien's OK." Harry shrugged. "He likes to talk, but so do a lot of guys. Appreciates his wife. Maybe you oughtta pick someone like him, Julie." Harry smirked to himself.

Julie looked aghast. "Don't be ridiculous, Harry. You must be crazy. The guy's only half my height for one thing." She pouted, drank some more martini and ate a little popcorn which the bartender had supplied a moment before – no charge. "So," she said with a bored sigh. "Did O'Brien divulge any interesting information? Any nasty little pieces of gossip that we snoopers like to hear?"

"Matter of fact, he seemed pretty keen to tell me about a piece of work he'd picked up." Harry nodded. He had almost finished his own beer now. He didn't really want another though. It was too gassy. "Hey, gimme a JD on the rocks, honey." He addressed the bartender who obliged swiftly. "Chasing some guy up from Colombia evidently. Polish name. Can't quite remember it." He put a thoughtful frown on his face.

"Really?" Julie looked interested.

"Yeah. Some kind of family trouble, I understand. Who knows what else? O'Brien's talking to a guy called Juan, so he tells me." He was speaking casually, but watching her carefully, surreptitiously. He noticed a slight reaction in her mouth and eyelids when he mentioned the name. "O'Brien said they were looking all over the south west for this guy. Seems like quite an operation for some kid who ran out on a family business. What was that name? Began with a B." He pushed his fringe back out of his eyes, ran his hand to the back of his head and scratched it, frowning and twisting his mouth to one side in a pretence of trying to remember.

"Wouldn't be Byszewski by any chance?" Julie asked. There was a cynical twist to her own mouth.

"Yeah!" Harry grinned in fake surprise. "That was it! Byszewski. How did you know that?"

"I'm on the same case," she explained. "Been checking Phoenix out for evidence that the guy was here. First name's Ecuador. Pretty odd. Most people know him as Joe in fact." She drank from her martini glass with pretty relish. She had almost emptied it again. "You make a *divine* martini, Melanie, honey. If a little small. Jeez, do I have a thirst on me this evening!"

"I could make you a larger one," the bartender offered.

"Wonderful!" Julie smiled greedily.

Harry thought he had better be quick about getting the facts out of her. At this rate she would be incoherent any minute. "So you've met this Juan, I guess?" he asked.

"Yeah. He called me." She nodded. "I met up with him. Quite attractive. A little short for my liking, but I could make allowances."

"Did you get any of the background?"

"Hey! What is this?" She peered at Harry closely, leaning forward and sort of squeezing herself together with her upper arms to make the most of her already ample cleavage. "Why d'you wanna know?"

Harry shrugged. "Oh, just mildly interested. You know I had a little run in with some guys from down there a while back. I get a little nervous when I hear that there are things going on in my area, you understand?"

"Oh yes, I do remember that." Julie tutted. "I was *concerned* for you, honey."

"Yeah, well, hopefully it's all forgotten now," Harry said.

"Juan told me that this was some family thing – he didn't go into too much detail. I got a little suspicious because of the obvious connections, but he *assured* me that there was no cartel involvement. I mean, I explained to him that I got my reputation to keep up. You know we've got to watch our integrity, haven't we, Harry? We can't be seen to be getting tied up with anything on the wrong side of the law. So Juan says that this Byszewski guy had some big argument with his pop, and now Michael Byszewski – that's the senior guy – wants to get his son back so they can kiss and make up."

Harry nodded with interest and sipped his bourbon.

"Of course, it may just be a cover story," Julie continued. "I found Juan to be a little slick, if you know what I mean. Cute, but slick. Sure paying good money though. Hey, I gotta go to the john." She slipped off her barstool. Rather unsteadily, she made her way out of the bar.

Harry mused to himself, digesting this latest information. He felt uneasy. It seemed that Juan had altered his story to suit the situation. He hadn't wanted to put Julie Jefferson off the case so he hadn't told her about the cartel woman. Harry remembered O'Brien's description of this Juan. With what he'd just found out it seemed like the Colombian was definitely not a man to be trusted. So what was the truth about Byszewski and the family business? Why had he run out and entered the States illegally? Harry felt he was no wiser about that now than he had been four days ago when he picked up the case. He had the uncomfortable suspicion that his early doubts had been accurate and that he should have left well alone. He'd ignored his instincts all the way down the line here. Perhaps that was a foolish thing to do. It wasn't his usual style.

Julie Jefferson returned from the rest rooms. She had renewed her lipstick. Her mouth was like a crimson fly-trap. It scared Harry.

"Shall I call you a cab, Ms Jefferson?" the bartender offered politely.

"Don't know if I need one tonight, honey." Julie looked directly at Harry, her eyes narrowed in invitation.

"Yeah, well, I'd best be getting along." Harry stood up quickly. "Got an early start tomorrow. Nice to meet you again, Julie." He shook her hand. She held on to his after he tried to withdraw it.

"Hey, if you're free tomorrow, maybe we could do dinner?" she suggested.

"Er... I'm gonna be working *real* late tomorrow, Julie. And I'm expecting to be heading on home pretty soon. I can't really see us getting a chance to get together again this trip. Sorry honey."

"Yeah. Me too." Julie still had hold of his hand. "Hey, if you're here tomorrow evening any time though, I'll probably be around. We could have another drink at least." She pursed her lips and pouted at him.

"Well, maybe. I can't promise that." Harry tried to pull his hand away.

"How about a little kiss for old time's sake?" Julie put her mouth up towards him.

Harry pecked her on the cheek, finally extracted his hand and headed out of the bar at the maximum speed that politeness allowed. One place he knew he would most definitely *not* be the following evening was the bar of the Ramada hotel.

At seven thirty the next morning, Harry rang through to Tina Philpott's room.

"Hi Harry," she chuckled before he had said a word.

"Could have been anyone," he said with a laugh. "Anyhow, this is your alarm call. Breakfast at eight?"

"Of course," she replied lightly.

"Meet me out by the car," he told her.

He drove them to a Mexican diner in another part of the city.

"Why are we going so far away?" Tina asked looking puzzled. "There were plenty of places we could have eaten in back there."

"They do good *huevos rancheros*," Harry told her. "It's Mexican breakfast. You'll love it."

She looked at him quizzically. "There are Mexican diners all over the city, Harry. What's going on?"

He shrugged. "Wanna keep a low profile," he said and he wouldn't be drawn further. Tina was fidgeting with curiosity, and Harry was enjoying it. He was in a pretty good mood altogether this morning. He had had a dream about Tina Philpott which he remembered when he woke up, and which he had enjoyed a lot. It had set him up for the day.

The diner was dimly lit and quite intimate. It was easy to stay out of the way in there, to be unobtrusive. Tina tutted at Harry.

"You're obviously not English," she said. "Shunning the sunlight is not in their character. It's such a beautiful day, Harry.

142

Why are we hiding away from it?"

"It's *always* a beautiful day in Phoenix," Harry told her. "Now keep quiet and eat your eggs."

"Oh great," she said with a wry twist of her mouth. "First you want to hide me away, then you want me to stop talking. Why don't you just pack me up in a box and store me under the table?"

"Now that ain't such a bad idea!" he replied with a cackle.

"Tell me what you're up to, Harry Smith!" She threatened him with her fork.

"I'm hungry," he said. "I'll tell you in a while."

She glared at him in frustration. He put on an air of innocence and looked back at her, eating his eggs and tortilla, refried beans and salsa as slowly as he could. He was a great fan of Mexican food, especially *huevos rancheros*. It was good, cheap and filling. He had a second mug of coffee on the table and a cigarette in his hand before he would say anything more.

"Just after you left the bar last night, that other investigator turned up," he explained. "We were *very* lucky she didn't catch us together."

"You know her as well, do you? Quite a little coterie you've got round here." Tina looked sceptical.

"That's a big word for it," Harry remarked.

Tina shrugged. "I love words," she said. "Books, language, you know."

Harry looked at her. It was the first thing she had really revealed about herself apart from the family stuff. "Anyhow, she was out in LA too," he said. "After a little prompting, she admitted to being on your brother's case, but she lives in the vicinity of the hotel she told me. I didn't want her to spot us together. She might make a connection."

Tina nodded slowly. "I suppose I'll have to keep hidden then. Oh great, that'll be fun!" she said ironically.

"Well, I guess one of us ought to be at the hotel in case your brother turns up anyhow."

Tina made a huffing sort of noise. "Does that mean I'll have to stay in my room all day?" she demanded.

"Hey, it's up to you." Harry shrugged.

"And all evening?" Her eyes narrowed at him.

"It's possible Joe'll turn up, and then I guess you'll have new plans to make," Harry said patiently. "But if not I guess we could go out somewhere tonight."

"Well that's big of you," she said. "I'll wear a bag over my head, shall I?"

"It ain't my fault," he told her. "We'll just be careful. There'll be no problem."

Tina harrumphed at him and sipped her coffee, mug cupped between her hands.

"We'll have to be on the lookout when we do go out though," Harry mused, half to himself. "She uses that bar a lot she told me. She said she'd be in there tonight."

Tina eyed him suspiciously. "What's she like then?" she asked.

"Who?"

"Julie Jefferson," Tina said with exaggerated patience.

"Well, er... sort of tall, blonde, built. A little overbearing, if you get my drift."

Tina nodded knowingly. "After you, was she?"

"Oh I... I don't think so." Harry shook his head dismissively. "Nah! Shouldn't think I'm her type."

Tina was peering at him intently. He tried to look nonchalant, tried not to catch her eyes where he could plainly see mischief dancing. "She was, wasn't she?" She leaned towards him.

"She kinda overdid the martinis," Harry admitted.

Tina rocked back in her chair, smirking with evident glee. She had a knowing look in her eyes. Harry thought she was being rather forward.

"She went home in a cab," he said. "You can take that look off your face, Ms Philpott. I don't like the implications."

"Oh well, I *am* sorry." Tina made a contrite face, and then raised her eyebrows in an aspect of demur primness.

"As a matter of fact, I damn near had to fight the woman off," Harry growled, clenching his fists slightly. "That's one hell of a scary broad."

Tina's eyes widened. She sucked in her cheeks and screwed up her mouth in a tremendous and obvious effort to suppress laughter. Then she put her hands up over her face and her shoulders began to shake. Strangled yelps emerged from her as she tried to stifle her hysterics.

"What's so damned funny?" Harry demanded. "I guess it wouldn't be quite so amusing if things had been the other way around, huh? If it was the guy in pursuit it would be a pretty serious thing."

Tina stopped laughing and looked at him. She was still smiling, but there was kindness in her eyes. "You're right," she said. "I'm sorry Harry. I didn't mean to make fun of you. I just couldn't imagine you being scared of a mere woman."

"Yeah, well, this ain't no *mere* woman," Harry huffed. "More of a *mere* tarantula."

Tina tittered again. "But you must admit there's a difference," she said more seriously. "Men are usually stronger, aren't they? Physically, I mean. If it came down to it, in the end, you could knock her out or something – if it was really that bad. Women don't normally have that option, do they?"

Harry sulked a bit, considering what she had said. "I guess so," he admitted. "But I ain't at all sure in this particular case. This is a hefty broad. For all I know, she may be a mud-wrestler in her spare time."

Tina began to laugh again; hearty, dirty laughter. After a second or two of pique, Harry found himself joining in. He felt a strange kind of glow inside himself. Too much coffee, he supposed.

Tina paid their bill and they got up to leave. They were in no particular hurry. They stopped at the door and Harry looked out in an exaggerated 'on the run' kind of manner. Tina giggled at him.

Just inside the diner, not far away from the door, a man sat reading a newspaper, printed in Spanish. He looked Latin-American, quite attractive, perhaps thirty-five years old. As Harry and Tina passed by, indulging in their antics, he glanced up casually at them. He looked back at his paper, and then looked up again. He peered curiously at Tina, examining her closely, as though she reminded him of someone. He called the waitress over, paid for his breakfast and hurried out into the street, but by this time there was no trace of the pair. Cursing in Spanish, he walked around to the parking lot and sat in his car for a while, thinking.

nineteen

She feels so tired of all this worry and confusion. When he holds her in his arms, loves her with all the tenderness in the world, she can forget for a little while. But then the dreams come again and reality breaks through and all the cares come back. She thinks she knows what he's doing. He's not much good at hiding things from her. And how long will it last then? This life that's bound to end in tears?

He's gone to Geneva today. She doesn't think his trip has much to do with art. He hasn't painted much lately, and she's seen the worry, badly hidden behind his eyes, but there's no point in getting angry. She can't bring herself to discuss it openly, so she should remain reasonable with him. It isn't fair, she thinks, to pick on other issues and to skirt around the truth. She's trying to stay calm, to come up with some sensible plan for action.

She writes in the morning; concentrates hard on what she's doing. She got a cheque in the post first thing: royalties from an earlier effort. She knows they've plenty of money, but it makes her feel good to know that she can support herself. At lunchtime, she looks out and sees it's bright. For some reason, she feels suddenly optimistic. The Brouwersgracht looks fine today, picturesque and pretty with colourful jostling houseboats crammed closely together along its banks. It's not such a bad place, Amsterdam. This evening, Mari's coming over. They'll plan their trip and drink some wine and she'll try to put her worries aside. She feels oddly free. He won't be back until Saturday. She has two days of solitude. She smiles, surprised at the lightness of her.

After some lunch, she steps outside. December has just begun, but the weather is unseasonably warm. She has too many clothes on and grumpily she goes back inside for a moment to adjust her dress to the temperature. But the grumpiness is good-humoured and very temporary. She feels the fresh air fill her up, sees the afternoon sun sparkling on the water in the canal, and she walks slowly, contentedly, ambling aimlessly, letting her feet take her where they choose.

She finds herself on Kalverstraat, looking into shop windows, wondering about new clothes. He wouldn't have her shop here. He thinks she ought to spend her money in grander stores on finer things, but she was never one for swagger; never bothered much about fine quality or exclusive labels. She likes simplicity: clean lines and plain fabrics on her body, not too much decoration. She'd feel silly in frills. She remembers one Christmas years ago, going back home in tight black jeans and leather jacket, bright red lipstick on her mouth. She was only sixteen and had previously dressed in shapeless things. The look on his face when he saw her like that. She smiles at the memory and then she feels sad. Why did she have to grow up, she wonders. Why are promises so much better than their fulfilment? She remembers the stark, bright emotions of her youth. How real everything felt then; how intense. Now she sometimes feels anaesthetised. What's wrong with her?

Suddenly a thought comes into her mind. She thinks she is always waiting. All her life. Waiting for someone or something else to make things happen; to make things right. Waiting for joy to come to her. She has never sought it out, save once or twice, and even then she was frightened to state it plainly; scared her requests might be rejected so that she instead tried to manipulate the situation to her ends. You fool, she thinks. She sees herself as pathetic and weak. But knowing what she wants is hard for her. She used to think she knew. Now maybe her old desires are not enough; perhaps they are no longer valid. She decides that she will ponder on this and in the meantime she goes into a clothes shop and tries on a pair of jeans that fit her snugly, and a bright red sweater that caresses her breasts. In the pocket of her jacket is a tube of lipstick. She paints her lips and smiles at herself in the changing room mirror. She mouths the words 'sexy cow' at her reflection and smirks at another memory. It seems like a happy time in retrospect, but in reality she was bursting with teenage angst.

She buys the clothes and then finds a place to change into them. She throws the old ones into a waste bin and feels wicked. She will dress like this in future, she decides. She's been drifting around too long in rags. She lifts her head and walks with panache, drawing looks from here and there. In a café, she drinks cappuccino and nibbles on a sweet biscuit, and she feels excited.

As she leaves, as light begins to fade from the sky and the day starts to chill towards evening, she catches sight of him again: the tall man, like the one she dreams of, like the one who died because of her and because of him. He's not so close that she can make out his features clearly, but with her new-found attitude to life, she decides to pursue him. She walks quickly until she's ten metres away. His back is to her, his hands in his trouser pockets. He carries a London Times newspaper tucked under his left arm. She hesitates a moment and almost turns away. But no! She chides herself, and she determines to be relentless. She looks intently at merchandise behind some glass, but she's watching him and what he does. He's unaware of her, she thinks. He starts to move away. She follows him with a casual stride. The way he walks looks so familiar, but she doesn't altogether trust her memory. It can't be him in any case. She's simply having fun.

149

He's followed the Singel round in her homeward direction. That's convenient. He might have led her miles away. Outside the post office on the corner of Raadhuisstraat, a gaggle of people and bicycles obscure him. She loses sight of him, worming her way through the crowd, and then she comes out unexpectedly upon him waiting at the pedestrian crossing for the lights to change. Quickly, she drops back, crossing the road a way behind him, and she dawdles, letting him get ahead of her until she's a comfortable distance behind. Then he seems to speed up and she has to trot to keep up with the length of his stride. She's sure he doesn't know she's there. He doesn't look behind him and she cleverly anticipates his actions when he crosses another road. She's pleased with herself.

Before the Singel meets the Brouwersgracht, he turns off at Blauwburgwal to the west. Now he walks more slowly, glancing into shop windows. She wants to stop and look too, but she must keep her eye on him. The afternoon grows colder now. The sky turns pink with the advancing evening, and the light's changing wavelengths soften all the colours and sharpen the outlines and odd angles of the tall narrow buildings. Then, on a bridge across the Prinsengracht, he stops. He leans on green railings and gazes north towards Brouwersgracht and the Noordermarkt. He hasn't seen her, but now she's not sure what to do. She can see his face plainly in profile as she walks towards him, intending perhaps to pass by and then stop somewhere ahead, or to turn and take the west bank of the canal towards her home. He's so like the other man as she remembers him, that it's uncanny. She feels her heartbeat, violent in her chest. She draws up close, but still he hasn't noticed that she's there. He looks as though his thoughts are quite far away and very sad. She feels her emotions well in sympathy with his sorrow. She wants to stand alongside him and to say his name. She wants to cradle his head against her breast and to see him smile. She wants to soothe the world-cares out of him.

She walks behind him passes by and on. On the west side, she turns to the north and begins to head for home, but a few yards on she can't resist. She turns round to look at him again. He has come away from the railings. He is walking towards her, looking straight at her. She feels herself overcome with fear or excitement, she's not sure which it is. She can't move from the spot. It's like a dream where her legs won't work. As he approaches she gazes at his face and he at hers. He knows her. She's sure of it. There's a look in his eyes that takes her back in time.

"Anna!" A voice spins her round. It's Mari there, shocking her into the present. "I was on my way over." Mari brandishes a bottle of wine at her. "You're supposed to be at home waiting for me. What a fine friend you are!"

Anna shrugs and makes a guilty face. She kisses her friend on the cheek to make up for her badness. Then she turns around to check where the man is, but he's nowhere to be seen.

twenty

The morning dragged. Harry looked up a couple of old acquaintances in Phoenix, and drove around for a while somewhat aimlessly. It wasn't his favourite city. It spread out across the desert for miles and miles, mostly low-rise apart from the business centre. He thought it rather a dull place. But it was certainly hot. One of the buildings down town had a big meteorological display on the side of it. It flashed up the current temperature at 115 degrees Fahrenheit.

Just after midday, he picked up some sandwiches and took them back to the hotel. He knocked on Tina's door and announced himself.

"Come in, it's open," she called. She was lounging on a reclining chair, a book in one hand and a cigarette in the other.

"Brought you some lunch," Harry said.

"Good," she replied. "God, I'm bored."

"Why don't you go shopping this afternoon?" Harry suggested.

"What for?" she asked in surprise.

"Hell, I don't know. Women like to shop." He shrugged.

"*Your* women might," she said. "I feel like lounging about in the sun and taking a dip or two in a cool pool." She stubbed out her cigarette, put down her book and stretched herself luxuriously backwards. The black vest she was wearing parted company at the waist with her jeans and exposed a small band of smooth, tanned midriff. She turned slightly towards Harry, onto her left side, and threw her right arm languorously over her head. Her hair fell about like slithers of fine jersey cotton, and she pouted at him. "But of course, sunbathing in the desert is a particularly stupid thing to do," she sighed.

Harry sat himself down on the floor a little way from her,

arranging himself carefully to hide a pleasant but inconvenient reaction to her movements that had manifested itself in his groin. He admitted to himself that the thought of watching her swimming wasn't such a bad one either. He handed her a sandwich. She pulled the recliner into its upright position and slid down off it onto the floor where she sat cross-legged, quite close to him. He regarded her curiously.

"What's up with you?" she asked him with an engaging kind of familiar rudeness.

"Just thinking how much you've changed since we met," he told her. "Five days ago, was it?"

"I'm a bit wary of people I suppose," she said, nodding slowly. "All right when you get to know me though, eh?" She sniggered, screwing up her nose with a kind of self-deprecating expression.

"Hell no, I wouldn't go *that* far," Harry cackled.

"Oi!" she said, leaning over and slapping him quite hard on the arm.

"Ow!" he complained.

"So what psychological type have you got me down for now, Mr Smith?" She grinned at him.

"Well, let me see…" He took a bite from his sandwich and chewed, thinking of a suitable answer. "Clearly mercurial, touch of the dramatic, possibly borderline with psychopathic tendencies."

"Hmm. If I knew what any of that meant, I might have to hit you again, but I don't so you're probably safe. Hang on, did you say psychopathic?" She glared at him comically.

"I'd have to do tests to be certain." He nodded gravely.

"I wouldn't kill anyone," she told him.

"It wasn't the kind of test I was thinking of," he cackled.

"Anyhow, what about your pop? You don't like him too much."

"Oh, I can talk a good murder," she shrugged. "When it came right down to it, I wouldn't have the guts. I'm a coward at heart. There, you can put that on your list. Goodness, I'm not coming out of this very well, am I?"

"Lost cause by the sounds of it," Harry agreed.

"Oh well, I may as well give up trying to be good then." She smirked to herself. "So," she turned to him, looking at him rather directly. "Providing Joe doesn't show up today, where will you be taking me tonight?"

"Hey! I thought you were paying!" He raised his eyebrows, pretending to be indignant.

"Oh, all right, where am I taking you?"

"Surprise," he said. "I've got a few ideas."

Tina lifted her shoulders up to her ears and grinned gleefully.

In the afternoon, she swam for a while in the hotel pool dressed in a one-piece black costume that was more sporty than sexy in design, but nonetheless clung to her slim body, leaving little to the imagination. She wasn't a strong swimmer, but she managed a few lengths, with an easy, lazy kind of action. Harry didn't have any swimming trunks with him, so he sat beside the pool under the shade of a large umbrella and sweltered somewhat in the heat. He was pretending to read a newspaper but actually he was mostly watching Tina and rather enjoying himself. He remembered the dream he'd had in some detail and thought he had better turn the shower down to chilly before they went out later.

Carefully, at seven o'clock, after an afternoon doze in their separate rooms, and time spent refreshing themselves from the heat of the day, they sneaked out of the hotel into the car park where a giant

154

saguaro cactus erupted out of a patch of gravel, silhouetted, almost black against the deep turquoise of the early evening sky. They got into the back of a waiting cab which took them ten miles across the city to Glendale and an Italian restaurant that Harry knew. He liked Italian food as well as Mexican. It was a nice dark restaurant with intimate little tables which shielded them from too much contact with the other diners. Harry ordered pizza and Tina got some pasta with seafood. She insisted they have Chianti to go with it and called Harry a philistine when he suggested that American beer would be just as good.

"Anyone would think that we were the subject of one of your 'matrimonial investigations'," Tina said lightly.

"Makes it kinda interesting though." Harry grinned.

"I wonder when Joe will turn up." Tina looked pensive. "Do you think there's any danger, Harry? I mean, honestly, have you any idea what's going on?"

He thought for a moment. A candle on the table flickered causing shadows to play across Tina Philpott's face. Her eyes looked dark in this light, the pupils of them wide open, the long lashes of them silhouetted on her lids. She never wore make-up on her eyes, Harry noticed. She didn't need to. Tonight she had red lipstick on her mouth. It suited her, drawing attention to its shape and mobility. No fly-traps there. "I can't say I do." He considered whether to mention that Julie Jefferson's story had differed from O'Brien's. He was concerned that she would worry, that she might withdraw from him and that the evening would be spoilt. He decided not to tell her. He wanted them to have a good time. "All my information shows that your pop wants Joe to go back to Bogotá," he said matter-of-factly. "The worst thing that can happen is that they find him first. That's

155

what my feeling is. But I think we'll get there. I mean, he's gonna come to us, so we've got a better chance, I reckon."

"I hope you're right," she said. She ate some food, lost in her own thoughts for a while. Harry let her be.

After the meal was finished, they strolled out a block or two to a bar. This too was dark inside with sections of it partitioned off. They positioned themselves so that Tina was completely hidden behind a screen, but Harry could see people coming and going.

"I love to walk," Tina said as they sat down opposite one another. She had her black dress on again tonight. She looked very sultry in the dim light. "I do it all the time in London. It's a beautiful city, Harry. Have you ever been there?"

"Can't say I have." He shook his head. "Never been out of the States as a matter of fact."

"I can imagine that exploring this country might take a lifetime." She nodded. "But people think London's horrid and it isn't. It's magnificent. Even the nasty bits have their charm, you know." She smiled softly to herself.

"I find cities claustrophobic," Harry admitted. "I mean, I was born in New York, but I always felt kind of hemmed in there. I like Arizona. It's got a lot of space. You can get out in the desert here and it's totally empty and totally silent. I like the ocean too, but I don't get to it too often."

"I love the sea," she said. "It's always changing, and you're right, there's some feeling of freedom about it. I remember once. Something had happened to upset me – nothing important now. I'd been out to Switzerland to see Bolivia and... and her partner, and for the first time I went back to England by train and boat. Before that I'd always flown, always been terrified." She raised her eyes in exasperation at herself. "Anyway, I was feeling sad and the weather was rough, and I stood out on the deck of the ship as it crossed the English Channel, and the power of the sea was amazing. It kind of filled me up. It made me feel insignificant and yet whole somehow. It seemed to share my anger. I can't really explain. I felt like it healed me." Her eyes sparkled with the memory.

Harry was captivated. He said nothing.

Tina, coming back to the present, looked at him and laughed. "Sorry. Dreamy nonsense as usual."

He shook his head. "Not at all. I can understand it."

She smiled at him warmly, and then lifted her glass and looked at it indignantly. "How did that happen?" she demanded of him. "I've run out of beer."

"Well, I guess you must have drunk it," he told her.

"Such is life," she said, looking resigned.

Harry caught the eye of the bartender and ordered another for them both. By the time they had finished those it was just past ten o'clock. Harry felt OK. He asked Tina if she wanted another. She said she had had enough.

"What's this?" he teased her. "Stamina lacking?"

"I believe it has something to do with discretion being the better part of something else," she said, pretending to be bleary.

"Never was one for discretion." Harry pursed his lips, shook his head and lit himself a cigarette.

"Oh! And you with your job!" Tina chastised him indignantly.

"Well then, it's a matter of not disgracing myself."

"How might you do that then?" Harry cackled slightly.

"I might pass out under the table, for one thing," she warned him, raising her eyebrows. "It wouldn't be good for my image."

"I can see that," he agreed. "It's a little early though."

"Well, maybe we could go dancing," she suggested wryly.

"You want to?" He wondered for a moment if she was serious.

She giggled. "Good lord no. I was kidding."

He gave her a very meaningful and knowing look. "Well, you know that what the client says goes," he said conspiratorially.

She began to chuckle with that vaguely dirty laugh she had. She was trying not to, but her shoulders shook and gave her away.

"Now what have I said?" Harry pretended to be affronted.

They took a cab back to the hotel where they snuck back past the bar and bought coffees from the machine. Their rooms were close to each other on opposite sides of a corridor. They dawdled back to them, exchanging idle, ludicrous conversation, neither one knowing quite how to go on. Harry's resolve about not being to blame left him. Actually it had left him much earlier in the evening, maybe even at lunchtime. He knew that if she didn't ask, he would.

"I think there's an Indiana Jones movie on TV in a while," he said. He looked at his watch, and then sipped his hot coffee. He put his left hand into his trouser pocket and rested it there, fingering his room key. Neither he nor Tina had opened their door yet.

"Come and watch it with me," she invited him hesitantly. She was looking up at him, into his eyes. Her fine eyebrows meshed into a puzzled, worried little knot on her forehead. Her beautiful turquoise eyes pleaded with him not to turn her down. He smiled at her.

"OK," he said.

Harry Smith and Tina Philpott did not watch the movie. They did not even finish drinking the coffees they had just bought. Directly she had put hers down on the bedside shelf, he touched her arm just lightly and looked into her eyes, and she came up to kiss him with a

158

kind of passion that he hadn't felt from anyone in years. He was lost in her, and she felt like liquid sunshine in his arms. His body was lean and muscular and she explored it, fed on it, worshipped it, and he adored her and delighted in her; abandoned himself to her.

Later, he went out and brought back hot coffees to replace those they had let grow cold. They sipped them in silence, lying sidelong beside each other, both wearing unsuppressable smiles. They looked at one another, and then they laughed soft and long until they were intoxicated with it. Later still, they made love again gently, slowly, exquisitely until they could hardly bear the joy of it. So absorbed were they in each other that neither noticed the small red light that flashed dully on and off on the telephone which stood on the dresser, some way away from the bed. The little red light that indicated a message had been left with the reception desk at the hotel whilst they were out.

Instead, they held one another and slept, each one contented for a few peaceful hours.

twenty-one

Late on Saturday morning, he disembarks at Schiphol airport, picks up his small, neat, black Mercedes from the long-term car park and drives into the city. They have a private garage space for the car. It isn't cheap, but he doesn't care about that.

In the apartment, she's lounging around. She's sitting at the big window that looks out over the canal, scribbling notes about plot. He startles her with his silent entry, and she jumps up and offers him coffee. She looks happy and mischievous. She is wearing clothes he hasn't seen before. They hug her figure and suit her well. He admires them but says nothing for the moment. He wonders what she's been doing whilst he was away. He's suspicious of her good mood.

"How did it go?" she asks brightly, kissing him with an exaggerated smack of the lips. She wipes his mouth with her index finger. "Now look," she tuts. "Lipstick all over you."

"What's all this decoration?" he asks her. He can hardly summon a smile.

"I'm determined to be cheerful," she states. "It'll be Christmas soon. Do you remember that Christmas when I was sixteen?" She sidles up to him again, puts her arms around him and runs her hands over his buttocks, pulling him towards her suggestively. She gives him one of her feline looks. He feels glum.

"I'm sorry, Anna." He shakes his head and strokes her hair with his hand. "I'm tired and nothing seems to be going right at the moment. I missed you."

She looks crestfallen, and she releases him. She turns away and concentrates on making coffee. He feels wretched now. He's hurt her. He puts his arms around her waist, coming up to her from behind.

160

"I remember," he says softly, kissing the tip of her ear. "How could I ever forget? We almost gave ourselves away there. I could hardly keep my hands off you."

She wriggles in his grasp and giggles a little. He wishes he could match her friskiness. He has a lot on his mind.

He's pleased to sit down with rich coffee and a cigarette. It's another fine day. The apartment is bright and clean. Two of his works decorate the living room walls. They're her favourites. Full of fire and life she said they were. He likes them too, although he feels that his style has matured substantially since then. She won't have them changed for something later though. She likes to cling to the familiar. She doesn't take to the new too readily, he thinks.

"Did you see Mari?" he asks with all the interest he can muster.

"Oh yes. She came here Thursday evening." Anna nods and smiles happily. "We got as pissed as newts and had a brilliant time. She had to spend the night. We couldn't find the door!" She giggles uncontrollably at this thought.

He wonders how come women seem to have this ability to let go, to abandon themselves to pleasure. The cares of his world are heavy on his shoulders. They never let him be.

"So is it all arranged?" he asks, trying to keep disapproval – or is it jealousy – out of his voice.

"We think we'll go in January," Anna says more sedately. "Mari's busy at work for the rest of this month. She thinks she'll get time off more easily after Christmas. She's checking and we'll book it all next week if it's all right. I think the break will do her good. This thing with Jan is wearing her down."

"I'm not surprised. It's a bad situation."

"She needs some time to sort herself out." Anna nods, looking

161

thoughtful. "At heart, I think she's strong. I think she'll leave him in the end and recover some faith in herself."

Joseph shrugs. He smokes his cigarette. Mari's problems seem trivial to him.

"So what happened in Geneva?" Anna asks smoothly. She sips her coffee leaving lipstick traces on the cup. Joseph's attention is drawn by this mark.

"Nothing good," he says. "There's an exhibition of contemporary artists planned for next summer, but they specifically wanted to show some works that I can't get hold of at the moment. I wanted to show new paintings – ones that are for sale – but they weren't interested in that, damn them!" There's more venom in the curse than is appropriate. He can hear that himself. Should he tell her the truth? He's a feeling that she'll know soon enough. How will she feel about him then? He imagines her cold towards him, uncaring. The thought cuts him like sharp paper. He'd rather she was angry. He hopes she'll be angry, but he can't face it yet.

Anna takes another sip of coffee. She lights a cigarette with a red-tipped match. He wonders why she doesn't use the pretty lighter he bought for her. She looks at him quickly and then glances away as if she can't bear to look him in the eye for long.

"I don't suppose it matters very much. We're not about to run out of money, are we?" she says.

"It's not the point. I'd like to think I do something reasonably worthwhile. I don't want to just sit around being rich. If you never sold another book, would you be happy?"

"I wouldn't stop writing, but I suppose I might feel that my life was a waste of time. I suppose I'd want to find something else to do as well."

He says nothing. There is so much on his mind that he's not sure he can cope with ordinary conversation.

"Listen," he says after a minute or two of silence. "I'm feeling a bit low. I don't want to depress you with my mood. I'll take a walk and try to snap out of it."

"All right," she says.

He kisses her before he leaves and tells her that he loves her. She says she feels the same for him. She seems so strong today, so unaffected by him and his misery, that he's worried. Again he wonders if she's having an affair. He doesn't think so. He wonders if it's just her time with Mari that's made her happy. These women seem to strengthen one another somehow; to give each other courage and support. He doesn't have friends like that. His cronies talk of intellectual things. They'll commiserate about a broken heart, a lost love affair, for sure, but he relies on her to help him and on other women to stoke his ego. And now, in his hour of need, she can't come to his aid because she doesn't know what ails him. He's lied to her; broken a promise and he must pay the price. He feels the justice of it and curses himself.

He walks to his office in the afternoon sun. There are a couple of faxes on the machine. He tears them off and reads them, but they are nothing of importance. His answering machine shows two messages. He plays them back. The first is from Carlos asking that he make contact at his earliest convenience. The second is in Spanish but without the European lisp. It's not from Eduardo. It's not about the Vaquez accounts. It's something much more important. Joseph understands the words very well, although to any snooper, any spy or listener-in, they might sound quite innocent; quite friendly.

He hasn't heard from these people in a long while. It seems

163

they've found him. He thought he had eluded them, that they had been rounded up and dealt with. But there are always those willing to step into the shoes of dead men. And now he finds that he's been working for them, innocent and unknowing. They've been using him through layers of intermediaries. He curses himself again. He thought the trouble in Geneva was bad enough: blocks put on another set of accounts; some arrests made in Germany. Things are getting too close for comfort. But apprehension, trial and incarceration are the soft options. Those who left the message on his answering machine would laugh at such a liberal system of justice.

twenty-two

At seven-thirty a.m. the telephone rang. Harry Smith, having for once slept past his habitual seven o'clock, stumbled dozily out of bed and picked up the receiver.

"Yeah?" he said, still half asleep. There was a short silence at the other end, during which Harry remembered that he wasn't in his own room.

"Argentina Byszewski!" A malicious-sounding foreign voice spat the name at him down the line.

"Who?" Harry's brain churned for a moment. "Oh... yeah, she's here. Hold on."

Tina had woken up now. She was pulling herself out of bed. Sleepily, and with a sheepish little grin on her face, she wandered over to him. He handed her the receiver, but she put it down on the dresser, reached up to put her arms around him and kissed him. She stroked the back of his neck in a way that he particularly liked.

"Good morning," she whispered. "How come I get an alarm call even when you're in my room?"

Harry ran his hands over her back, savouring the smoothness of her. "I guess it's your brother. Sounds foreign anyhow."

Something happened to her eyes then. It was as though she had just felt something die inside of her. She turned away from Harry and picked up the phone. Harry walked back to the bed and lay back down, pulling the covers up over himself. Suddenly, he felt empty.

"Hallo?" Tina said.

The voice on the other end was loud enough for Harry to hear, but it spoke in French and it wasn't particularly clear. Harry had learned a little French at school, but his memory of it was sketchy now at best. Nonetheless, he made out some of what Tina was saying.

"Don't be silly, he's just a friend," he caught.

More angry words came down the line.

"He helped me find you... look, let's have this argument later..."

Harry couldn't understand the next bit.

The conversation ended. Tina replaced the receiver and sighed. "He says he'll be here in half an hour." She stood next to the dresser, naked, looking lost. Her fists were clenched.

"Come here," Harry said gently. She did as she was told and sat down next to him. He reached out and gathered her into himself. All at once she seemed to have turned into a frightened child. He held her close and she clung to him, but he could feel that she wasn't really with him any more. Harry wondered what hold this brother had over her. He was beginning to dislike the guy, and he hadn't even met him yet.

At eight o'clock, practicalities like packing and payment hastily completed, Harry Smith and Tina Philpott walked into the reception area of the Ramada Hotel. The promised convention had, it seemed, already begun. People with loud voices and louder clothes swarmed heartily around, greeting one another with shrieks and shouts of pleasure. Harry preferred to start his days in a quieter way. The noise grated on his nerves.

Harry and Tina picked their way into this maelstrom and looked around but, even though the place was packed with people, it was easy to spot Ecuador Josef Byszewski.

He was only medium height, but he had a weird kind of presence about him. He exuded confidence and importance. People did not get in his way. There was a similarity to his sister, but

166

everything about him was harder, more symmetrical and angrier. He wore faded Levis which fitted him as though they were tailor-made, and a black shirt which was loose and expensively cut. His skin was tanned deep brown and on his wrist was a black watch with a black face. There were no numerals, just hands glinting thinnest gold.

He noticed them at once. His eyes, similar to Tina's but without the glints of green and about a thousand times colder, ran dismissively over Harry and then settled on his sister. And as she looked back at him, it seemed to Harry that everyone else in the room, including himself, simply faded away. He couldn't read what was in those two pairs of eyes as they approached one another, but it was clear that no one else existed for either of them at that moment. Perhaps he imagined it, but Harry thought a sudden hush descended on the crowd. He saw people staring, open mouthed at the pair, caught and silenced in mid sentence. It only lasted a second, and then the hubbub broke out again, but Harry felt unpleasant chills travel down his spine.

Tina Philpott was wearing blue jeans and a simple red vest. Her brother reached out to her and touched her upper arm. The touch was a caress, so sensual and intimate, yet lasting just a moment or two. Harry had thought the women he'd spoken to had over-reacted to this man; made too much of him. Evidently not.

Tina and her brother spoke quickly to one another in French. It wasn't possible to hear much of what they said. The crowd around was babbling and the separate words were indistinguishable although the foreign sounds stood out from the American twang. One word came through though: 'putain'. Harry knew what that meant. It was fired by Ecuador Byszewski at his sister and her cheeks turned crimson in response. Harry felt angry.

At last, Tina smiled broadly in a terribly icy kind of way and,

167

taking her brother's arm, she led him over towards Harry, who recoiled slightly, feeling that he would rather be someplace else.

"This is Harry Smith," Tina said slowly in English. Harry felt strange with two pairs of those eyes looking at him. One pair was friendly, gorgeous, almost turquoise; the other were a deep, bone-chilling blue, and as full of hate as he had ever seen anything in his life. "He is a private detective who helped me find you, recommended by great uncle Clive. He has been very good to me." She winked at Harry, who thought it best not to react. "Harry this is my brother, Joe. I think he's a bit overwrought at the moment."

Harry held out his right hand to the other man and said: "Hi, pleased to meet you," but the response was a sneer, and then the guy advanced towards Harry and pointed a finger at him. Ecuador Byszewski was four inches or so shorter than Harry, and seven years younger, but Harry did not feel at an advantage.

"Never touch my sister!" he growled in a voice that was heavily accented, low and powerful.

Harry shrugged. "Up to her, pal," he said, wondering who the hell this guy thought he was.

Tina intervened. "Wait for me here, Harry. I'll be back in a little while."

Harry nodded and sat down on a chair which was part of a row backing onto a wall. The convention people had started to disperse, making their way off to their meeting room or wherever they were going, and the foyer was nearly empty now, apart from one or two stray souls. It was bright in there, a cheerful kind of yellow. Harry lit a cigarette and wished his mood matched it.

After a time, Tina returned, looking wistful. "I've put him in the bar," she said. "Pity it's not open. Your friend Julie might have

168

come in and taken charge of him."

Harry laughed.

"I'm sorry about him," she said, shaking her head. Her own accent seemed a little stronger now. "He's crazy. Too long in Colombia. Gone mad, I shouldn't wonder."

"He seems a little weird," Harry admitted. "Possessive about you…" He wondered about them then. Was there more to this than a straight brother-sister relationship? It was a nasty suspicion to have. He kept it to himself. It was none of his business.

Harry finished his cigarette and both of them stood up. Tina took hold of his hand and led him to the most private area in the foyer – a corner by a cigarette dispensing machine.

"Thank you for last night," she said.

"I guess it wasn't very professional of me," Harry looked to the side, feeling slightly embarrassed.

"I don't care about that. Look, would you kiss me please?" she asked him with that delicately knotted brow, that troubled, worried look that he found completely irresistible. He obliged her, tenderly at first, then passionately, holding her as close as he could. It wasn't his style to make such displays of affection in public, but he knew this was probably his last chance and he wasn't about to let propriety deprive him of it.

She pulled away at last and looked up into his eyes. He could see passion in hers; an intensity he had seen the night before. "I…" she started and then shook her head. "Maybe some things are better this way," she said.

Harry nodded and kissed her again. He felt for a moment that he was losing something of himself, like she was stealing something from him that he might never get back. "It's been a *real* pleasure,

Tina," he said gruffly. He felt a touch embarrassed but... "I would have liked some more time with you, babe," he added.

She looked up at him with a smile that was full of trust. "Me too," she said. "Harry, I..." she tutted and bit her lip. "Oh, you're just gorgeous," she told him, chortling and grinning gleefully, and then she slipped out of his arms.

"You too, babe," he called after her. She laughed and waved, and then she was gone.

Harry Smith walked out of the hotel into the wall of heat outside. He unlocked his car, opened the door and got in. It was baking in there, but he didn't start up the engine or the air conditioning system yet. He still hadn't finished his work.

Ten minutes later, he saw Tina and her brother leave the hotel and get into a waiting taxi cab. Then he started the engine, turned on the air conditioning full blast and followed the cab out onto the road. It took the route to Sky Harbour airport, and so did Harry. When he got there, he parked up and walked into the Departures area. He looked around carefully. He didn't want the Byszewskis to see him. He wondered if they had managed to get tickets to London at such short notice. Then he spotted them, walking towards the departure gates, Tina looking terrified and he assumed they had. She didn't see him. He went to the ticket desk and said he was trying to contact a Ms Philpott; that he believed she was flying out to London shortly.

The desk clerk said he would check, and looked on his computer. "Oh yes," he said. "Sir, she is booked on the 10.30 flight to Los Angeles, connecting to the 14.00 flight to London Heathrow. First class, sir, would you like me to page her?"

"No, no, that's just fine," Harry said. 'First class?' he thought. That was some serious money. "I wonder..." he said. "I need to call collect to England. Is there a phone I could use?"

"Sure, sir. Right over there by the waterfall."

Harry looked and saw a concrete structure with water drizzling down its facades. There were some payphones next to it, under yellow hoods.

"Oh, and what time does the LA flight arrive in London?" he asked.

"Let me see sir... Eight a.m. as scheduled, sir."

"Thanks. That's great."

Harry made his way over to the payphones. He dialled the operator and asked for the reverse charge call, reading the numbers that Tina had given him a few days ago out of his notebook. In a while the call was connected.

"Mr Mason, sir, sorry to reverse charges like this, but I'm in a payphone at the airport," he explained.

"That's quite all right, Harry, what can I do for you? Is there some news?"

"Well, you asked me to stick with Tina until she left the country, so..." He related the flight details.

"That's marvellous, Harry," said the elderly cheerful voice at the other end. "Good job. I'll send you the fee we agreed. You can't do any more now. I should get on home, my lad. I expect you've had a bit of a time of it with our Tina."

"Er... yes sir. She's just fine, sir. I enjoyed her company."

"Good. Well, cheerio Harry. All the best to you."

Harry Smith left the airport, picked up his car and drove to the Metrocentre shopping mall where he wandered around for a while. He thought he might pick up a little gift for Suzie, but he couldn't concentrate on the task. He found himself staring at emeralds in a jeweller's shop window. A printed card alongside labelled them as 'Finest Colombian'.

Harry pulled himself together, made his way back to his car and then drove slowly out of Phoenix and up the highway towards Flagstaff, Arizona.

twenty-three

Just because he was carrying an English newspaper doesn't mean he's English. Lots of Dutch people read foreign papers. He could be American. It's more difficult to get the American papers here. Perhaps he had a twin brother. He never said he did. He told her about his family. He would have mentioned it. She's got to stop thinking about him. She can't get him out of her mind. It's like an obsession.

He comes back late in the afternoon looking so unhappy she can hardly bear it. She steels herself and makes a promise, and then she goes out to the supermarket and buys fresh fish and white wine which she hopes will be chilled enough in time. Maybe a few minutes in the freezer will do the trick.

Later, she sautés the herrings in butter, and steams tiny potatoes with colourful vegetables. He compliments her on the food and approves her choice of wine, but he's miserable. She can't make him talk much. After the meal is finished, they sit together on the sofa. He cradles his brandy bowl. The amount of brandy in it is unusually large. She has decided not to drink anything except coffee. She wants to keep her wits.

She breathes deeply five times and still feels anxious.

"Tell me what's wrong, Joe."

He's startled by the question. His thoughts were somewhere else. "I'm just feeling down." He shrugs. "It's the time of year, I expect."

"I know there's something more." She tries to keep an even placidity in her voice. She doesn't want a fight.

He shakes his head. "No. There's nothing else, Anna.

173

Honestly."

She sighs. "I'm sorry Joe, but I think you're lying." She brings in firmness now. Firm but still calm. "I think you've been lying to me for a while. I don't like it, but I'm not going to get angry about it. There's no point. We may as well discuss it and see what's to be done."

"I'm tired Anna. And you're wrong." He lays his head against the back of the sofa, eyes closed. He doesn't want to admit it. Is she wrong then? She feels frustrated. How can she make him tell her the truth? She tries to imagine how it would be if he weren't lying now. If all he has said to her recently were true. If there were really nothing to worry about. Everything would be all right then, wouldn't it? No. It doesn't fit.

"I think you've got involved again," she says with trepidation. "In the old business."

He opens his eyes and glares at her. "Why are you pestering me like this?" he asks angrily. "Can't you see I'm tired? Leave me alone."

"No!" She's annoyed now. "Do you really think I'm so gullible that I believe all this rubbish about exhibitions in London and Geneva and the rest and nothing ever to show for it?"

"So you don't trust me?" He sounds bitter.

"No," she admits. "I don't think I do, Joe. I'm sorry. It sounds terrible to me that I don't but it's true."

"Well thank you very much!" He lights a cigarette irately. "It seems to me that you're the one who can't be trusted, Anna. You're the one who talks of someone else in your sleep. He may be dead but he still haunts you, doesn't he?"

She recoils from him. "I don't know what you're talking

about!" She tries to be indignant, but feels her face flush hot. "Don't try to turn things round onto me, Joe. If you've got a bone to pick with me, do it another day. We're talking about you at the moment."

But he's not listening to her. He looks as though a penny just dropped. He shakes his head. "It can't be," he murmurs. "Juan always did a thorough job."

"What are you talking about?" Her voice is raised. She's almost shouting at him. "Who's Juan?"

"What?" He looks at her but it's clear he's thinking about something else. "I think I'll go out for a while. I could do with a walk."

"I thought you were tired." She's puzzled; angry and upset.

"My head's aching," he explains. He doesn't seem to be annoyed any more. He's preoccupied. "I need some air."

He's gone. Out of the door and away. She lets out a frustrated little scream and thumps the seat of the sofa with her fist. Why is he so stubborn? She's worried though. Worried that her dreams reveal themselves. But maybe he's right. Maybe he's hit on the truth without realising it. The tall man could be a ghost. But why should he come back now? At this particular time? Why? After these peaceful years?

twenty-four

Michael Byszewski was tired. Tired of the violence in this country, and of the life that he led. Sometimes he looked back on his time and he regretted that he hadn't made a normal home for himself and Jeanne and the children. He could have avoided all this mess if he hadn't been so ambitious; if he hadn't loved money so much, but it was his nature, he realised that. And it hadn't been so bad early on, when he was a young man with more energy and enthusiasm. The odd bit of extra cash going through the company added a fresh dimension to things: money destined for one of the many accounts he controlled in Switzerland and the rest of Europe. A favour for a friend.

He remembered when he used to love the business; to thrive on it. He delighted in finding new ways to move money around until its origins could not be traced. He was good at that. That's why they came to him. It still held a fascination for him – when he was in the mood for it.

He remembered when he had brought his son out to join him. He had kept Ecuador on the legitimate side of the business at first, but the boy wasn't blind. He saw how people came prying sometimes and invariably ended up dead not long afterwards. Favours on both sides. Ecuador had not wanted to get involved in anything illegal to start with, but he was an intelligent boy; easily bored. He'd been fascinated by it, drawn in despite his youthful integrity, and eventually he had become a master at it himself; as cynical as the next man. It was a shame in a way, but Michael saw it as part of growing up. He didn't believe there was any alternative.

But now Ecuador had gone. Disappeared. Michael Byszewski knew his son wasn't over-fond of Colombia, but he had thought that the boy might settle down one day. That he would find some girl to marry and raise a family, but it didn't seem to be in his nature. Michael didn't blame him for leaving. Things were looking grim at the moment. Even if you weren't directly targeted, you might get caught in some crossfire or blasted by some bomb. It wasn't the safest place in the world to be. He didn't want his son harmed. He didn't wish ill on any of his children. He loved them all in his way, even little Argentina, although he knew he would never win her round. He wondered where Ecuador had gone. He still had his son's passport. He had retrieved it a little while after Argentina's wedding in the hope of controlling the boy's movements, but Ecuador had clearly had enough; got scared by the cartel's murderous behaviour; made a run for it and hoped for the best. They reckoned the States, his sources. Arizona. There were connections there.

It was Friday. September 22nd. Just over a month since Ecuador disappeared. Michael Byszewski had expected more information by now. He had to decide what to do, if anything. If the boy got talking to the wrong people about the wrong subjects, he could get himself into trouble. If the cartel thought Ecuador might cause them difficulties then nothing Michael Byszewski could do or say would protect him. He could even get problems himself. It was tiresome.

Michael's secretary called through to tell him that Juan was there. He didn't like Juan much; didn't altogether trust him. He was a sneaky little bastard, but he was good at finding things out; at taking care of business.

"Hola, Señor Byszewski!" Juan smiled as he came in. He was around thirty-five years old. Good-looking. As slippery as a snake.

"Buenos días, Juan. What have you got for me?"

177

Juan sat down on the comfortable, leather-upholstered chair on the other side of Michael Byszewski's large desk. He offered Michael a small cigar. Michael refused it. Juan lit one himself, puffing out a cloud of strong, acrid-smelling smoke into the room. "Loads of stuff, Señor Byszewski. All the gen." He grinned with white teeth and well-positioned laugh-lines. His eyes were dark marble-grey.

"OK," said Michael. "Carry on."

Juan pulled a notebook out of the inside pocket of his jacket, licked a finger and flipped through the pages of it.

"Ah... Your boy was in Phoenix on August 28th. He went travelling around and got back there night of... September 8th. A woman, name of Maria Laughton – used to be Gomez, worked for you a while on the accounts..." Juan grinned again, then sucked his lips in over his teeth. "She got him false papers, name of Joey Diaz. He flew out to London Heathrow on September 9th. One way ticket. First class. He was accompanied by a woman, name of Tina Philpott who was making a return journey. Maria Laughton said his sister had been looking for him, and some private detective, name of Harry Smith."

For a moment, Michael Byszewski's brain didn't make the connection. Then he remembered where he had seen the name Philpott before. Argentina! Jesus! Still? No, surely not, he thought. He mustn't jump to those conclusions. But then he remembered something. Two years ago, maybe a little more, Ecuador told him that Argentina had moved. He had given him the new address. Michael had assumed that she'd moved with her husband but, come to think of it, Ecuador had seemed mighty pleased about something at that time. He'd been a lot happier since then, until just recently when he had seemed to be preoccupied for reasons that were obvious now.

"Took a little effort to get the information out of Maria," Juan

178

was saying. "She denied everything to start with. We had to get a little bit heavy. It was a nasty accident. Lots of people have accidents in their pools in Phoenix. Common thing." He rested his left ankle upon his right knee, shook his head and tutted. Sucked on his cigar.

"Did anyone talk to the private detective?" Michael Byszewski asked. He remembered Maria. The boy had had a little thing going with her once. Not for long. She'd been a nice enough girl. Shame. Still, these things often happened.

"Nah!" Juan waved his cigar dismissively. "What more could he tell us? He just helped the girl find your boy. However," he added. "I think my friend in Medellín might be interested in him. I seem to remember a little difficulty we had a while ago. His name's come up before. Now this thing with your boy. Maybe he's too much trouble?"

Michael Byszewski shrugged. "I don't give a damn what you do about him. It's no skin off my nose."

"So, your boy's in London, eh?" Juan nodded thoughtfully. "London's difficult for me. Long way to go. Don't know people there. It would be expensive."

"Yes, well, I'm not paying for you to go to London, Juan. You can forget that idea. Leave it with me now. Thanks for what you got. See Theresa about the bill."

Juan left. On the way out, he presented his bill to the secretary, chatted her up for a while, and made a phone call to his friend in Medellín with whom he had a short and unsatisfactory discussion about Harry Smith. Some people just didn't understand what costs could run to in these cases.

Michael Byszewski sat and thought for a while. He was starting to accept that Ecuador was a lost cause. He couldn't see much point in

179

chasing him halfway around the world to bring him back to a place he didn't want to be.   Maybe if they could have discussed things beforehand, perhaps some arrangement could have been reached. They could have set it up for the boy to work out of Europe if that's what he wanted.

But neither of them had ever talked about their feelings to the other. Michael felt overwhelmingly sad about it all. He had hoped that he might have got on better with his son. Once again he regretted not spending more time with the boy when he was younger. He could see that he was at least partly to blame for the outcome.

But now, what about Argentina? Surely all that old stuff was over? The girl had been married. The two kids had lived normal lives for eleven years or so now. She would have grown out of all that; thought better of it, surely?

He felt weary. The effort of pursuing the matter felt like too much trouble. He still felt bad about it, still thought it was his duty to check up and stop anything untoward, but how? The kids were grown up now; thirty and twenty-eight years old. They had to make their own decisions, he supposed. But the thought of it saddened him. Maybe that was his fault too. He wished he could go back and change his life.

Michael Byszewski checked his diary. He fancied a break somewhere. Cali, he thought. He had some good friends there. It would be nice to see them again. He liked Cali. It wasn't too hot and it had a nice atmosphere about it, especially in the evenings. He was tied up until the end of November. He called his friend who said he would be very welcome to stay for a few days, he and Amalia. Amalia was the woman who Michael lived with now. He was content with her. Comfortable. She wasn't like Jeanne had been though.

He remembered when he first met Jeanne. She was sixteen and more beautiful than any other woman he'd seen before or since. She was full of passion. He and his elder brother, Peter, had bumped into her on Bastille day in Rouen, must be thirty-nine years ago now. Peter had always been the one for the girls, always the one with the twinkle in his eye. But Jeanne had fallen for him, Michael. He hadn't been able to believe his luck. Until later, that was. Years later, when Peter won again. Michael felt bitter, but he knew that this too was his fault. After those first couple of years when he had spent a lot of time in Europe, his father became ill, and he'd neglected her. He had never tried to understand her.

He called a travel agent and booked the round trip to Cali, flying out on November 27th with Air Avianca; flight 203. He jotted the details down and then he phoned home to tell Amalia the good news.

At two o'clock that afternoon, the telephone rang in Juan's apartment. In fact, both the apartment and the telephone number there were recorded as belonging to his girlfriend. It was a convenient arrangement. Juan kept a low profile.

She answered the call and then passed the phone to Juan who was relaxing with a cup of strong coffee and a small cigar, after a prolonged and enjoyable lunch.

"Joey! My man! Been looking for you, my friend. You gave me the slip, you bastard." He cackled happily then listened for a moment.

"I understand, my friend. You want to keep your whereabouts a little quiet. That's OK my man. It's no problem... Oh, Joey, you're a generous man. I always said it. A true prince among thieves, ha, ha!"

He concentrated on what he was hearing, frowning.

"Sure, Joey, no problem at all. Consider it done my friend. You know the terms. My friend in Medellín won't be sorry to see him go, I can tell you. Have a nice life, Joey!"

He replaced the receiver, rubbed his hands together and grinned at his girlfriend. "Nice little job," he said. "Only take a day or so. More lovely money, my pretty lady. It's a great business."

It was Sunday evening. Harry Smith was watching a movie on TV and drinking a beer in his apartment. He felt restless. He lounged along the lumpy sofa, head propped on a cushion which he had pummelled into place between the arm and the back of the settee. The cushion was limp and inadequately filled. It didn't protect his head from the hard edge of the arm. He had to keep moving to stay comfortable.

Since he had returned from Phoenix two weeks ago, he hadn't picked up any major work, although the money had come through from Clive Mason as promised. There had been a couple of routine, five-minute jobs of little consequence, but that was all. He wondered about a change of scenery. He had moved out to Flagstaff originally because he wanted to be in a smaller place, but now he had to admit that there wasn't generally as much work here as in the big cities. He couldn't decide where he wanted to go.

He felt undecided about Suzie too. He couldn't honestly see their relationship continuing for much longer. They had met up a couple of times since he got back, but it was clear that some fundamental change had taken place. Harry had to admit that he was beginning to find that her company bored him. He had tried to talk to her and found himself bringing up subjects that he wouldn't have bothered with in the past; things he might have liked to discuss with

Tina Philpott, for example, but Suzie hadn't been interested. She'd accused him of getting serious, so he had shut up and tried to behave like he used to, but it didn't seem to be enough any more.

A memory came to him. He could only have been fourteen years old. There had been a girl in his class at school. She'd had beautiful, long, curly, auburn hair and amber eyes like pools of light. She was intelligent too – top of the class in several subjects. Her mother and father were English and Lorraine was her name. Harry had been entranced by her and, to his surprise and delight, she had been interested in him too. They had got to know one another and spent hours discussing things. She had even let him kiss her once or twice. Then one day he had overheard her talking to a group of older boys. She was flirting with them, being admired by them. He had heard his own name mentioned, and then laughter; her calling him an idiot, saying how dull and stupid he was. He remembered the pain of it. He had forgotten that until now. It was a long time ago.

Around thirty minutes earlier, Harry had ordered a pizza to be delivered. He could cook for himself all right, but this evening he couldn't be bothered. He hadn't been to the store, and he didn't have much food in. He wondered what was wrong with him. Normally he was pretty well organised. Just this last couple of weeks, he'd let things slide a bit; gotten kind of lethargic.

The door entryphone buzzed. He hauled himself up off the sofa, loped to his apartment door and pressed the intercom button. It was the pizza delivery guy. Harry released the lock on the main entrance to the apartments and waited, standing, hands in pockets, staring at the TV screen.

A minute or so later, there was a knock on the apartment door. He opened it. Two men came in, pushing him backwards. They

183

didn't seem to have any pizza with them. One of them had a gun with a silencer fitted to it in his hand. He was Latin-American, around thirty-five years old. Quite good looking. Harry thought he'd seen him somewhere before.

"Mr Smith?" he asked politely in a heavy accent. The other man shut Harry's front door behind them.

"What's the problem?" Harry felt more puzzled than scared. He thought there must be a mistake.

"I got some friends, Mr Smith," said the man with the gun. "And they don't really like people interfering in their business, you understand me? You know where Medellín is, Mr Smith?"

"Sure, I…"

"Of course you do, Mr Smith. My friend there has a good memory, you see. He remembers some trouble in Los Angeles with a man called Harry Smith. He wasn't very happy about that."

Harry shrugged. "Hey, that was seven damn years ago. Isn't it a little late to come demanding retribution?" He had a very bad feeling about this. "Anyhow it wasn't anything personal. In actual fact…"

"My friend in Medellín won't be interested in excuses, Mr Smith. He has an exceptional memory. Maybe he could have let it go. He's not an unreasonable man. No, no, not at all, but you see you got involved in his affairs again. You've made some enemies, Mr Smith. It isn't just my friend in Medellín that's upset with you. There are other people who don't like you interfering, Mr Smith."

"I had no idea…" Harry began, raising his hands in an exasperated, angry kind of gesture.

"Sorry, Mr Smith." There was a small noise, almost obscured by the entryphone buzzer sounding again. Harry felt the impact of a bullet in his chest. He felt surprised for an instant, and then he fell down onto the floor. He remembered an image. Two exquisite blue-green eyes, pleading with him not to turn her down. There was nothing more.

twenty-five

On Monday, he's awake early. For once before her. He's managed to avoid the subject so far. She knows then, but he can't admit it. It's such a confession of unworthiness. He creeps around the apartment, trying to be out and away before she's up, but he fails. She, yawning, wanders out of the bedroom, stretching herself in her silky dressing gown. Her nipples show through it, but sex is the last thing on his mind.

"You're up early," she says. He hears a note of malice. "Got a few more deals to do, have we?"

"It hurts me that you won't trust me, Anna," he says curtly.

"It hurts me that you lie to me," she replies. "I thought I meant more to you than that. I thought we were important to one another; that you wouldn't take risks that might hurt us."

"Why won't you believe me?" he asks her angrily.

She comes and stands in front of him; looks into his eyes. She reaches up with her hand and touches his cheek. The touch stings him with its softness. "You've always been everything to me," she says in a voice no more than a whisper. "How could you do this to us? To me? I trusted you." Tears fall out of her eyes and sparkle on her cheeks. A ray of morning sunlight steals in through a window, catches her liquid eyes and picks out traces of emerald.

It's too much for him. He can't bear this. He turns away from her and hurries out of the apartment, out onto the street.

Soon he is in his office. The look in her eyes is with him. He tries to put it aside. He can't afford emotion at the moment. But he doesn't know what to do. If he could just get through these current troubles, then maybe he can drop the business; bow out and cease to trade. He wants to have the last part of his life again so he can make a better job of it. He says a prayer although he doesn't believe in salvation. He asks for help, for some inspiration, to get through this and to have another chance. He wants one last opportunity to prove himself worthy of her. He swears on the graves of his father and his dead sister that he'll never gamble with their future again.

He makes himself some coffee, smokes a Gitanes, and then he calls Carlos. Carlos is not a happy man.

"I don't like these delays, Mr Mason."

"My apologies. I had some urgent business to attend to in Geneva."

"So I hear." The voice of Carlos is bleakly unemotional.

Joseph is concerned. "Oh?" he queries.

"I understand that there have been some, shall we say, difficulties?"

"A few minor problems," Joseph says amenably. "Nothing too serious."

"I heard it was quite serious," Carlos disagrees. "I can't regard imprisonment as a minor problem, Mr Mason. It's not a minor problem that I wish to encounter."

Joseph doesn't know what to say. How does Carlos know this? How far has the knowledge spread? He thinks quickly. "I'll admit that there have been some troubles with a couple of clients. They were a little, how shall I put it? Over-enthusiastic in their usage of accounts. One always has to be careful about attracting attention in this game, Carlos. You understand."

"I don't consider it to be a game, Mr Mason. I consider the care of my money to be absolutely serious. I'm afraid I'm going to have to find someone else to take care of funds. I can't take the risk. Your operation is too high-profile, Mr Mason. I'm sorry, but we won't be requiring your services. Good day to you."

Joseph replaces the telephone receiver and lights another cigarette. He's not so worried about losing the business, but he's concerned that knowledge of the Swiss problem seems to be common. And then there's the other matter: the telephone message. He's not sure what to do about that. He dials the number they left. There's no reply. Of course not. They're about five hours behind. He'll have to speak to them later.

At lunchtime he visits a nearby café. He eats a cheese sandwich and drinks a glass of beer. He feels that he needs it today: something to wash away some of the tension that's in him. After this, he takes a walk, trying to calm himself. He strolls along the Kaisersgracht a little way. He stops and sits for a while, smoking, staring at the water. Idly, mind blanked by a jumble of problems, he watches people passing by on the other bank of the canal. With a start, he realises that he recognises two of them. There is Frans, walking, ambling slowly, smiling in a satisfied manner, and with him is the man with the London Times. The man he saw in the restaurant and at the swimming baths. The man he thought was following him. The man who looks like the one in Anna's dreams.

They haven't noticed him. He watches intently. He only met the American for a moment – hardly enough time to remember him clearly – yet there's no doubt that this one's like him. He wonders if she has seen him too; if that's why she dreams of him now. He hates the man, just for looking like the other. And what have he and Frans in common? His suspicions are aroused. Is this some kind of game they're playing? If that man, hands in trouser pockets, tall and dark-haired, is not the dead one, then who is he?

Back in his office, at two-thirty in the afternoon, Joseph dials a long number. The person who answers is no one he knows, but they know him. They call him by a name he hasn't used in six years. They tell him that if he hadn't wanted to attract their attention, he should have kept his nose clean. He knows that now. It's pretty obvious. He remains polite. They're asking a very big favour of him. They laugh when he says he's not interested; that he's decided to stop trading. They tell him he should have thought of that earlier; that he doesn't have that kind of freedom of choice. They tell him their terms. They terminate the call.

Joseph sits with his head in his hands.

After thirty minutes have passed, he raises his head. He opens a desk drawer and searches through papers until he finds an old diary. Dated 1989, he looks in the back of it at scribbled telephone numbers, and finds the one he wants. It's English. He checks the international dialling code, and then dials the number. A male voice answers, elderly, pleasant and well-spoken.

"It's Joe Mason," Joseph says. "I'm having some problems. I could do with some help."

"What sort of problems, my boy?" asks the man.

Joseph explains. It pours out of him in a flood. He can't stop it. There it is, all his treachery laid out before him.

The old man is silent for a moment. "When I helped you before, Joe, you promised me you'd leave this stuff alone. You promised her too, didn't you?"

"I know. I thought it wouldn't matter."

"Does she know now?"

"She suspects," Joseph admits. "I haven't told her."

"What makes me saddest is that you're putting her at risk," says the old man. "That makes me very sad indeed. I trusted you, Joe. I laid aside a lot of reservations and I trusted you to look after her. You've let me down. I can't tell you how angry that makes me. I can't begin to explain. I've had a lot of influence in the past," the old man continues. "Been able to pull a few strings and the like, but I'm not above the law, my boy. I don't know what you expect me to do."

"I hoped you might be able to get me another passport," Joseph says. "Another ID."

"We had a deal, Joe, do you remember?" the old man says. "You gave us information and an undertaking. We gave you a future. But you promised me something else, didn't you? You said you'd look after her. You agreed that you'd take care of her. You've gone back on your word, Joe, and now you come to me again, and you ask for more. I'll be eighty years old soon, you know. Can't expect to be around much longer. Who will you turn to next time you're in trouble, eh? Next time you think a few little deals won't do any harm? Your father had the right idea, you know, running the business where he did. Europe's not the same sort of place, my boy. Not the same sort of place at all. You can't expect to bribe a few people in high places and walk away scot-free here Joe. I should have thought you had more sense."

"What can I do?" Joseph asks. "I've let her down. I want to make amends. I've let you down. There's nobody else I can turn to." He feels pathetic and emasculated. He's also annoyed at having to crawl like this; to beg for help. He never thought he'd sink so low.

"I don't know, Joe," the old man says. "The government here have been trying to stop the trade through Europe for years now. They've always got people watching, always vigilant. I told you to stay out of it. I can't get papers without inside help, and I can't get inside help without a good reason. I know we're related, my boy. It makes me very sad that I can't help you, but there it is. You're a grown man, Joe. You've made your choices and you must live with the consequences. I'm sorry."

"OK." Joseph understands.

"Oh, by the way," the old man adds. "If you tell her about this conversation, then give her my love, won't you boy? I miss her a lot, you know. I wish you luck, Joe. You'll need it. Good bye."

Joseph puts down the receiver. He puts the old diary back into the drawer. He puts his head back in his hands and for the first time in twenty years, he cries.

twenty-six

There he goes again, walking out on the truth. She's crying but inside her she's as angry as a wasp in a web. There's something else now besides the deals he's been doing. Something he's said has given her another terrible suspicion. She wants to find out more, but she can't do it from here. The telephone bills show the numbers dialled. She wants to keep it quiet.

In the morning, she tries to write, but her worry is pervasive and her mind too jumpy. After her lunch, she takes a shower and makes herself nice, working hard to make it a habit. She walks with a purpose and buys a card for the phone. She finds a kiosk and dials the English number that she hasn't forgotten in all this time, but the number is engaged. She tries again, and then once more, but they're still talking, whoever they are. She'll go and buy coffee; come back in a while.

A miserable face she sees in the window; it's her own reflected in the glass, staring moodily out at December. Children pass by outside, their faces painted like Black Peters for Christmas, laughing and shouting with the joy of the season. She tries to make herself look less unhappy; she glances around to distract her attention from what's inside her head.

Her heart almost stops when she sees him. He's there in the corner with coffee at hand and pencil poised above the newspaper crossword. Has he seen her? Should she run away or stay? Her bottom is glued to the chair, her cup held still in mid-air en route to lips painted red. She watches him, engrossed in his puzzle, examining every detail of him. His hair is flecked with a little grey at the temples. That fits with the forty-three years that he'd be. If it were

192

him.

Frustrated at a difficult clue, he raises his head and sees her stare. She feels her face warming and looks away quickly, out of the window, all frightened and fumbly. She can see him out of her eye's corner. He's risen and is coming towards her. She thinks she will faint if he speaks.

"Pardon me," he says, vague twang of New York. "Do I know you?"

She raises her eyes to look at the kindly brown of his, elevated eyebrows with asymmetrically wrinkled forehead.

"Is it you?" she asks. "How can it be?"

"Is it you?" he says. "Despite reports to the contrary, I survived the incident." He sits down opposite her without invitation. There are so many things to say, but none of them will come out of her open mouth.

"I'm so sorry," she says eventually. "It was my fault."

"Did you hire the guy with the gun?" he asks her with that old half-smile.

"No, no, but…"

"Then I don't think you're to blame. I've always made my own choices. I knew the score."

"Neither of us knew all of it." She shakes her head. "But what are you doing here?"

"Oh, just travelling." He calls for more coffee, pulls a cigarette from a packet with a camel on the label and lights it with a lighter with a camel on the front.

"I'm not the same woman any more," she tells him.

"Well, maybe I ain't the same guy either," he says. "Life doesn't seem quite such a simple thing as it once did. I used to think I knew my own mind, knew what I liked and what I wanted. I ain't so sure any longer."

"I know," she says. "The past comes back to haunt me, the present is a nightmare, God knows what the future holds."

"I was in England," he tells her. "I met that old guy there. Your…"

"Clive!" she exclaims. "Is he all right? I was just trying to phone him."

"Still going strong." He smiles. "Almost eighty years old, mind as fast as a jaguar."

She smiles too and then she begins to cry.

"Hey, don't do that." He reaches out. She lets him take her hand. "Let's go," he says. He pays the bill for him and for her, and guides her out into the street. A taxi stops at his call and drives them to his rented apartment in the Jordaan, not too far from her home. She follows him upstairs to his door. She hardly knows what she's doing. A few things of him are scattered about inside but not much. Nothing sentimental. No photographs or mementoes. She takes off her jacket. She is still full of woe.

The apartment is a studio, with the bed in the main room. She looks around her uncertainly.

"D'you want a drink of some kind?" he asks her.

She shakes her head, no, and stands awkwardly until he invites her to sit beside him on the sofa. She perches there. It feels so odd. He's been in her dreams so much lately that it feels as if she knows him like she did before, but it's been such a long time. She thinks he's probably forgotten things about her. She remembers everything about him.

"We knew each other for such a little time," she says. "But

when Clive told me you were dead, I couldn't bear it. I cried for days. I felt so much to blame."

"He told me you cared," he says.

"What happened then?" she asks him. "Why did they say you'd died?"

"A pizza delivery guy saved my life. He found me and got me to the medics just in time but, considering the people involved in the shooting, it was decided to put out word of my demise and for me to lie low. So I got a change of name and travelled around looking for a different kind of life. I went up to Canada for a while and indulged myself in a little more education. See, at college I skipped classes and didn't do too well. Never realised my early potential, as folks like to say. So I went back and learned some more. More psychology and English too. A little math thrown in for good measure.

"But I liked my old job, meeting people and finding stuff out. One day, on a whim, I decided to go further afield. I remembered you and old Clive, and I gave him a call. He was happy to see me and put a little work my way."

"Really?" she says. "You worked for Clive? Doing what?"

"Spent a little time in the West country looking into a smuggling ring last spring and summer. Nice kind of place down there. Good people."

"Drugs again?" she says with a smile. "I'm surprised…" and then the smile fades from her face. She begins to shiver, not with cold. "Oh my God," she says in quavering voice. "You're not here on holiday are you?"

He looks at her with concern and sadness. "It's a kind of working vacation, you could say," he admits.

"Oh God," she says again, covering her face with her hands. "I don't know what to do."

He gets up from the sofa and goes to the refrigerator, pulls out two bottles of Amstelbier and removes their tops deftly with a hand opener. He gives one to her. "You need a glass for that?" he asks.

"No." She accepts the beer and takes a swig from the bottle. It's fizzy and cold. "You've been following me, haven't you?" she accuses him. "Me and Joe. You're here to… What are you here for?"

"Not to cause trouble," he tells her.

"But you know about us!" She realises it in terror. "You must loathe me. Oh God!" She begins to cry again, this time sobbing and out of control. It's her worst nightmare, but she doesn't know why. What does it matter what he thinks? They knew each other for a week six years ago. He means nothing to her. He means everything to her. She realises it with a shock. How can that be? And of course she means nothing to him. He's there to follow her for some reason. Just as he worked for her before, now too he is doing a job. He's no feeling for her. She's lost. She knows now what's been happening to her this last month or two. She's been falling in love with a memory.

He reaches out to her, but she recoils, gasping with tears.

"Listen," he says. He sounds earnest and urgent. "I don't loathe you at all. Quite the opposite in fact. Saying this is real hard for me. I'm not a guy who talks about his feelings easily, but I'll admit that meeting you changed my life in more ways than one. I tried to shrug off how I felt as some kind of intense desire that'd fade away in a week or two. But I couldn't forget it. Maybe the incident sealed it into me, made it all the stronger. I can't tell."

Through her tears, she can see how it pains him to say this thing. She doesn't know how to respond. A tiny sprig of hope is growing inside her. She's still scared and angry too, but these feelings

196

have no focal point.

"Give me a minute," she says. She puts down her bottle of beer, gets up and walks away to find the bathroom. There she sits upon the toilet, resting her forehead on clenched fists, elbows on her knees. There must be an answer to all of this; a solution to the situation. She can't see what it is. She breathes deeply and tries to find some point of equilibrium, but her anchor has gone. She's drifting through deep waters made murky with white powder and dirty money. Down in some uncharted reach of her, she knows where the blame really lies, but she can't face the implications of that. Not yet.

In a while, she stands and washes her face. There's a shelf running along the wall above the basin under the window. On the shelf, which is covered cheaply in white melamine, is a razor and a can of shaving foam. And there, a little further along, a postcard which startles her. The picture on it is a reproduction of 'Nighthawks' by Edward Hopper. The picture in her room. The picture she's always had on her wall since she went to London eighteen years and seven months ago. Except for a little while when she couldn't bear to look at it. The time when she first thought he was dead, and it reminded her too much of America. And he's out there now, alive and real. Outside this door. How queer she feels.

She picks up the postcard and turns it over. All that's written on the back is a telephone number. The one she was dialling earlier this afternoon.

She walks back out. He's still sitting on the sofa. He looks at her. She stands, looking back at him.

"I suppose I'd better go," she says, not knowing what else to do.

He stands and walks towards her until he's quite close. "Don't go yet," he says softly.

She can see sadness in his brown eyes. Suddenly she can't stop herself. She reaches up and takes hold of his face, pulls it down to hers and kisses him with all the love she can find. He puts his arms around her and holds her tightly, kissing her back passionately. She wants this. She wants it so badly. She wants to be looked after; to be told what to do and how to go on. She doesn't want to be grown up any more. She feels she no longer has any strength of her own. It's used up and squandered; thrown away on a wasted vow. She clings to him, kissing him, drowning in him. She feels the years fade from her. Soon they are lying together naked, although the apartment is not that warm. He makes love to her gently. His tenderness makes her tears return.

"I'm sorry," she snivels. "I feel quite stupid blubbing like this. I've been in a bit of a state recently. I suppose it's all coming out of me."

"I don't mind," he says, holding her like a baby.

For a little while, no more is said. She lies in his arms feeling peaceful in this sanctuary. She strokes his body with her hand, smoothing him down. She kisses his funny forehead and runs her fingers through the fringe of his hair. She cradles his head, holds it against her breast and brushes his hair back from his face.

"I'm so glad you didn't die," she whispers. "So glad."

"I'm pretty happy about it myself." He smiles, catching hold of her hands and kissing her lips. "Now, tell me about yourself," he says. "I think I'd find your life very interesting, Mrs Mason."

She narrows her eyes at him. "How much do you already know?" she asks.

"A little. Clive told me some. He knew I'd find out anyway, and I had my suspicions in any case."

She feels a strange thing; an odd lightness. Though he said it before, the full implications of it just dawn on her now. He knows her past and doesn't hate her. She's nothing to hide from him. The relief of it nearly overwhelms her. For so long now, she's been living in half-truths with no one she can talk to freely. She realises just how difficult it's been, how much it has worn her down.

There's a clock by the side of the bed. It's half past four. "I can't stay now," she says. "He'll wonder where I am. Can I see you again? Would you mind? Are you too busy? I think I'd like to talk, but I don't want to be a nuisance."

He laughs. A quiet little laugh. "I can't think of much I'd like better."

She walks home slowly. Every emotion in the world seems to be mixed up inside her. She passes by a telephone kiosk and remembers. She whips in and dials the number before she can have second thoughts. He's so pleased to hear from her she thinks he'll cry. She almost does herself. It's been so long.

"I've called for a favour," she explains, when they've run out of love to tell each other about. "You must refuse it if you want."

"How could I angel?" he says.

"You don't know what it is yet. It seems silly now I come to ask. Just me being silly. Perhaps I shouldn't bother."

"Out with it, old girl," he says with stern humour.

"I expect it's nothing," she goes on. "But yesterday Joe mentioned someone called Juan. I've heard that name somewhere before... I can't remember... oh, this is stupid. Sorry."

"You want to know who Juan is?" The old man is serious now. "It's a common Spanish name, angel. It might not be easy."

"He said: 'Juan always did a thorough job'," she remembers.

"Oh, this sounds so bad!" she cries. "Going behind his back, checking up... I..."

"You're having problems, darling?" The old man sounds so kind.

"I expect it'll be all right." She tries to calm down.

"You need someone to talk to, old girl."

"Yes," she says. "I think I've found someone."

"Good," he says. "I can't tell you how glad that makes me, angel. I can't begin to explain."

twenty-seven

It's late in the evening and he hasn't been home. He doesn't know how to face her; how to keep his cool. He's been trying to find things out about Frans and the tall man, but he's had no luck. He knows he'll have to talk to her, but what will the words be? He thinks they'll have to leave Amsterdam. Get in the car and drive; desert this life that they've lived comfortably. His fault.

He has eaten a little food, drunk a little beer. It's ten-thirty when he finally walks through the door. She's watching television and he's surprised as she hardly ever does. They're showing 'Brief Encounter' on one of the channels. She's looking at it wistfully with traces of tears.

"Hello," she says. She's quite off-hand. She doesn't seem to care how late he is. He wants her to question him tonight. He wants her to start the show, but she's no interest in him.

"Why are you watching that rubbish?" he asks shortly.

"It's not rubbish. It's one of my favourite films. I used to go to the cinema quite often in England. I think I might do that again."

"How's your day been?" He starts to make some coffee.

"I'll talk to you when this has finished. Let me just watch the end."

Angrily, he walks over to the screen and turns off the television.

She glares at him. "What do you think you're doing?" she demands.

"I want to talk. You don't watch television."

"You can wait, and I can change my habits if I like. You've walked out on me a few times when I've wanted to talk, Joseph Mason, so you can damned well wait now." She turns the TV back on

201

with the remote control. "Get out of the way, please." She states it strongly. He is standing in front of the screen.

"I want to talk, Anna. It's important." He switches off the television again.

"When I want to talk, you walk out the door. When you want to talk, I have to listen. Is that how it is, Joe?" She's very angry now. "How nice for you. How marvellous that your way should always be the right one."

This won't get them anywhere. He turns the television back on. "Call me when it's finished," he says. He goes into the bedroom and closes the door behind him. He lies down on the bed with his hands behind his head and stares at the ceiling. He's not really angry with her. He's just impatient to get moving, to do something. Whilst he's inactive, he can dwell on his troubles.

Eventually, he hears the closing music of the film. He springs up and goes out into the living room. Deliberately, she waits until the final copyright notice appears on the screen. Then she switches off the television. She moves herself, sits at one end of the sofa, cross-legged, facing the middle of it. She lights a cigarette. She looks inscrutable with undercurrents of a hurricane. He sits at the other end of the sofa and turns to face her, one leg crooked up upon it, his arm along the back.

"I think we have to leave," he says.

"Really?" She draws on her cigarette and blows the smoke out in a white fountain. Clearly she has no plans to make this easy for him. He looks at her. He remembers the trust that used to be in her eyes. He hasn't seen that for a long, long time. Once upon a time he thinks he deserved it. But he sees how many times he's failed her, always with a good and logical excuse. Why did she trust him so much? It's not his fault he's human. How could anyone live up to her ideals? She'd like to live in wonderland; inside her storybooks. She isn't cut out for the real world.

"You were right. I've been doing some business," he states, all matter-of-fact and straightforward. "I'm sorry, but there it is."

"So, I'm not the only one who breaks promises then. That's good. That makes us even." She smiles. It's deadly.

"I've been set up." He's not sure it's true, but it's nice to deflect a little blame. "There are investigations going on. Some difficulties. Unfortunately this has alerted people to our presence here. People who I would rather didn't know where I was. So it looks like we'll have to go somewhere else. I'll have to lie low for a while until... well, for a while."

"Oh," she says. "That's nice. First I'm required to give up my family and friends in England and now, having made a life for myself here, I have to throw that away too, because you're too stupid to stay away from trouble. Why did you do it, Joe?"

He shrugs. "It's interesting. I was bored. I didn't think there would be a problem. There's not much point in going over old ground. The situation is here and now, and I need to deal with it."

"All right. If we stay here, what will happen?"

"I should think they'll get to me pretty soon. I'll probably be arrested. But that's only if I can stay sweet with the Colombians. If I upset them, I could be in big trouble."

"Where do you want to go?"

"I don't know. Just take our stuff and drive somewhere."

She thinks for a moment. "They'll trace the car. They'll find you."

"Australia then," he says. "We could lose ourselves there."

"We'd need visas to get in, I expect. We'd leave a massive trail of documentation behind us."

"Well, what do you suggest?" he asks. He feels annoyed. She's right. All avenues of escape seem traceable.

She shrugs. "I've no idea. Give me some time and maybe I'll think of something. I'm tired now."

"Anna, this is urgent," he tells her. "I haven't much time. I want to leave tomorrow."

She looks at him sharply. "Oh no." She shakes her head. "I'm not leaving tomorrow. I've made other plans."

"What plans?" he demands of her. "What plans are more important than my life, Anna?"

She looks at him for a while, not answering. He can't read what's in her mind at all. There doesn't seem to be any feeling in her eyes. "Understand me now," she says. "I don't suppose you can even begin to imagine how angry I am about this, Joe." The words stab him. He hears an echo in them. "It's the most profound feeling I've ever had in my life. That should make you happy. If I didn't love you then I wouldn't care, but I do love you. Our blood demands that of me, Joe. Maybe I understand now how you felt when I married David, when I broke my promise to you. The disappointment is almost unbearable.

"I've suspected your dealings for a while, and I've been quite sure of them just recently, so I've had a little time to consider what I feel about it.

"When I got married, I thought it was over between us. I'd waited for you for five years or so whilst you screwed every woman you could get your hands on and even lived with someone. All right, you didn't marry her. I couldn't see the difference. But I believed we

204

were finished. At the time I had no prospect of you coming back to me, and I couldn't see any point in pining my life away for nothing. David Philpott was a nice man. Maybe he wasn't quite right for me, but at least he wasn't in Bogotá.

"This thing that you've done seems to me to be quite different, Joe. Quite different. We had each other. At last. After all those years. Eleven years. And you've risked everything. You've risked getting yourself put away and leaving me alone again but, worse than that, you've risked your life and probably mine too by implication. Do I really mean that little to you, Joe? You'd throw all we have away because you got a little bit bored?" Her voice has risen to a strident pitch. It hurts his ears. The truth of her words is like knives in his head.

"I can't see much point in running away at the moment," she says more calmly. "I don't know where we could run to. Maybe you could go back to that nice apartment you first stayed in in London. Hah!" She lets out a mirthless little laugh. "I don't suppose they'd have you now. I expect they'd say you'd had your chance. I wouldn't blame them." She picks up her cigarettes and her box of matches and stands up. "I'll give the problem some thought," she says in a businesslike tone. "But I'm not leaving tomorrow. I'm going to bed now. I don't want to be disturbed."

She goes to the bathroom, and then to her room, leaving him sitting, feeling like a scolded schoolboy. There seems to be a power in her that he hasn't seen before. He wonders where she got it from. But doesn't she realise how serious this is? He starts to go after her, intending to pull her out and make her listen, but he thinks better of it. Instead he turns on the television and turns the volume way down. He switches the channel to CNN on satellite. There's a picture of Bogotá on the screen, or rather a map of Colombia with Bogotá marked on it. He turns the sound up slightly. What's happening there? Something that'll get him off the hook?

International outrage, says the presenter, at the release of a group of gangsters from prison. They were put away six years ago or so and now bribery and corruption mean they're on the streets again.

Joseph feels sick. Things he thought were as bad as could be have just got worse. Juan's out of jail.

twenty-eight

Oh why did he have to pick this time to make his confession? She understands that he's in danger but what can she do? Wherever he goes it will be the same, and if she's with him, she'll be in the boat too. Does she want to die with him like Bonnie and Clyde? Like Cassidy and the kid? She doesn't think so but her brain won't think about it properly. It keeps slipping off the issue.

She wants to be out before he's up, but he's awake early, sitting at the table with coffee and tobacco. No food for breakfast. He looks as though he's been awake all night. Not much sleep in this apartment last night then. She tossed and turned herself.

"Anna, please," he says as she sits down with tea and toast.

What?" she asks.

"I've got to do something."

"Then do it," she says, shrugging her shoulders, biting into her toast. "I've an appointment at nine. I'll be out all day."

"What appointment?"

She looks at him and doesn't answer.

"Anna, for God's sake!"

She can see that he's nearly frantic. "The safest thing for you to do," she tells him. "Is to hand yourself over to the police and ask them to lock you up. I can't see any other way out, Joe. That's my best suggestion at the moment."

"But they'll put me away for years!" he says. "And when I do get out, I'll be in the same position. And what about you?"

"It's kind of you to think of me." She smiles as sweetly as she can and sips some tea. "It's nice of you to take me into consideration. Such a pity you didn't do it earlier. Oh, look at the time. I'd better get going."

She rushes away to brush hair and teeth, put lipstick on her mouth and the nice red sweater on. She wishes him breezily goodbye and flies out of the door with no kisses. She walks along the canal bank, breathing in cold crisp air, looking at the beautiful pale winter world with thoughts whirling around in her head. Should she feel guilty leaving him like this when he's in such despair? Something in her won't let her care any more. It's not just his dealings with drug money and his women – disappointing enough in themselves – that concern her now. The other thing that she suspects – the thing she phoned Clive about the night before – makes those misdemeanours seem almost minor. In the sleepless hours of the night, she's dwelt on it and come to a terrible conclusion. She feels a snake of hatred growing, writhing inside her. It might not be true. She should wait and see.

She thinks about the other man, the one she'll see in a minute. She remembers when he came to her room in San Francisco and she, fresh out of the shower and naked, threw on the first clothes that came to hand, not noticing how much they revealed of her until his eyes told her. His eyes. Those eyes that made her feel desirable and beautiful. She had liked his kindness before; his easy way of talking to her that made her feel comfortable in a strange land; his lack of fuss on the plane when she had felt so frightened. But it was then, in that moment in her room, that she knew she wanted him. She knew then that she had no right to at that eleventh hour when she was about to have the thing she thought she had always desired. Something changed in that moment. Ever since then a part of her has pined. She's lived with regret.

She's reached his door. She rings his bell and he lets her in. He seems a little shy of her. She questions him with her eyes. They go up to his apartment and he stands a little awkwardly, hands in trouser pockets, looking at her.

"Will you kiss me?" she asks him. "Do I always have to make the first move, or will you do it one day because you want to?"

He grins at her and gives her a peck. "I'm scared of you," he says. "You could bite."

She laughs in surprise. "Good lord! How can you be scared of such a pathetic creature as me? If only you knew what went on in my head..."

"Then tell me."

"There's a price to pay for knowing," she says quite seriously.

"Oh?"

She smiles wickedly and begins to unbutton his shirt.

"At this time in the morning?" He raises his eyebrows in pretend disapproval. "It's a hard life sometimes."

But in the end he doesn't seem to mind at all. He calls out her name in his moment of passion. The name she used to use. She loves the sound of it in his mouth, with his accent. She whispers his own name back to him, tells it to him as though she loves him; as though she never knew proper love before.

In a while, he makes them some coffee and comes back to bed, lying beside her, hands behind his head whilst she sits upright, propped up by pillows and the headboard and begins to tell him her story.

"After I was born, my mother fell ill," she says. "I suppose it was some post-natal thing. My brother and two older sisters went to stay in France with our grandparents. They didn't come back until I was five years old. They were strangers to me. My father always worked in Colombia. He came back twice a year to see us. Perhaps he did a little business. We were innocent of all that then. The governess, Olga, looked after me. Despite having four children, my mother never took much interest in us. When she was young, she lived in Rouen in France and her life was a whirl. Then she met father. He got her pregnant, married her and stuck her away in a remote farm in Switzerland. I think she just vegetated.

"Anyway, when my brother came home, he was delighted to have a little sister to look after. The older two bossed him about – especially Bolivia." She giggles slightly, and then grows more serious. "I didn't like her much when I was little, but in later years we got on well. I haven't seen her for a while."

"I guess you miss the rest of your family," he says softly.

The emotion this little sentence evokes takes her by surprise. She gulps and catches a tear on her hand. "Sorry," she says. "Yes, I do. Very much. I get to see them sometimes. Maman and uncle Peter, and Livvie – Bolivia – but Joe doesn't like me to. They don't know about us. He's scared I'll let something slip."

"Sounds like a pretty tricky existence," he whistles. "How do you keep it quiet? Do they know you both live here?"

"They don't know Joe does. Nobody except Clive and Caroline know that. The rest think he's still in Colombia. He never kept in contact with them anyway, so it's not hard to keep that secret. But of course when I see them, I have to pretend to live alone. I'm quite good at it now though I don't like lying. I was going to go to England with my friend in the new year. Joe's really worried about that. He thinks we'll see my aunt and my other cousins and Mari will mention him and then there'll be trouble."

"He could be right, I suppose."

"I know." She thinks for a moment, and realises something else that's been growing. She's wanted them to find out and give her an excuse to leave. She thought that this malaise began when she first saw the man lying next to her now in the café here two months or so ago. But that's not true. It started long before, when reality did not live up to her expectations. Quite early really after they settled here in Amsterdam. But she had fooled herself that her feelings would pass and she knew that she must stick to her promise this time, whatever the cost. She's been living a lie. She's been lying for years when she has only ever wanted to tell the truth. But what is she? An author: a liar by profession. She despises herself for her weakness. Why could she not have just faced the truth and gone back to England years ago? She doesn't know. What a high price she's paid for her indecisiveness and deceit. She sees how much it has taken out of her. She remembers herself when she went to America. She remembers a sparkiness, a brightness, some optimism that has gone. She mourns her younger self and wonders if she can ever get it back.

"Who's Peter, then?" he asks.

"Father's brother," she explains. "He used to travel widely. He's a teacher. He came to stay with us when I was eight years old and never left again. My mother was glad to see him. He took father's place in more ways than one. Of course, I didn't realise that then, not until much later, although it's obvious with hindsight."

"So what did your pop do?"

"He turned a blind eye, I suppose. He couldn't do much else. He wouldn't give up the business and come home, and he didn't want to move us over there, so he was stuck with it. It was odd actually. He was always quite stubborn, quite sure of himself and his opinions and yet, with Peter, he'd crumble away and defer to him. I found that

211

strange. Peter was older, but much less intransigent. Mother and father separated when I was sixteen. They sold the house and she and Peter went to live in Geneva where they still are. So you see I lied to you again." She hangs her head. Another falsehood.

"The truth might have been a little complicated to explain." He nods. "Especially on such a brief acquaintance. I won't hold that one against you." He grins and kisses her on her left breast which is quite near to his face. "See?" he says. "I can do it of my own accord."

She laughs at him. "Are you bored yet?" she asks.

"No, but I need the bathroom if you'll excuse me for a moment."

She says of course, and he gets up and lopes off towards the other room. She looks around. She decides that he's not a very tidy man. Bits and pieces are scattered about: an item of clothing here, a damp towel over there. She's fond of order herself. She likes things neat and clean and uncluttered. She wants to tidy up, but she knows she mustn't interfere with him.

He comes back in and makes some more coffee to keep them warm. It's in two mugs that don't match. She smokes one of his cigarettes because she likes the picture on the packet.

"We didn't go to school as I probably told you," she says. "Olga taught us at home, so we never mixed much with other kids."

"So you and your brother never had outside distractions."

"No." She shakes her head. She finds it quite hard to talk about this. It's been a secret for such a long time. Only Caroline and Clive knew the truth. And her father – but he wasn't told. "My oldest sister, Venezuela, went to live in England when she was eighteen – not long before Peter came to stay. Bolivia was a loner, and she was fanatical about horses. She liked them more than people I think, although she

212

and Olga were very close. They became lovers later."

He lets out a whistle. "Jeez," he says. "Maybe 'interesting' ain't an adequate word for this."

"I know." She bites her lip. "It's all a bit sordid really."

"Hey, I never said that," he says. "I ain't the kind of guy to make judgements on people's private lives. So long as they aren't hurting anyone else, I can't see it matters what they do. That don't mean I'm not deeply *interested* of course." He grins with a slightly lewd and comical look and she smacks him on the arm in play.

"Joe and I… It was when I was thirteen," she says. "It was my fault really. I'd become aware… you know… of things, and I used to dream about him. It was his fifteenth birthday. He came to my room and I offered to… I didn't know about incest. I didn't know there was anything wrong with it. It seemed quite natural to me."

"So when did you find out about it?" he asks.

"Oh, Joe knew," she says. "He told me then. I thought it was silly and, because it was forbidden I suppose it seemed more exciting."

"But it didn't stop him."

"Well, no, I…" She stops. "I always thought it was my fault," she says.

"Why try to blame someone?" he asks.

"It carried on until father took him away to Colombia when he was sixteen," she says, remembering. "Everything seemed very simple then, very pure and full of truth. Somewhere along the line it began to get complicated. I don't know. Anyway, I was devastated when he went, but he came back for holidays and we carried on. He promised me when he left that he'd never get married, that we would be together one day. He made me promise the same thing.

"When I was sixteen, I went to England. That was in May. In

that July we met up in Tourettes-sur-Loup – that's a little hill-town in the south of France. We were going to stay there for a month, but father turned up at the end of the third week and caught us in the act and that was that."

He looks concerned. "That must have been a bad shock. He suspected you, I guess?"

"It was horrible," she agrees. "That was Joe's fault in a way. He told father where he was going, but he didn't tell him that I was going too. Father went back to Switzerland for a week or so to see mother and Peter and to sort out their situation. It seems funny that he waited so long to do that, but I suppose he left it until all the kids had left home. Anyway, I mentioned to mother that I was going on holiday with Joe. Father obviously put two and two together. He wasn't so blind as I thought. He took Joe back to Colombia and confiscated his passport. The next time I saw him was at Venezuela's funeral."

"She was your oldest sister?" he checks.

"Yes. She was really beautiful, like maman," she remembers. "But when I saw her in England it shocked me. She looked so tired and ill. She took a lot of drugs, you see. She was a bit wild, like mother had been. She died of an overdose when she was twenty-eight.

"Father and Joe came over for the funeral. Father took a great delight in telling me that Joe had a girlfriend. I didn't believe him at first, but Joe wrote and told me it was true. He said it made no difference to us but that a man has needs, or some such rubbish!" The bitterness of what she says surprises her. She shakes her head. "Sorry," she says.

"You thought he was making excuses," he says.

"Yes! Yes I did. I thought I could have waited forever for him.

I didn't see why he should be any different. Why is it different for men?" she demands of him.

He puts his hands up, implying surrender. "Hey, I didn't say it. I don't know if it is or not. I ain't ever been a broad."

"Broad!" She's angry now, not particularly with him, but she wrestles with him and he fights her back gently, and when he has control of her he kisses her.

"I may be a dumb old guy," he tells her. "But you're causing certain parts of my anatomy to behave like they're eighteen years old."

She looks to see and giggles. "Oh yes!" she says. "Can I put that somewhere for you?"

Later, after some sex that is dirty and delightful, inhibitions diminishing, he dozes for half an hour or so and she watches him sleeping. Then he rouses himself, gets up and cooks her a little lunch. He boils some pasta and makes a quick tomato sauce. He won't let her wash up. He believes, he says, that dishes are best left a day to mature.

"Tell me the rest," he says. "If you want to."

"You're kind to me," she tells him, kissing him.

"The rewards for that are pretty good I'd say." He puts his hand on her bottom and savours the shape of it.

She looks quizzical. "Does that make one of us a prostitute then?" she asks. "Or both?"

"Seems pretty symbiotic to me," he laughs.

"That's a big word for a dumb old guy," she tells him, kissing his nose. "I think dumb old guys are my favourite sort. Where was I?"

"You were getting indignant at a man's needs." He grins.

She narrows her eyes. "Ah yes. Well, I fumed about that for a

215

while, then went to bed with my cousin."

At this point he hoots with laughter. "This ain't Caroline, I assume?"

"No!" She giggles. "I never tried that! Trevor was her brother. We were good friends and it was just a laugh. We weren't serious; it was a giggle. But a few weeks later, I found that I was pregnant. I had to have a termination, of course. Even if he hadn't been related to me I would have. The thought of having children always horrified me. Perhaps it was because of Joe. Maybe I thought they would be born with the tail of a pig or something..."

"Ah hah!" He says. "Gabriel Garcia Marquez. A very appropriate writer."

"Ooh!" She grins. "Not such a dumb old guy after all. It wasn't really that though," she admits. "I always felt so bound up in my self and my situation that I couldn't spare anything for them. I thought I might end up like maman, bored out of my skull, and I thought there were enough of my family around already. Bringing more weirdoes into the world didn't strike me as a particularly responsible thing to do.

"I wrote Joe a letter and told him about it, just to teach him a lesson. He ignored me for a while and then I found out he'd been living with someone. I gave up then. I thought it was over and the promises we had made were just childish dreams and perhaps it was all for the best anyway. I decided I had better forget about it and get on with my life. I met David a year or so later. When he asked me to marry him I felt nervous about it. I thought living together would be enough, but he wanted things done properly so I went along with it. I felt comfortable with him, as though I'd always known him. Looking back now I don't know if I ever fell in love with him though. I don't know if that's important in the end. I was twenty-two then. Joe turned up on my wedding day and told me exactly what he thought of me. I couldn't believe how bad I felt. I thought I was over him, but when he was standing in front of me, saying how much I'd hurt him, I knew I was wrong. He had some power over me that I couldn't escape. I thought I never would."

"I guess some people set a lot of store by those vows," he says.

She shrugs. "Maybe if he'd invited me to his wedding, I'd have felt the same," she admits. "But he was right in a way. I mean he hadn't broken his promise and I had. He was always so certain of himself, so sure he was right, so honourable. At least I thought he was. I thought he was infallible: a hero. I was always prepared to accept that I was in the wrong.

"I didn't see him again after that until we met in Phoenix. An event at which you were an unfortunate witness." She smiles.

"Oh, I don't know. The event had its good points. But how did you get from there to here?"

"He got arrested when we got back – directly we got off the plane at Heathrow. I don't know how they knew which plane we were on. I didn't tell anyone." She looks puzzled.

He strokes her arm and looks at her with concern. "I've a confession of my own to make," he says softly. "I told Clive. I followed you to the airport and checked it out. Clive asked me to, you see? When I called him he asked me to stick with you until you left the States. I didn't know they'd arrest Joe, but he paid me to do a little more than you wanted."

For a moment she's confused. "He paid you to stay with me?" She feels lost. "I thought… I thought…" She can't say it. Has she been such a fool? "Did he pay you to screw me then?" She asks

217

bitterly. "And now?" She turns away from him, distraught. She feels used. She thought he liked her. She hoped he did. Just a little bit.

"No," he says firmly. "I told you yesterday how I felt. Don't fish for more compliments. Don't make me out to be that callous. I don't like it. Once upon a time I didn't much care about the women I hung out with. They were just a bit of fun. You changed that. I told you so."

For a minute or two, she considers this information, and then she sees that he's right and that she's being foolish. Perhaps she's transferring her misplaced love for Joe onto him before he's ready for such a thing. She doesn't yet know him inside and out; all his foibles. She's rushed to him as though he's her sanctuary, the answer to all her problems. She sees it's not fair of her. She turns back and looks at him, into his kind eyes that have taken now a look of firmness, of no brooking of silly childish games. "I'm sorry," she whispers, and she tries to explain what she's just been thinking. It's difficult to say, she can't use her clever words in the way she'd like. She feels clumsy and inarticulate.

"I know," he says. "Remember I learned a lot about psychology. I understand these things. I'm taking risks too, you know. You might recover from all this and throw me aside after all. We can't know what the future holds, neither of us. We've gotta just see how it goes. But I never 'screwed' you. I wouldn't do that."

She looks at him. She can't imagine casting him aside, but he's right, she knows it. "I'm sorry," she says again. "I'm not sure I understand these things as well as you. Would you teach me about them?"

"Sure," he says. "But not today. Come here." He pulls her to him quite forcefully and kisses her, holding her tightly for a while.

218

"Now go on with your story. What happened after the arrest?"

She lies down again, looking up at the ceiling which is cracked in a couple of places. A small-bodied leggy spider lurks in one corner, minding its own business, not doing anyone any harm. "I had no idea what was going on. They kept him safe for a time, trying to get information out of him. I suppose he must have given them some because after two weeks they let me see him, and he told me he'd been allowed out once or twice. He told me then about the money laundering side of the business. He told me it was mostly father. He said he never had much to do with it. I believed him. I..." She looks across at him with a worried twist to her eyebrows.

"Don't worry," he says. "I doubt there's anything you can tell me on that score that I don't know already. Clive gave me a pretty full account."

She sighs. "I suppose he was lying. I wanted to believe him but, over these years, I've realised that he wasn't telling the truth. It's hard to bear when you trusted someone..." A tear escapes her and she brushes it away angrily.

"I know," he says softly. He strokes her arm with the back of his hand, and she sees the concern in his eyes. She remembers something that she wants to know.

"How did Clive know about you?" she asks. "You know, when I first met you. It was him who gave me your name. I meant to ask him but, what with everything else, I never got round to it."

"Secret." He taps the side of his nose and grins, but she fights him, tickles him into surrender. "All right, all right," he gasps, holding her wrists to stop the assault. "D'you remember when we saw that MacArthur guy in San Francisco?"

She furrows her brow, and then it comes back. "Oh yes! My

219

favourite man!"

"If you recall, he mentioned me having had some dealings with the Colombians."

She ferrets again in her memory. "Vaguely."

"About seven years before I met you I was working out of Los Angeles on some routine kind of case, but it got out of hand and had connections that led me into the middle of a cocaine-smuggling operation that was being run out of Medellín. I never wanted to find things like that out. Too damned dangerous! But there I was plum in the middle of one of the biggest courier rings in the South West.

"Course, I couldn't pretend it wasn't happening so I got the CIA involved and a lot of arrests came out of it. I got commendations for it and a great deal of work came my way afterwards. It gave me a good reputation in certain circles – I guess that's where Clive got my name – but a somewhat precarious one in others. I was scared for a time that they would come for me. Course, they did eventually, but that was after we met."

"I suppose that was because Joe was working for the same people," she ponders. "I remember now that Clive said you'd had some other involvement. That was when he was trying to comfort me, to convince me that it wasn't my fault, but it was! I drew attention to you again by employing you!"

"Well, that may be true." He says. "But you weren't to know. Tell me what happened when you and Joe got back together."

"Being with him then was odd," she explains with a sigh. "I felt we'd changed, the pair of us. He was still serious, still ardent. He still took himself very seriously, whereas I'd become more light-hearted I thought. It was difficult not to be with people like Caroline and Clive around." She smiles. "I miss them."

"You'll see them soon, if you go back in the new year."

"Yes!" She considers it with some glee. "I can't wait."

"Good," he says.

"But there was a kind of chemistry between us," she remembers. "When we were together it was as though no one else existed. It had always been like that. Then, when I thought everything was all right again, Clive came in and told us that Maria was dead. They weren't sure at that point whether or not it was an accident. I had an idea it wasn't and I was so worried that you would be next, but Joe seemed totally callous about it. I couldn't understand why he seemed to hate you so much. I tried to phone you when I got home; tried to warn you. I kept getting your answering machine. I was too late…" She catches her breath with the pain of the memory.

"Hey, but it's OK." He cuddles her, chuckling softly. "I'm the one that got away, remember?"

She clings to him for a moment, still not quite able to believe the joy of the fact that he's alive; still hoping that it's not some cruel dream like those she's had just lately where he's been there and then she's woken and realised the truth. At least the truth as she thought it was. "I didn't see him again until November. I didn't want to. But when I did he had changed. He seemed much more loving and understanding; more like his old self. It was as if we hadn't been apart for all those years. It's funny. I remember him saying to me that I must have loved you because I was so upset, but how could I? We only knew each other for a few days. I told him I didn't but… well, if I hadn't thought you'd died I suppose it might have been different. Perhaps I'd just have remembered you as a nice kind man and, by the way, a remarkably wonderful fuck." She giggles.

He makes a face of mock embarrassment and says "shucks"

with a chuckle.

"But because of what happened... oh I don't know. It's like you said yesterday. It made it mean more somehow. When I first saw you here, when was it? Mid-October? It all came back to me. I couldn't stop thinking about it, about you. I kept dreaming about you. He knows I did. He told me I said your name in my sleep."

He puts his arms around her then, holds her tenderly a little while, strokes her hair and kisses her head. She smiles and closes her eyes.

When she opens them, the light has changed to late afternoon.

"You've been sleeping," he says, kissing her eyelids.

"I'm sorry." She's surprised, waking up in his arms.

"Confessions are tiring," he says.

"I didn't sleep much last night," she explains. "What time is it? I'd better go home. I don't want to. Things are very difficult."

"Can you come out later?" he asks.

She considers. "I don't see why not. What's good for the gander, after all. I'll try. If I'm not here by nine, I can't come."

On the way back, she calls England again, like she said she would.

"Angel, we're in luck with your Juan fellow," he says, sounding pleased with himself. "There's been a bit of bother over in Colombia. They let a lot of people out of prison a few days ago. One of those was a Juan Rodriguez. He went in as part of the round-up at around the time of Gacha's death. I think he may have been one of the ones Joe helped put away actually. I didn't deal with that part of the goings-on myself, angel, you understand."

"Oh," she says. "So he worked for the cartel in Medellín, did he?"

"Not exactly, darling. He was, shall we say, freelance. He used to investigate things for anyone who paid him. He'd track people down who had got on the boss's wrong side. And a little bit of hired killing now and then. We're actually pretty sure he was the one who shot Harry, darling. Got a description from a pizza delivery chap which fits quite nicely."

twenty-nine

It's five thirty p.m. and she comes in looking pensive. He's been there all day, unable to do much except sweat. He's smoked three packets of Gitanes. The apartment reeks of them.

"Hi," she says, not coming near him. He sees there's something changed. She looks dreamy and vaguely unkempt. There's a great calmness about her; a peace and tranquillity. He wonders what she's been doing.

"How's your day been?" he asks suspiciously.

"Quite nice," she says. "I'm going to have a cup of tea. What would you like for supper?"

"I'm not hungry," he snaps. "I can't eat with these problems."

She makes herself a mug of tea, and sits down on the sofa, cupping it between her two hands as though she's cold. He sits down next to her. She makes no move towards him, rather withdraws herself with a little movement.

"What shall we do, Joe?" she asks. At least she doesn't seem to be angry any more. "I haven't thought of anything but if you do want to try to run, you'll have to go alone. I'll go back to England for a while I think. It'll be easier for you on your own."

He's horrified. "What? You can't. I need you with me, Anna. You know what you are to me."

"We can be apart for a while. Perhaps it would do us good. Things haven't been so good lately, have they?"

"I don't want to be apart from you. Eleven years was enough. When I said we'd be together, I meant forever, Anna."

"Yes, but you promised me you wouldn't get involved in the business too," she explains calmly. "All this trouble puts a different face on things, don't you think? I'm sorry Joe, but I just can't handle this. I need to get away from it and I want to go home."

"So, you'd run out on me; withdraw support when I need you most?" He's incredulous.

"You put yourself in the position, Joe. I can't see why I should pay the price for that."

"Then you don't love me." It's the only conclusion he can come to.

"Of course I do. You're my brother."

"Is that all now?"

She looks at him, examining him, a puzzled look in her eyes. "You've hurt me a lot in my life," she says. "You left me to start with, and then were unfaithful. You lived with someone yourself, then raged at me for getting married. You've never let me forget it, have you? And lately you've let me down very badly. You've let yourself down too, Joe. It hurts me to see you're so human, but that's my problem, not yours. Maybe I expect too much from people."

"So I'm not good enough for you?" he asks, angry and frightened.

"In some ways, no. But maybe no one ever could be. Not completely. All my life I've been in love with a dream, Joe. I have to step back for a while and see if I can still love reality; if I can lower my sights and accept the truth without casting blame."

He feels desperate. He can't believe that she'll leave him to face this alone. He's always needed the certainty of her. It's true that he wanted to get away when he was young; to have some years of freedom. It was a risk he felt he should take. A risk that he thought had backfired when she married that man. But he knew that wouldn't last. He knew that when he saw her at her wedding. He knew she'd come back to him eventually.

It wasn't like that with the American. He had decided then that the time had come for them to be together. He was certain she would come for him, and she did. He'd left those clues for her to follow; dropped hints to help her worry about him, to make sure that she would still care. But when he saw that self-satisfied smile on her face in Phoenix; saw how little his anger affected her, and the look in her eyes at the mention of that man's name, he'd known what must be done. He wanted the American out of the picture. Completely. He thought he'd got his wish. He wonders if Juan made a mistake.

"Please, Anna." He feels his unusual tears again. "I don't know what to do." He looks into her eyes but there's nothing there for him. No love. No desire. No hope. He can't even see compassion. It's his worst nightmare.

"Neither do I," she says. "I think I'll have a shower. I'm going out later."

"Going out?" he yells, incredulous. "Where are you going?"

"Don't question me, Joe. You know I don't like it," she says in a vague imitation of himself. She stands and starts to go to get some things. A towel, her dressing gown et cetera. He leaps up from his seat and grabs hold of her.

"You don't care, do you?" He's holding her arms tightly. She's wincing with pain. He wants to kill her if she doesn't care. She can't exist separately from him. It isn't right. It isn't how things should be.

"You're hurting my arms, Joe," she says calmly. "Please let go."

He does as he's asked. He still can't bring himself to hurt her physically. She's such a precious thing.

"Whether I care or not makes no difference," she tells him.

226

"My caring won't save you from jail or from crooks in Colombia. I could stay here and mope about it with you. Worry, fret and have a really bad time, or I can go out and try to enjoy myself while it's still possible."

"I'll come with you," he decides. He's serious. Maybe she's right. Go out, drink too much, pretend it isn't happening. He feels momentarily cheerful.

"No. I'm going alone. Go out if you want to but don't come with me. Find another girl to make you feel better tonight, Joe. I don't mind." She gives him a little smile which is polite, and then she goes to perform her ablutions.

At eight, she leaves. He's beside himself with anger and despair. After a moment or two in which his mind is blank with rage, he pulls on soft warm shoes and his leather jacket, and he follows her out onto the street.

He sees her to the right of him, on the old swing bridge crossing the canal. Her hair shines red-black under a street lamp. She stops for a moment, turns and throws something into the water. It drops with a soft plop into the icy blackness. Her shoulders are hunched slightly against the cold, and she hurries on. Where is she going? Joseph follows her carefully. It isn't too difficult to stay out of sight at first. The moon is hiding behind ranked oil-black clouds and it's quiet round here tonight, but soon she enters streets strung gaudily with Christmas lights and he must stay further back and take more care. He's intent upon watching her direction; obsessed with her pursuit. He doesn't notice that another figure dogs his own steps. A man of medium height, perhaps a little smaller than Joseph himself, slips between shadows. He's better than Joseph at this job. He's done it many times before.

thirty

She takes him to a bar she likes: wooden tables and games to play. Tea lights in green glasses brighten their faces from below. Ajax are playing soccer in the European Cup and almost every face is turned upward, captivated by the TV screen in the corner. But these two won't watch the game. They drink cold beer from half-litre glasses and say cheers.

"I didn't see him again until Christmas," she says. "I thought Clive was messing me about, giving me the slip. I was very cross with him. But actually they were sorting things out. My father was killed in a plane at the end of November. Do you remember that flight from Bogotá to Cali that was blown up?"

He nods. "They were trying to kill Gaviria – the presidential candidate who took over from Galan. So they got your pop instead?"

"Mmm. As you know, I never liked him much so I can't pretend I was too upset. Then Gacha was killed in December, so Joe seemed to be off the hook."

"Everyone thought he was the head of the Medellín cartel," he recalls. "Actually it turned out to be Pablo Escobar." .

"I know, but Gacha's lot were the ones my family worked for. Joe didn't think that he knew anyone who worked for Escobar so he wasn't particularly worried about him. Anyway, Clive got us some new IDs and we came over here at the start of 1990, almost six years ago."

"Did Clive ever try to talk you out of it?" he asks.

She drops her head. "Yes he did. Well, sort of. He dropped a lot of hints. I don't think he wanted to tell me what to do. He isn't like that. I think he believes in people finding their own way. I'm sure he hoped I'd grow out of it or something. I thought it was what I wanted though. I can be quite stubborn, you know."

"Really?" he says with a grin and a cackle.

She looks back at him wryly. "I called myself Anna because my middle name's Anastasia, but I like it when you call me Tina. Will you call me that?"

"Sure thing, ma'am," he says, smiling at her. She thinks how much she likes his smile; how much she likes the whole of him. "And now things aren't so good?" he asks.

"It was exciting at first." She runs long bare fingers around the rim of her glass. No rings now. Thrown into the Brouwersgracht. And the emerald. Loose the chains. She steals one of his cigarettes which he lights for her with an indulgent scolding tut. "Of course I missed England and my friends and family there, but being with Joe… Well, it was all I thought I wanted. I always knew there would be a price to pay. For a while, it was great, but after a year or so I suppose the novelty wore off. I don't know. He has a hard side to him. He was always sure of himself, stubborn and determined, but he'd grown harder in Colombia – quite opinionated and self-willed. There! Who am I to talk?" She smiles ruefully. "Anyway, he likes his women too." She shrugs. "He says it's the way things are in Colombia, that it doesn't mean anything to him. It's just an ego trip. I didn't like it much though. I tried not to mind, but…"

"You felt kind of hurt, I guess?" he offers.

"Yes, I did. I know that sex doesn't mean very much on its own, especially to him. And he's very attractive. You see women go sort of gooey around the edges when he looks at them in a certain way he has. They lose control of themselves. He's tried it with me once or twice. Hah!" She takes a drag on her cigarette, and then blows out the smoke with a fast puff. "But I know the game. He likes to feel he's in control of things. He can't have that with me so he goes out to get it elsewhere. It's like a little fix. A drug."

She sees his eyes distracted by the opening of the door and looks around herself to see. She freezes in her seat. Joseph sees them in a moment, strides to their table and leans forward, his two hands splayed out upon its surface. He glowers with a dreadful menace and speaks, not to her.

"Come outside. We have something to discuss."

The tall man stands, agreeing in silence.

Outside, the three of them stand, close to the water's edge. They wanted her to stay behind but she wouldn't. They couldn't force her to. She lurks between them and a little to one side. She's frightened. Joseph lights a cigarette, glaring, shifting between feet, edgy.

"Who the hell do you think you are?" he asks the taller man, who loiters, hands in trouser pockets, shoulders slightly hunched.

"You know my name, I guess."

"What are you doing with my wife?" As he says it she sees uncertainty in his face. He must realise that the American knows the truth of the situation.

"Having a beer for old time's sake. Do you have a problem with that?"

"I suspect there's more to it." Joseph nods with anger. He looks around at Anna who wants to speak but can't think what to say. "Why?" he asks her. There's a light comes up off the canal. A rippling reflection runs across his face and catches at his eyes, filled with pain.

Something grasps at her heart. All her life she's loved him. All his life he's loved her. She knows what she is to him. No matter how he lies and breaks the promises he makes, she knows he thinks he can't survive without her. She feels intensely guilty for her treachery; this blithe disregard with which she's treated his love lately. She feels at fault. She looks at him and wonders how she'll ever let him go. How foolish she's been to think she might; to think this little fancy might take flight. There's safety in him despite his deals with love and money. She knows he'll never leave her, that she'll never have to prove herself worthy, that he knows her, good and bad, happy and sad, joy and pain. There's safety in him. Security of love. Perhaps he's right and they could run. They'll go to the east; slip away into the orient, find another life to live. She knows he won't fail her again. He's learned his lesson this time; she can see that in his eyes. Her age-old love still lingers, printed on the stuff of her; programmed into her DNA. She looks at him and sees the happy, ardent boy she used to know. She sees the truth and honesty she saw when he was seventeen. She sees his love for her that's greater than anything she could ever hope to find again. She can see all of her life in his eyes. She walks towards him, into his waiting arms.

Joseph grasps her to himself and holds her so tightly that it stops her breath. "I'm sorry," he says. "I'm so sorry. I won't let you down again, I promise you."

She looks up at him, but he raises his eyes away from hers to see the other man still standing there. A sneer crosses his face.

"I thought you were dead," he says, contemptuous and triumphant.

And then she remembers what he really is. She turns to look at the tall man. He appears to be quite calm. He makes no reply but just looks back at them with some sadness.

The pain and love that were in her heart have fused together into a shard of ice. The snake is full grown. She knows she is not choosing between one and another. The American has made her no promises. She remembers that he doesn't like commitments. There's no comfortable future in that direction. She is choosing between herself and a murderer. She's astonished at how difficult this seems to be.

As Joseph's hold on her relaxes, she takes her chance and slips out of his reach. He starts after her, but there's a sound around behind him. There is a confused moment. Before she's sure what's happening, the tall man has hold of her, and another man is standing with them. The man looks Spanish or Latin-American, in his early forties, quite good-looking. He regards the three, cackles slightly and then focuses his attention on Joseph.

"Hola Joey my friend. So nice to see you after all these years! And Mr Smith!" He sucks his lips in over his teeth, and then he lights a small cigar. A light breeze blows up off the water and snatches away the brown smoke that trickles out of this. Smuts of it dance for a second in the air and then take flight, whipped up and away. "Not like me to miss my target. *Pero*, considering how I got paid for the job, who cares?" He cackles merrily.

"Hey, Juan! You're a long way from home." Joseph turns to the man, opening his arms in greeting.

"So, you're pleased to see me, eh?" Juan grins quite nastily.

Anna is frozen to the spot. So this is the man, intertwined with their crossing paths, who did dirty work for her family and anyone else who paid him. She doesn't know whom she loathes the most, and yet now Joe's in danger and her instinct's aroused. She wants to save him from this, but she's frightened. She looks up to Harry for help, but he's watching carefully, holding her loosely in a way somehow protective but not overt.

"Of course I am, my friend." Joseph smiles a smile that she's never seen. It's so cold and calculated that you might mistake it for malice.

"Well, that surprises me," Juan says. His grin has gone. His mouth is like iron. "You must realise that I've come to collect my reward, my friend. The debt you owe me. The price you must pay. I spent six years in jail to save your sweet skin, Joey. How do you *feel* about that, man?"

"Hey, Juan, it wasn't my fault!" Joseph shrugs in exaggerated fashion. "Nothing to do with me. I was locked up myself."

"If you was locked up, then how come you called me?" Juan's mouth stretches around the words unpleasantly.

"I got lucky. Got access to a phone."

"Yeah, Joey, sure. And to buy your own freedom, you tell tales on your friends." Juan puffs at his cigar and blows the acrid smoke into the face of Joseph. "You should have been more like your father, my friend. The man had a little *integrity*, you understand me? He wasn't some poisonous fucking little rat." The words drip with quiet and deadly venom. Anna is shaking. Harry holds her more tightly and whispers something to her that she doesn't catch.

Juan turns towards them. "Are you interested in this, Mr Smith? And this young lady. I seen your face before. I got a good memory. See, Mr Smith, I got this problem. I'm about to end the life of my friend here and I don't really want no witnesses to this, you understand?"

"You don't have to do that, Juan," Harry says quietly. "Save yourself the trouble. I've a feeling he won't be on the streets much longer anyhow."

"Oh?" Juan shows exaggerated interest. "Got himself into some difficulties, eh? What a terrible shame. What a foolish thing." He cackles nastily. "But you see I'm an impatient man, Mr Smith. I don't want to wait for justice and besides, I got a *grudge* against my friend."

Because Juan is looking at them, Joseph is trying to edge away. Anna sees this with her peripheral vision. She tries not to react, but a flicker of her attention gives the matter away. Juan turns back to Joseph who stands still now on cobble stones, one leg next to an *Amsterdammerje* – a bollard – there to stop cars parking too close to the bridge.

"Going somewhere, Joey?" Juan asks. From inside his jacket, he pulls out a small gun and a silencer. He fits one to the other and waggles the coupled thing around nonchalantly.

"You won't get away with it here, Juan," Harry says quite firmly. He doesn't seem to be afraid, yet Anna's teeth chatter in her head with cold and terror. "You'll never get out of the country. Leave him to the police."

"Don't interfere, Smith," Juan sneers. "I'll be out of here while your corpse is still warm, man. You don't have to worry about my well-being."

The moon comes out, lugubrious and full from behind ragged ink-coloured clouds that leave strands of their substance across its face. Its light falls upon the heads of Joseph and Juan, shines blue and silver on their similar-coloured hair. It glints off metal on the little barrel of the gun that Juan now points at Joseph with a hand steady as stone. His other moves to its top side to make it ready. A car, old and noisy, pulls up at the exit from a side-turning and, accelerating away, backfires. Anna screams in fright. Juan turns, distracted, and Joseph jumps, down into the cold, black water. He dives down under and can't be seen.

"Run," says Harry.

Juan is shooting bullets into the water. They zap and hiss, but the gun itself doesn't make much noise. Anna doesn't move. She can't. Harry roughly grabs her arm and pulls her with him, along the street, along the bank of the canal. Her feet fumble and then find their way. Juan shouts and fires the gun again. Harry lets out a gasp and stumbles but catches himself. They run around a corner. Harry is limping but still going. She looks at his face and sees pain written into it, looks down, sees blood darkening the leg of his trousers. There are running steps following them. How many shots will the little gun fire? Do they need to be reloaded these days? And where is Joe? She knows he swims well, but the water's so cold in this season. She finds she can't think of him. There's someone she cares more about. Someone whose life she'll save this time if she can, whatever the cost.

They turn around another corner. The tall houses lean in towards them. Gables and tie-beams, stark outlined, black against the moon-grey sky, glower inwards over their heads. There is a little alley to their right. They run across and down and it opens into a wider square, but it's a dead end. Her brain works like a machine. She pulls him after her, down some steps and around and underneath the arch above which leads to the main door of the property. There they nestle, in amongst rubbish and bad smells. Their breath makes white vapour in the cold air and she wishes it wouldn't. She looks at him. His eyes are closed, and strain shows in the lines of his brow and in the hardness of his jaw. She sees his trouser leg is soaked with blood. She listens hard and hears no sounds of creeping feet or running shoes.

Have they eluded him? How long can they wait to find out? Harry needs help. She's never learned first aid.

A minute more passes and still no sound above. She moves herself out of the stiff position she's been in. Harry still has hold of her hand. His eyes are still closed and his face looks pale. She reaches up to touch it, and his eyes open. He looks at her, frowning. "I'll be OK," he whispers, quiet as he can.

"I don't want to leave you," she tells him. "But I have to get help. You're bleeding so badly."

"Looks worse than it is, I expect," he says.

She pulls her hand out of his, reaches up and takes his head between her palms. She kisses him. The kiss contains all that she has to give him, and he looks at her with a question in his eyes. She smiles and creeps away.

Slowly, slowly, up the steps, raising her head above the parapet. She looks to left and right. No sign of Juan. Did they give him the slip? There are lights on in the house next door. She ponders for a moment, and then pads back down the steps. There's an ugly hat in the pocket of her jacket. She wears it sometimes when the cold's too much to bear. She pulls it out and stuffs her hair up under it so none is showing. Then she takes off her jacket and gives it to Harry to protect him more. She's freezing, but that doesn't matter.

Now she walks up the steps as though she's lived there all her life. She emerges casually onto the pavement. As she turns to go to the next house, she catches sight of a movement on the street corner. It's Juan there, vigilant and waiting, damn him. For a moment her anger's so great she thinks she'll just go and strangle him with her bare hands. Perhaps best not, but the emotion gives her courage. Head raised, purposefully striding, she walks the few feet to the next front door.

Juan notices her and watches. She sees but ignores him. She thinks he isn't sure. She rings the bell and waits, praying.

"Ja?" The door opens a little way.

She puts on the kindest smile she can find. An elderly lady looks timidly out. Anna searches her head for the Dutch words to say. They arrive in her mind in her moment of need. "I'm sorry. My friend is sick. I need some help. Can I use your phone?"

"English," the lady deduces.

"Ja," says Anna.

"I don't know." The lady's undecided

"There's nobody else in your house?" Anna asks. "I don't want to make you frightened. I'll try next door." She can sense that she's being watched. She glances away and sees that Juan has got closer.

"I'll get my neighbour," the lady says. Leaning around the door jamb, she presses another bell above her own. Anna did not see this one before. A minute later, a stout woman in her late forties is with them. Words of Dutch are gabbled back and forth. Anna waits with outer patience. Juan is just across the square. Now she's scared to go inside in case he decides to investigate down under the steps where she's been.

"What's wrong with your friend? Where is she?" the new arrival says too loudly.

"I think that man is following us." Anna tries to indicate Juan without him seeing. "My friend is hiding." She whispers this. "Would you call the police and an ambulance for me?"

"The station's not far," the first lady says.

"I know, but I'm scared that man will hurt us," Anna pleads.

"Phone them, Marta," says the younger one. "I'll stay here with her. Just get them to come here quick."

Marta scurries in to do as she's told. The stout woman comes outside and peers across Anna's shoulder at the lurking Juan. She indicates to Anna to step to one side, and then she folds her arms across her battleship bosom and glares at Juan solidly.

He lingers for a minute, and then, lighting a small cigar impatiently, he turns and walks quickly out of the street, around the corner and out of sight.

Anna lets out a squeak of laughter and hugs the woman who tuts and splutters in surprise, then grins and says: "Let's get your friend. I've been a nurse in younger days. Maybe I can be some help."

homeward

Harry sits in the small and uncomfortable seat of an aeroplane thirty thousand feet or so above the North Sea. In a while the plane will be landing at Heathrow. It isn't a long journey. The London Times is on his knee, folded open at the crossword puzzle. A new one he's about to start. He bought the paper at Schiphol airport. It gives him some little pleasure – a fresh crossword with no clues yet completed. He delays starting it a little longer. He looks forward to it. He learned the skill while he was in England and now he's hocked. He shifts in his seat to make himself more comfortable. His leg still hurts him where they took the bullet out. He's got two holes now. He hopes there won't be any more.

Next to him, looking remarkably relaxed, is Tina Philpott, or Argentina Byszewski, known lately as Anna Mason. He looks at her face. She's gazing out of the aeroplane window watching winter clouds piled up beneath them. He thinks she looks a little older than her thirty-four years. There are hollow places under her eyes, and that little line around one corner of her mouth looks deeper than he remembers it. He doesn't mind. He doesn't mind at all. She'll always be beautiful to him, same as the first time he saw her back in Flagstaff, Arizona, USA.

And now he's completing the task the old man set him; doing what he went to Holland to do. "Find out what's going on, would you, Harry, my boy?" the old man said. "And if there's trouble, bring her home. I've a feeling Joe Byszewski is going to get into difficulties and I want her out of it."

Harry didn't relish the prospect then. His own feelings concerned him. And hers. But he liked the old guy. Liked him a lot.

He was willing to take the risk. He hadn't reckoned on Juan turning up of course, and he's quite aware of how close he came to failure. But still, she's with him now and out of danger and that's all that really matters in the end.

He thinks he'll tell her the full story soon. All about his brief and how he's been manipulating the situation a little bit. He's pretty sure that she won't mind. He's pretty sure she knows how he feels about her. There are some things you just can't fake after all. And he had nothing to do with her brother's troubles. Byszewski got himself into that mess. Harry's only involvement in the laundering operation was to meet up with Frans Hendriks on a couple of occasions to get an update on the situation. That investigation was nothing to do with him.

So he's taking her home. Cleared things up in Amsterdam and bringing her and her belongings back to England. Back to where he hopes she'll be happy. He's surprised at how little she has. Apart from the books and her desk that will be sent later, when she's found a place to stay, there's only a bag or two, and the picture, wrapped up carefully down in the hold of the plane. The picture whose name they chose for this operation. He and Clive.

She turns and sees him watching her. She smiles at him with a question in her lovely eyes. He remembers when she smiled at him once before on a plane. Like a cat coveting cream.

"You don't seem to be too scared today," he says.

"When Joe and I came back from America he saw how terrified I was of flying," she explains. "He told me I was frightened of the future. I suppose there's nothing to be scared of any more."

He puts his hand on hers and holds it.

They found her brother's body some days after he dived into the water, swept out and then washed up on the shore of the sea. Afloat and bloated, killed by the cold and a shot that found its target – not deadly in itself, but no aid to strong swimming. She had to go to identify him and Harry was worried, but she coped remarkably well. It wasn't him, she said. His body, yes, but not the boy she knew, the man she loved. It was a stranger in his shell, a surrogate that had supplanted the original. Just a cruel and nasty caricature.

But sometimes he catches sight of her pain, when she thinks he isn't looking. He sees the strain in her eyes as she tries to keep control. He's not surprised. He knows she might have problems for a while. You can't give up on years of dreams without a little emotional turmoil. He thinks that's inevitable. And it's fine. He'll wait for as long as it takes. He's changed his mind about a lot of things.

He thinks it's sad that her friend reacted badly when she told her the truth. There was no sympathy, just disgust. He supposes that these taboos run deep in some people although, with what he's learned in recent years, Harry can see that it was not a surprising outcome of their situation, and not quite as uncommon as people might think. He saw how much Mari's reaction hurt her though. That made him angry. He wanted to give that woman a piece of his mind at the time, but he could see that she didn't understand. It would have done no good.

She's turned back to the window now, looking peaceful. He's glad. When he first saw her again, back in October, she looked so troubled and weary that it almost broke his heart.

He looks down at the crossword puzzle, prepares his propelling pencil, poised about the page. He reads the first clue. One across:

'Hopper bids Howard sweet dreams (10)'

Laughing   softly   to   himself,   he   fills   in   the   answer.

www.ingramcontent.com/pod-product-compliance
Lightning Source LLC
Chambersburg PA
CBHW050513260626

47157CB00004B/1307